Murder at Beulah Crest

RUSS SMITH

This is a work of fiction. Names, characters, organizations, places, events, and incidents are either products of the author's imagination or are used fictitiously.

ISBN: 978-1-09832-908-2 (print)
ISBN: 978-1-09832-909-9 (ebook)

ACKNOWLEDGEMENTS

Many thanks to Dwight and Barbara Reed, and the team at *The Bookstore* in Frankfort, for their support and advice. I encourage my readers to support their local independent bookstore. It's a great place to find the right book and to meet interesting people.

Also, thank you Deborah Meyer and Steve Wynkoop for helping to point out the many errors in the numerous drafts of this book.

CHAPTER 1
The First Murder

Elsie Taylor woke early Tuesday morning, as is her habit. She's the first person awake at Beulah Crest and often the last to call it a day. Nothing happens or is rumored to have happened at Beulah Crest Cottage Park that Elsie doesn't know about.

The park sits on land above Crystal Lake in the Village of Beulah, in Northwest Lower Michigan. There are 20 modular homes in the park that the residents call "cottages".

The sun was bright as Elsie emerged from her cottage to take her morning walk by the lake. As she started down the stairway through the forest from the crest to the lakeside trail, she found herself thinking, *I won't let anything cast a shadow on this beautiful spring morning.* While deciding whether to walk into the village to get a bagel at the local deli or in the other direction toward the boat ramp, she had thoughts about the park and her friends and neighbors who lived there.

The park changed as it grew over the years. Nigel Piddlemarsh and Spencer Butcher, the park owners, added a pool a few years ago. Last year they opened a coffee shop in the small house that was on the property when Spencer inherited the otherwise vacant land. The little house, usually referred to as the Mouse House, also contained the park office and a small studio apartment for the resident park manager.

The resident red fox, that some residents called Arthur, watched as Elsie approached. Wild foxes are usually skittish around people, but Arthur had learned over the years that some people were a threat and others were a source of food. Arthur's ears perked up as Elsie began talking. Elsie often talked to Arthur when she had something on her mind, even though the fox never responded. He sat patiently while Elsie talked, waiting for her to give him a treat.

"Arthur, today's the anniversary of my move here from Ann Arbor. Life "Up-North" has been good. This view can't be matched anywhere in the state, don't you think?"

Elsie paused to take a leftover sandwich from her pocket and tossed it to the fox. "Don't get me wrong, Arthur. It isn't the park itself or the lake, but the people and sense of community we have here that makes this place special. I've greeted and welcomed each new resident as they moved into their cottage. The last cottage went up only a few months ago and now, with only a few homes exchanging owners each year, the park is complete."

Arthur appeared to listen intently to Elsie, when in fact he was wondering if she had anything else in her pocket. She often had more than one treat.

"I don't have any children, Arthur, and Daniel died the year before I moved here, so the residents of Beulah Crest are my family."

Elsie threw Arthur the other half of the sandwich and continued with her walk. As Elsie approached the lakefront and noticed the first lilacs of the season starting to bloom, she thought again about her neighbors. One of the newer residents is that peculiar physicist, Xander Wolfe, a professor at Northwestern University in Chicago. He only comes up on occasional weekends, so she didn't expect to see Xander today. Then she remembered that Katie, his sister, was visiting, so he'd be up all week.

Arthur didn't usually follow Elsie down the stairs to the lake. So, as Elsie picked some lilacs, she asked, "What do you want, Arthur? I'm out of food and I have too much going on to talk more. There's Max's lunch and then I want to go to Frankfort. The Bookstore owner, Barb, called to tell me the book I ordered, 'Table 29', is in. It's about the murders on the ship Katie and Xander took to England a few years ago."

After Arthur finally ran off, Elsie started to think about the other people who lived at Beulah Crest. She knew every resident by name and could tell you about their families and interests. She worked as a librarian at the University of Michigan for thirty years before retiring and she knew that her mind acted like an old card catalog system. In her mind, each resident of the park had imaginary cards containing information collected over the years. Once she placed it on a card, the information would not be forgotten, and she could easily retrieve it at any time.

Everyone in the park would say they knew Elsie, and a few would even consider her to be a close friend. Most would describe her as looking like a middle-aged clerk or bank teller who always dressed in gray as she walked around the park wearing flat shoes. She wore very little makeup and the only jewelry she wore was her wedding ring and a small broach fashioned out of local Petoskey stone. Her appearance and personality were somehow disarming and encouraged people to talk and share things they wouldn't share with anyone else. Most people in the park understood Elsie's love of gossip, but they assumed she would never tell anyone what they had told her, "in confidence".

Elsie's cottage, one of the nicest in the park, sits on a large corner lot where Hummingbird Lane turns to the right to become Ridge Drive. There is a large deck overlooking Crystal Lake along the side and back of her cottage. From the corner of her deck she can see the Village of Beulah in the distance on the eastern shore of the lake.

She volunteered one morning a week at a hospice near Manistee and another morning at the Maples nursing home in Frankfort. On summer afternoons and evenings, when not otherwise occupied, she tended her garden or walked around the park and talked with her friends.

On her walks through the park, Elsie picked up tidbits of information from and about her neighbors. Her training and experience as a librarian told her that accuracy was an integral part of any cataloging system, so initially she found it difficult to filter out things she couldn't be sure were true. After her first year in the park and after six families had moved in, Elsie decided she needed to change how she kept track of her neighbors and started to keep two imaginary cards in her mind for each resident.

The first card only included facts. This included things she had observed or verified. For example, she frequently saw Albert Pankhurst leave his dog, Greta, outside all night. While having tea with Xander Wolfe she learned that he was a vegetarian who liked to cook in his spare time.

The other imaginary card contained the things heard over the years that had not yet been verified. For example, Bonnie Campbell's 2nd card included the gossip that she was having it on with the mailman and the recent comment from someone that the mailman rumor wasn't true because Bonnie was sleeping with Gus, the man who sold fresh duck eggs from a stand in front of his house on Lake Street.

Elsie kept track of all such stories and would occasionally share them with others in the park. Before sharing, she would usually say, "I'm not one to gossip, but did you hear...?"

Elsie loved the park and enjoyed collecting information about her neighbors, but she had another passion - the game of bridge. She learned to play while she was a student and began competing in duplicate bridge tournaments with Daniel before they were married.

A year after moving into her cottage, Elsie found a new bridge partner, Babs Tucker, who bought a cottage a few doors down on Ridge Drive. Babs and Elsie played several times a week and frequently entered regional and national tournaments. Elsie's encyclopedic memory served her well in the world of bridge. She's one of the highest-ranked duplicate bridge players in the state.

Elsie thought about Babs and how she bid an interesting bridge hand on Monday as she picked the white lilacs. After picking the flowers, she remembered that Babs always warned her not to bring them in the house because it was unlucky to do so. Elsie wasn't superstitious, so she collected a large bunch to put in a vase on her kitchen table.

Superstitions and all, Babs was Elsie's best friend. When Elsie had stopped by Babs' cottage to welcome her to the park over eight years ago, with a plate of brownies, they instantly became friends. They had similar interests, were both recently widowed, and they looked surprisingly alike. At bridge tournaments, most people thought they were sisters.

When Elsie finally got home with the flowers, she noticed that the door was open. She hadn't locked the door. People in the park rarely did. One of the neighbors must have stopped by to return something they had borrowed.

She entered her cottage and called out. "Say Babs, is that you? I've got lilacs for the table. I don't want any of your nonsense about them being unlucky. We better get moving if we're going to make it to Max's birthday lunch on time."

After seeing the mixer Babs had borrowed sitting on the counter, Elsie thought to herself, *That's strange. Babs usually locks the door if she's been here when I'm not home. I'll give her a call after I put these flowers in a vase.*

While arranging the lilacs, Elsie heard Albert's dog, Greta, barking outside her kitchen door. "What are you all excited about, Greta? Did Albert forget to feed you? You never bark, so something must be going on?"

As soon as Greta realized she had Elsie's attention, she quickly padded along the side of the cottage and around the corner. When Elsie came around the corner, she could see Babs on the deck and a chair knocked over next to her. As she approached Babs, Elsie was horrified to find Greta licking blood off of Babs' forehead. Elsie shouted. "Stop that, Greta! Now sit, over there while I help Babs get up." Shocked by Elsie's loud voice, Greta meekly obeyed and sat quietly where Elsie had indicated.

"Babs, what happened? Did you lean over and fall? Are you OK?"

Elsie quickly realized that Babs was not OK. There was a pool of blood collecting on the deck near her head and she wasn't breathing. Elsie checked for a pulse but couldn't find one. It took a few moments to sink in, but it was clear that Babs was dead. Elsie wasn't usually one to panic or scream, and it hadn't hit her yet that she'd lost a close friend and bridge partner. She couldn't help Babs, so she focused on what she needed to do.

First, she took her cell phone from her jacket pocket and called the emergency services by pressing 9-1-1. When she got through, she gave her name and address and then calmly told the operator, "I believe there's been a murder. My neighbor is lying in a puddle of blood on my deck."

After hanging up, Elsie started asking herself questions. *Did I just tell the police that Babs was murdered? Maybe she just fell. Who would want to kill Babs? Of course, she must have fallen. She tripped over something. Who would kill Babs?*

Elsie sat on the chair on the other side of the deck, next to where Greta was patiently waiting. While petting Greta, Elsie's thoughts shifted to her friendship with Babs and fond memories of things they had done together. She remembered the first time they played bridge and then started to wonder who would organize the park potluck dinners that Babs always coordinated.

The sounds of the approaching sirens broke Elsie's train of thought. She told Greta to stay where she was sitting and returned to her kitchen. *The police will be here soon. I'll make some coffee. Yes, I'll make them some coffee.*

It seemed like it took a long time for the police to arrive, but once they did, it was like a swarm of locusts had descended on the park and Elsie's cottage.

***

How could I make such a mistake? Elsie was the first person on my list. There are others, of course, but the way Elsie likes to gossip is just not acceptable. I've been thinking of doing this for over a year, and now, when I finally act, I kill the wrong person. What a way to start my work of cleaning house at Beulah Crest.

Poor Babs. She wasn't even on my list. They look so much alike, don't they? Why was she sitting alone on Elsie's deck? She must have been waiting for Elsie, who usually has a cup of coffee on her deck around this time if she isn't off at the Maples or that wretched hospice in Manistee. So, I assumed she was my target.

Babs was a kind and gentle soul who truly appreciated the quiet life, the beauty of Benzie County, and the lake. Nothing like Elsie, who's the biggest gossip I've ever met. Being a gossip isn't the only reason Elsie needs to be taken care of, but the park will be a better place once she and the others on my list are no longer around.

I'll need to be more careful when I take care of Elsie and the others. True, I couldn't tell it wasn't Elsie from behind when I struck Babs in head with a hammer, but I should have been sure of her identity before I acted. I was careful when I bought the hammer at a rummage sale in Traverse City so it couldn't be traced, and I put on an old lab coat and latex gloves when I struck, but it's obvious I wasn't careful in putting the hammer to its intended use.

Looking back, I can see I acted quickly so I wouldn't have time to change my mind. When I got behind Babs, I just hit her with the hammer, using all my strength before seeing who my victim actually was. After I made the fatal blow, the chair tipped, and Babs fell over. She looked at me, wondering what just happened for the few seconds before her life slipped away. She somehow knew I was the one who struck her, but it appeared that she couldn't quite process why I would do such a thing. I live in the park and I know she considered me to be a kind and helpful person. Only last week I helped her take some old dishes to a rummage sale at the Methodist church down in Frankfort.

I can hear the sirens of the approaching police cars and the ambulance. They will surely send an ambulance, just in case Babs is still alive. Fortunately, I was able to get into the woods to a place where I can observe things with the pocket binoculars, I always carry with me. I was lucky to get away before that wretched dog, Greta, found the body and started barking. I wish Albert would keep her on a leash, or better yet, in his cottage.

I still have the hammer, along with the lab coat and gloves in my shopping bag. I'll need to dispose of everything before I head back home. Or should I? Perhaps, I should keep it all for Elsie? The lab coat and gloves are covered with blood. I need to get rid of those for sure. I don't want them to be found.

I can see Elsie through her kitchen window putting the coffee on for the police. So typical. She'll be pumping them for information as soon as they arrive. I expect she'll also share a boat load of park gossip with them.

Well, I better get back to the park. I'm sure the police will want to question everyone who lives there. Wait, … I left my car parked behind the village hall in Beulah last night when I walked home from the council meeting with the folks from the park. Oh well, it's only a short walk into Beulah. I'll go pick up my car there up first. I'll throw the gloves and lab coat away on the way in the trash bin next to the pickleball court in the village park.

Hold on! It must be the shock of killing the wrong person that has me acting so haphazardly. Today's the day people from Beulah Crest are meeting for lunch at the Cold Creek Inn for Max's birthday party. It's supposed to be a surprise party, but there are no secrets in the park, are there? Since my car is already in town, I'll just walk to the restaurant. It's almost noon, so everyone should be arriving about now. It's not the perfect alibi, but once everyone has a few drinks, who'll remember exactly when people arrived? I'll put the hammer in the trunk of my car before I join the others.

CHAPTER 2
The Investigation Begins

S pencer was on the terrace of the coffee shop at the Mouse House when he saw the police and emergency service vehicles rush past with their sirens blaring. "Not another fight," he said to no one in particular as he watched the cars race past. There was a fight after a late-night party at one of their parks in England last month, but that was after midnight and the people involved had quite a bit to drink. Since this was a Tuesday morning, and the police were stopping in front of Elsie's cottage, this had to be something else. Anyone in the park could tell you that Elsie never drank more than an occasional sherry.

As he approached Elsie's cottage, a sheriff's deputy who was marking off Elsie's cottage as a crime scene stopped Spencer. "I'm sorry sir, but this is a crime scene and I must ask you to go no further. We're just getting set up here and the first thing we need to do is secure the area."

"I'm Spencer Butcher. Nigel Piddlemarsh and I own the park. What's happened? Is Elsie all right?" Lord Piddlemarsh and Sir Spencer never used their British titles while in the U.S., as American's never seemed to know what to make of them.

The officer handed the roll of yellow crime scene tape to one of his colleagues before he responded. "I can't tell you much Mr. Butcher. Mrs. Taylor is ok, but someone was attacked on her deck, over on the side of the cottage that faces the lake. I can't tell you anything else. The sheriff is on the way over. With something like this, he'll be involved in the investigation."

Before he could learn anything else from the deputy, Spencer noticed Elsie approaching him from her cottage. It was obvious that she was rattled. She wasn't walking with her head held high like she usually did, and when she spoke, her voice was much lower and hushed than usual. "Oh, Spencer! It's Babs. Someone's killed her. She's lying in a puddle of blood on my deck. It's just awful." Her acquired Midwest accent seemed to fade as her native Brooklyn accent surfaced.

Elsie, who was often the one to provide comfort to others in the park when they shared bad news, allowed Spencer to put his arm around her shoulders. While she held back her tears, Spencer took charge. "Let's go up to the coffee shop and get you a cup of tea. You can tell me all about it."

Elsie responded while holding back a tear. "I put the coffee on for the police, but they said they might be awhile and that I should wait somewhere else until they finished."

As they walked up the hill to Mouse House, more police vehicles drove past on their way to Elsie's cottage. When they arrived, a small group gathered outside to watch the arrival of the emergency vehicles. Since most of the park residents were at work or in the village at Max's birthday lunch, only Albert and his dog Greta were there, along with Ben Welden, the groundskeeper and

Ian De Vries, the resident property manager. Albert helped out as a volunteer in the coffee shop. Ian and Albert asked Spencer at the same time. "What's going on?"

"Let's all go inside," Spencer answered. "I'll tell you what I know, which isn't much." Once they were seated and had their tea or coffee, Spencer shared what he knew. "Babs Tucker is dead. She was found on the deck of Elsie's cottage. The police are investigating the incident. I expect they'll want to talk to all of us, so it might be a good idea if we all wait here until they arrive."

While the small group waited at the cottage, Spencer used his cell phone to call Nigel, who had gone ahead to the Cold Creek Inn to get the lunch started. When Nigel answered, it was obvious the birthday luncheon was well attended because of the background noise. The line got quiet as Nigel headed outside so he could talk. "Where are you Spencer? Almost everyone else is here."

"Some bad news Nigel. They found Babs Tucker dead on Elsie's deck. Elsie thinks she was murdered."

"Babs, murdered! In the park? I can't believe it!"

"I don't have many details yet, but the police are here. There's a swarm of them. They've got crime scene tape all around Elsie's cottage."

"Is Elsie OK?"

"She's fine. A bit shaken up though. She found the body when she came back from a walk down by the lake."

"Poor thing. At least she'll have fresh material for when she makes her gossip rounds."

"That's kind of harsh, isn't it?"

"Probably. It's the shock, I guess. Now that I think about it, I feel sorry for the old dear. Anyway, should I come back? Do you think I should tell everyone here?"

Spencer thought about it for a minute. He was always the one to plan things. "Why don't you stay there, and I'll check with the police and see what they want to do. I'll call you back after I talk to them."

Spencer hung up and got up to leave the group and check with the police. Ian followed him out and pulled him aside as he walked onto the front porch of the cabin. "Spencer, I'll join you when you talk to the sheriff. It might make things easier."

"What do you mean?" Spencer asked.

"You and Nigel may have more money than God himself, and you own the park and a 'McMansion' on the other side of the lake, but you're both outsiders. Foreigners to boot. The sheriff doesn't like foreigners. I might not have any money, but my family goes back a long way here in Benzie County. The sheriff might talk to me. I know he won't have much to do with you or Nigel."

"I know what you mean," Spencer replied. "Nigel's family name goes back countless generations back home. He's treated like royalty while I'm still seen as the guy who grew up above a grocery store in Newcastle."

"The sheriff will treat you both as worthless outsiders, so you and Nigel are on even footing here. It's fortunate that you're not a migrant farm worker, or he'd arrest you right away."

The sheriff arrived a few minutes after most of the officers in his small department made their way to the crime scene.

Murders were an infrequent event in rural Benzie County, especially those without an obvious suspect. Jake Summerlin, a retired patrolman from Kalamazoo, who worked part time for the department, was manning the entrance to the park. Sargent Nick Townsend, who had experience investigating violent crimes, was managing the crime scene and starting to plan how the investigation would progress. He already had two junior deputies walking around the park looking for evidence.

The sheriff, elected by the citizens of the county to run its police force, got out of his brand-new police cruiser as Ian and Spencer approached. He straightened his gun belt and put on his large brown sheriff's hat as he considered how this event might impact his re-election campaign. Quickly solving a violent murder case, especially if the killer was one of the migrant farmers he was known to target when pulling over motorists, would provide some good publicity.

The sheriff was about to address Ian when he noticed Jennifer Reynolds, a reporter from the *Benzie County Record-Patriot* standing by the front gate of the park. Before Ian could say anything, the sheriff turned and walked toward the reporter. Sheriff Van Dyke was not one to miss an opportunity to talk with a reporter from the local weekly paper.

Ian pointed to the front gate as he provided Spencer some more insight about the sheriff. "That's a reporter from the local paper. Sheriff Van Dyke will be more interested in spinning a good story than finding the actual murderer."

Ian and Spencer walked over to the crime scene and talked to Nick Townsend. Both knew that Nick would lead the investigation, anyway. When they approached Nick, he was just getting off the phone with the medical examiner.

When Nick saw them approaching, he put his phone in his pocket and then warmly shook Ian's hand and then Spencer's. Nick always started out with a bit of small talk at a crime scene. Sometimes he could get a feeling about potential suspects by how they reacted. "How's your dad, Ian? Is he home from the hospital yet?"

"He's home and driving Mom crazy. Nothing new there. How's Sheri and your son doing?"

Ian and Nick continued with the small-town gossip for a few minutes and then Nick finally asked a question related to the case. "Have either of you been up on Elsie's deck?"

Spencer answered. "No, Elsie told me what happened and then I told Ian. We' been up at the Mouse House with Elsie, Ben, and Albert waiting for you to arrive. I think everyone else who lives in the park is either at work, school, or over at the Cold Creek for a birthday lunch."

Ian then asked a question. "I noticed Jake's watching the front gate and keeping people from coming into the park. Should we tell Nigel to have everyone who's in town stay there for a while or should they head back here after lunch?"

Nick thought for a moment, then responded. "How about you have them stay there for an hour or so after they've eaten. That'll give us time to check the grounds and talk to the few people who are here."

Sheriff Van Dyke walked over and interrupted. "How's it looking, Nick? I hear it was Babs." Before Nick answered, he told Ian and Spencer to go back to the Mouse House and that he'd be over in a few minutes.

"Let's walk over to Elsie's cottage and I'll show you what we've got. When they got to the deck, Nick continued. "Looks like one heavy blow to the head with a hammer or something similar. Probably happened in the last two hours or so. I'll narrow that down as soon as I talk to Elsie and of course the medical examiner will weigh in on the time of death."

"Do you think it was it a robbery?"

"Not likely. Her purse is on the table. There's over $100 in it, along with her keys and credit cards. It doesn't look like anything was taken from Elsie's cottage. The medical examiner will have an opinion, but I'm thinking that someone snuck up from behind and struck her before she had a chance to get up or struggle."

The sheriff didn't like what he heard. After Nick shared what knew and left to talk to the people at the Mouse House, the sheriff thought to himself about the case. *We usually solve a drugs deal that went bad or a domestic violence killing in a day or two and then there's a nice story in the paper about how the case was quickly solved. This one looks different. With no obvious motive or suspect, this case could remain open indefinitely. I won't let this be like the murder in Frankfort back in the 70s that they never solved. The press made the police look like fools. Nick's a good detective, but if he doesn't solve this case quickly, I'll find a suspect.*

While the sheriff was pondering the political implications and opportunities of the murder, Nick got to work and began questioning potential suspects and witnesses. He asked the others to wait in the coffee shop and started with Ben, the groundskeeper who he found planting flowers in the garden next to the house. Nick knew Ben as a "local" who grew up in Honor. He still talked about his football hero days at Benzie Central High School in the 1990s. Ben lived in a trailer on Homestead Road with his wife Constance and his two hunting dogs, Maxwell and Irma. When he found Ben, Nick asked, "Got a few minutes to talk Ben?"

"Of course, Nick. It's a nasty business. I can't tell you much more."

"That's ok, Ben. How about if you tell me about how you heard about the incident?"

"I've been over here all morning working in the garden. I was talking with Ian about the Huskie's chances this fall when Albert and Elsie came over and told us about Babs."

"When did you start work today?"

"I was here early, about 7am. I want to get all these flowers in before it rains."

"Did you notice anything unusual or any strangers in the park?"

"Can't say I seen anything unusual. People going off to work, the school bus at its normal time, and then the rest of 'em headed into Beulah for lunch. A birthday party for Max Silver."

"Did you see any visitors come into the park?"

"No, but then again I might have missed them. Check with Ian. Spencer had him install a camera at the gate when they put in the new barrier a few months ago. I think it takes a video or photo of every car that enters. Not sure if it tracks who leaves though."

"Can you think of anyone who might want to kill Babs?"

Ben thought before answering, as he pulled another tray with petunias and marigolds from his truck. "You know Babs. She's the kindest person in the park, or at least was. She might not have been born around here like you and me, but she was good as. She and Al built that big gray house on Crystal Avenue, just past Lake Street, back in the 70's? She sold it and moved here after Al passed away."

"It's a nice house. It surprised me when she sold it and moved up here to the park. It's on the best piece of lakefront property in the village."

"A niece, from Ohio, I think, bought the place. She talked Babs into selling the place to her for half of what it was worth. A year later, the niece flipped the house and made a killing. Maybe she was after whatever else Babs has."

"Can you think of anyone else who might have a motive or be angry with Babs?"

"No, I never seen anyone get angry with Babs. You might check over at the bridge club though. I've heard stories about those people getting into fights over that silly game."

"Any other thoughts, Ben?"

"No. I'll be burying Babs, you know. She'll be my first. I took the sexton job over at the township cemetery last week. Connie lost her job at the casino, so the extra money will help."

Not wanting to hear Ben go on about his wife's troubles, which could keep Ben going all day, Nick ended his questioning of the groundskeeper. "Well Ben, if you think of anything else, let me know. I appreciate what you've shared."

Nick let Ben get back to planting the petunias and went inside to talk with the others. When he walked in, Albert and Elsie were sitting in the coffee shop petting Greta. It looked like Greta was doing more to comfort Elsie than any person could. Ian was working at his desk in the small office at the back of the coffee shop. Nick stopped to pet Greta and told Albert and Elsie he would be with them in a few minutes, after he talked to Ian.

Nick had been friends with Ian's parents, Jenny and Rick since childhood, so he knew Ian as a smart kid who always had several jobs going at once. Ian graduated at the top of his class at Benzie Central and went to Ferris State for a year, but university life didn't work for him. When he came back to Benzie two years ago, he started working for Spencer and Nigel at the park.

When Ian saw Nick approach, he got up and greeted him. "I can't understand it, Mr. Townsend. Babs was like a grand-mother to me since I started working here."

Nick could see that Ian was upset and was trying to hold himself together. "I know, Ian. She'll be missed." Rather than a handshake, Nick gave Ian a hug.

Nick decided to open the discussion with something other than the murder until Ian was a bit more settled. "So, what have you been doing since you got back from Ferris? I haven't kept up with your parents as much as I should have?"

"The classes at school were a bore, so I got my real estate license up there for something else to do. When I came home, I started working here. I manage the property, collect the land lease rents, handle the few rentals we have, and try to get the real estate listings if anyone sells their cottage. The owners, Nigel and Spencer, are here only here a few weeks a year, so between Ben and me, we keep the place going."

"You still have that band? What's it called?"

"The Blind Visionaries, yep. It's actually doing quite well. We play once a week at the Cabbage Shed in Elberta and once or twice a week at a new place in Traverse City. I also work a few shifts a week at the new micro-brewery in Beulah."

Nick let Ian go on about his band for a few minutes and then got back to the matter at hand. "Tell me about this morning Ian. When did you get here?"

"I started late this morning, just before Elsie Taylor and Spencer came up here and told us what happened. I worked last night at the micro-brewery. I'm glad I have the little studio apartment here at the back of the Mouse House. No commute."

"Did you notice anything unusual or any strangers in the park this morning, or over the past few days?"

"Nothing out of the ordinary. I was just looking at the tapes to see if I could see anything."

"Ben told me about the new camera at the entrance. What kind of setup do you have?"

Ian led Nick into a small alcove off of his office where he kept the video monitors and related equipment. "It's simple, but pretty good. As a car approaches the gate, the video camera is activated and records until the car passes through. A second camera gets a shot of the license plate from the rear, after the car goes past. The system deletes the video after a week. I can give you a copy, but I don't think it will be much use."

"Why do you say that?"

"First, Mr. Townsend, the camera is obvious. Everyone knows it's there. Second, there aren't any other cameras in the park. You can take the stairs up from the lake or walk over from the condos on the west side of the park or the forest on the other. There are no fences or natural barriers."

"You're probably right, but please make me a copy. Have you got any idea of who was in the park this morning, before everyone left for lunch, or work, or whatever?"

"I can't tell you for sure, but I can give you a list of the people who only come up on the weekend and the summer people who haven't opened up their cottages for the season. Between the two groups, that's about 10 or 11 of the cottages that are empty now. By the end of the month most of the seasonal people will be here."

"That should help. I'll stop back and get the list and the copy of the video after I talk to Elsie and Nigel.

"No problem. It will only take a few minutes to pull everything together for you."

Before Nick approached Elsie and Spencer, he called Deputy Kathy McGregor on his cell phone. Kathy, the only woman officer in the department, was with her colleagues searching the grounds of the park. He asked her to come to the cottage to and sit with Elsie so she wouldn't be alone while he was questioning Spencer and Albert.

After Kathy sat down with Elsie in the coffee shop, Nick asked Spencer to step outside, so they could talk. After they sat down at a table on the front porch, Nick started with his questions. "Mr. Butcher, when did you come to the park this morning?"

"Spencer, please, Detective. Nigel dropped me at the park about an hour before you arrived. I wanted to check a few things with Ian before lunch. Just as I was about to leave for the lunch party, I learned what happened to Babs."

"Can you think of anyone who would want to harm Babs?"

"I can't, Detective. Although I liked Babs, I can't say that I knew her well. Nigel and I are only in Beulah for a few weeks, about twice a year. I know that Babs and Elsie were very close friends though."

"So, what's the story with this park, Spencer? I was working down in Lansing when you started it and missed all of the local gossip when you got it going. It's unlike anything around here."

"I know. We rattled some cages when our plans became public. I inherited the land and the Mouse House from a distant cousin I'd never met. It was a total surprise when I got a letter from a lawyer in Detroit."

"Nice surprise. This land has one of the best views of the lake."

"At first, we wanted to sell it. I'd only been to America once before, so I had little interest in doing anything here. Then a friend, Xander Wolfe, who went to school at Interlochen, suggested we develop the place, like our parks in England. Nigel and I own a number of similar parks in England and Wales, although most of them are quite a bit bigger."

"How did you get the permits to build this place? This is the highest density housing in the area and it's right on Crystal Lake."

"Since we invested nothing to buy the land, we had a lot more flexibility. We met with the Village of Beulah and worked with them to annex the land into the village, with the understanding that we would contribute to the rebuilding of their sewer system. In return, we negotiated for permission to build. We made some enemies in the process; I can tell you. Few people living on the lake were happy with what you Americans call a 'trailer park', even though there's seasonal one in the Village of Beulah on the lakefront."

"Do you think there could be anyone angry enough about the park to kill one of your residents? Have there been any threats?"

"I can't think of anyone. There haven't been any recent threats. The park sponsors a lot of local activities and charities, so most people accept us now. There were a few threats ten years ago when we started, but nothing since."

Nick was about to ask Spencer about the residents in the park and if he knew of anyone who might have a motive when an ambulance, with its sirens blaring, came through the gate and approached the Mouse House. As they watched the ambulance pull up, Ian came out onto the porch and told them what happened. "Mrs. Taylor had some kind of an attack or seizure. Deputy McGregor had me call 9-1-1 while she tried to help her."

It took the Benzonia Township paramedics ten minutes to stabilized Elsie. There was nothing for Nick and the others to do but watch the professionals do their lifesaving work. After stabilizing Elsie, the paramedics put Elsie in their truck and took her to the hospital, without giving Nick the chance to question her. After they departed for the hospital in Frankfort, Nick asked Kathy what happened.

Kathy finished writing some notes in her notepad while she gathered her thoughts and put her emotions in check. "After Mrs. Taylor finally settled down, we sat quietly while Albert got us each a cup of coffee. Then she asked me whether she herself might be the intended victim, since the murder took place on her deck. Before I could answer, she got agitated again and started having a seizure. I comforted as best I could and shouted to Ian to call 9-1-1."

Nick thought a moment before he responded. "Elsie has a point. We may have to look for a suspect who didn't specifically target Babs or, maybe one who didn't know either of the women. The sheriff won't like this. He's after a suspect he can arrest quickly."

CHAPTER 3
Max's Birthday Party

While events were unfolding at Beulah Crest, many of the residents were arriving at the Cold Creek Inn in nearby Beulah to celebrate Max Silver's birthday. The first to arrive was Nigel Piddlemarsh, the co-owner of the park.

Nigel had a special skill for fitting in and getting small communities to accept him and his real estate developments. Prior to building of Beulah Crest, no one in Benzie County would have thought it possible to get permission to build any housing development with 20 units on the edge of Crystal Lake. The condo development on the land next to the park was built almost thirty years ago and people still complain about how the views from across the lake were ruined.

Events like Max's birthday party were the type of things Nigel and Spencer did to create and strengthen a sense of community. There was always a party or event of some type for park residents when Nigel and Spencer were in town and usually some type of visible activity to promote the park. For example, there would be a big float in the Fourth of July parades in Beulah and Frankfort. When Nigel and Spence were at home in England, the responsibility for promoting the park fell to Ian.

Shortly after Nigel arrived and confirmed the arrangements at the Cold Creek Inn, other park residents came into the restaurant in a steady stream. Some walked from Beulah Crest, while others drove into town. Some, who worked in Beulah, Benzonia, or Frankfort, took extended lunch breaks to attend. Within 15 minutes, everyone who was expected had arrived, except for Spencer, Elsie, Ian, and Babs. People gathered in natural groups and found seats. Since some people had to get back to work after lunch, Cora, the waitress, and Nigel prompted everyone to find a seat and place their orders.

Nigel sat at a table with Herb and Dorothy Cooper, both retired veterinary surgeons from Ohio. They set aside a seat for Spencer, who was expected to arrive soon. Max Silver sat at the large table in the center of the room with several of his friends. Xander Wolfe, who usually wasn't in town on weekdays, sat at a table with his sister Katie, who was visiting. They held seats for Elsie, Babs, and Ian. Albert Pankhurst never attended such events. He said the noise of a crowded restaurant sets him on edge.

Just as Cora finished taking orders, Nigel's phone rang, and he received the news about Babs from Spencer. His first thought was to hold off sharing what he learned until after everyone had eaten, but he realized that anyone else in the room might receive a call from someone at the park. Best to get the news out as calmly as possible.

Nigel stood at the front of the restaurant and tapped his fork against a glass. Everyone quickly became silent, expecting one of Nigel's humorous speeches. "I just received a call from

Spencer. I'm afraid he shared some bad news. There's been an incident at the park. Babs Tucker has passed away. The police are at the park sorting things out and have asked that we all stay here for the time being."

There were gasps throughout the room and there was then a long silence as people took in what they just heard. Xander was the first to break the silence. In his early 30s, Professor Wolfe was one of the youngest people from the park at the restaurant, but one of the most distinguished. People who didn't know the suntanned Xander when they saw him ride his skateboard into town would never guess that he had recently received a Nobel Prize for his breakthrough work in solid state physics. Because of the silence, Xander didn't need to shout when he called over to Spencer. "Are Elsie and Ian OK? Other than Spencer, they are the only two expected today who aren't here."

Nigel responded to the group. "They're both fine. Elsie's a bit rattled, but she's being looked after by Albert and Spencer. Ian is also OK. Spencer will call when things have settled down a bit and we can return to the park."

Max then rose and addressed the group. "Let's just have a quiet lunch and dispense with the happy birthday nonsense. I don't think any of us are in a mood to celebrate. I'm certainly not. Perhaps Reverend Parker could lead us in a short prayer for Babs."

Although the Parkers only moved to the park two years ago, Hortense Parker was well known in the community. She retired last year after serving for over thirty years at one of the many congregational churches in the county. Her husband,

Derek, who was semi-retired, was at her side. He still worked a day or two a week at a small dental clinic in Frankfort. After Reverend Parker shared a short prayer, Cora began serving lunch and everyone began talking quietly at their tables.

Xander and Katie were at a table by themselves, which gave them time to talk. Katie was only visiting for a few days, so they both wanted to spend as much time together as possible, before Katie returned to Germany. After Cora brought Katie's bacon cheeseburger and Xander's veggie burger, Katie asked, "So, what's going on? Who's this Babs woman?"

Xander finished nibbling a few fries before answering. "You've met Elsie, the park's collector and distributor of local gossip?"

"Yes, I talked to her yesterday, while you were running. Sad thing really. I get the impression that she is lonely. Don't you?"

Before Xander responded, he flagged down Cora and asked for some mayonnaise. After Cora left, he answered. "Elsie is an odd character, I admit, but harmless. Anyway, Babs is, or I suppose was, her bridge partner and probably her closest friend. Unlike Elsie, Babs was special. Everyone in the park, and from what I gather, the county, knew and liked her. She was always there to offer help and encouragement to anyone who needed it."

"Wait, a minute. When I was up at Interlochen this morning, I saw a new fountain dedicated to a Babs Tucker. Is that her?"

"So that's where you were all morning. I was worried you'd miss lunch."

"Me, miss a bacon cheeseburger at the Cold Creek? Never! Anyway, was that her?"

"Yes, that's her. I really liked the old girl."

"What do you think happened? The police wouldn't be there investigating if this Babs just fell or had an accident."

"According to Elsie, the source of all local gossip, the unpopular sheriff is up for re-election and is desperate for some positive news coverage. Perhaps he's just making a show of things for the publicity."

Katie was about to ask Xander a question when she noticed the room fall silent as Cora turned up the volume on one of the large televisions in the restaurant. The TV station from Traverse City had interrupted the network Detroit Tigers pre-game show with a news alert.

Sheriff Van Dyke appeared on the screen. He was wearing his distinctive sheriff's hat and presented a sense of urgency as he talked. "I'll make a short statement now, and that's all. There's been a suspicious death here at the Beulah Crest Cottage park. I won't release the deceased person's name until her family is notified. A young Hispanic man was seen walking down Crystal Avenue shortly after the incident. The focus of our investigation is on identifying this person of interest. If anyone has any information, please contact the Benzie County Sheriff's office. Rest assured that I will not rest until we solve this."

When the TV station switched back to the baseball pre-game show, Cora turned down the volume and everyone in the room began talking about the news story. Nigel asked the group at his table how the television news could have possibly got the story out so quickly.

Derek Parker answered. "I'll bet it's that reporter, Jennifer, oh what's her name? Anyway, that one from the *Record Patriot*. I saw her drive into the park as I drove past on my way here from Frankfort."

Hortense Parker interrupted. "Oh, don't be ridiculous, Derek. She's just a small-town reporter for the local newspaper. That sheriff probably had someone from his office call the news station."

Max joined in the discussion. "Possibly Reverend, but Jennifer often sends video clips to TV stations, and she also posts them on the web. I'm guessing she was in the right place at the right time to grab the story and she used the Internet and her contacts at the TV station to get her story on the air. Fast response media coverage comes to Benzie County."

Bonnie Campbell, a retired Frankfort High School English teacher then asked a question. "What's with this Hispanic suspect on Crystal Avenue? That's nonsense. I saw Pablo Sanchez on my way into town. That idiot sheriff couldn't mean him, could he? Pablo cuts the grass at several cottages along the lake."

Derek, who believed all the rumors about Bonnie's sexual adventures and who secretly hoped he might have one with her someday, responded to Bonnie's question. "You're probably right about the sheriff, Bonnie, but how do you know Pablo? Is he a friend of yours?"

Bonnie, who was unaware that her sex life was the subject of park gossip, answered. "No, but I wouldn't turn him away. Too bad he's 40 years younger than me."

Similar discussions continued at all the tables during the lunch and while they served dessert. Some of the other customers having lunch in the restaurant or seated at the bar stopped by to chat or ask questions. Everyone knew and respected Babs. Soon after lunch, the people who had to get back to work left, while the others remained at the Cold Creek sipping coffee and talking while waiting for Spencer to call Nigel with an update.

* * *

Good God in heaven! Can you believe the mouth on that Bonnie Campbell? The whole restaurant can hear her going on about Pablo. Why would he want anything to do with an old trout like her when he's been seeing that cute waitress at the Cherry Hut. That slag Bonnie has been with every low-life scum in the county and now she's after Pablo. I wish I could find a way to keep her from attending the funeral.

Now wait a minute. Bonnie is on the list, but she's not at the top. What if I moved her to the top? Let's think about this… Who better to be at the top than Bonnie? She's trailer trash through and through. True, we all live in a glorified trailer park, but one does have to draw the line somewhere. She smokes, she drinks, and she sleeps with any man she can corner. How she kept her job as a teacher all those years is a mystery to me. Oh, and that raspy smoker's voice of hers. It drives me to distraction.

What about Elsie? I wanted her to be first, for several reasons. But now that I think about it, she could be useful to me as I take care of the other troublesome residents in the park. True, her tendency to gossip is deplorable, but given my mission, she could be an unwitting ally. She knows everything that goes on in the park and will probably make it her business to learn everything she can about the investigation. The police will line up at her cottage door for doughnuts and coffee. They'll think she can provide them with information about people in the park, when in reality, she'll be the one pumping them for everything they know about the investigation.

Yes, it's decided! Bonnie goes to the top of the list and Elsie moves to the bottom. I'll need to make a point of establishing a better relationship with Elsie. She knows I'm not very receptive to hearing her chatter. That will have to change.

Now to the question at hand: how to take care of Bonnie? Since she was at the bottom of the list, I have put little thought into how to take care of her, and then there's the other issue, Babs' funeral. If Bonnie is there, the whole event will be a spectacle.

Bonnie and Babs were friends, so Bonnie will want to be there. She might even want to say a few words to the congregation. Elsie would be the natural choice to give a eulogy, but she'll be too nervous to speak in front of a full church, so that task may fall to Bonnie. We can't have that, can we?

No, I can't have Bonnie speaking at Babs' funeral. That just wouldn't be right. She must be taken care of before it takes place. Hopefully, the coroner will keep the body for a while, so I'll have time to sort out how to take care of Bonnie.

Ok, it's decided. Bonnie is next, and she has to go before the funeral, but I still need to decide how, when, and where to do it. Somehow, using the hammer doesn't seem right, does it? It's covered with Babs' blood. Come to think of it, I think it's best to get rid of that hammer. Perhaps I should throw it in the lake on the way home.

As to where to take care of Bonnie, I wonder if I should do it at Beulah Crest? That wretched dog, Greta, alerted people much too soon after I killed Babs. I barely got away in time. If I kill her in the park, I'll need to do it inside Bonnie's cottage or in another cottage. I need to think about this some more.

Well, you've made some decisions, but you better re-engage in conversation with people before the luncheon breaks up. You always seem to provide comfort to people at times like this, so you better hug a few people and act as if you care about them. You don't want to act differently, today of all days. Decide on the next steps later, after talking to the police and Elsie. Perhaps they can give you some ideas.

CHAPTER 4
The Investigation Continues

After the ambulance left with Elsie, Sheriff Van Dyke pulled Nick aside and asked how things looked. Hoping to prevent the sheriff from doing something that would embarrass the department, Nick tried to sound positive when he answered. "There are no obvious suspects, but the crime scene is fresh and undisturbed by anyone or by bad weather. This one will be solved by forensics. Fingerprints and DNA will lead us to our suspect."

"You better be right," the sheriff responded. "I won't have this stretch out all summer. I'll take matters into my own hands if you don't clear this up soon."

While the sheriff and Nick were outside talking about the case, Ian was in his office on the phone with Elizabeth, who managed a social media site focused on solving crimes. Ian had met Elizabeth, along with Conner, Roscoe, and Megan, at a summer computer camp at Michigan State while he was still in high school. On the first day at camp, they were randomly assigned to form a team to work together to build a website as a project. When asked to give their team a name, they noticed that the first letter of their names, Conner, Roscoe, Ian, Megan, and Elizabeth provided a good start. Given only 10 minutes to come up with a name, they called their group, and their website, Crime Spartans.

The Crime Spartans website went public a week later, and to everyone's surprise, it quickly became popular. People could post information about unsolved crimes and make comments about their local police force, and pretty much anything about the crime investigation process. The website also gave its five creators a reason to remain in contact and maintain their friendships after the computer camp ended.

After a few months of the site being on-line, the team realized that designing the site was the easiest part of the project. The more difficult and time-consuming task was moderating and managing the site. Without proper management, there was the risk that users would post inappropriate things and the site would lose its focus.

Something that surprised Ian, and his friends, was the fact that the site was generating enough hits to make it possible to generate revenue by posting advertisements on the site pages.

Ian, the most entrepreneurial member of the team, put together a business plan that called for a full-time site administrator/manager once revenue grew to a certain level. Elizabeth, who was a part-time computer science major at Northwest Michigan College (NMC) in Traverse City was the only member of the team interested in managing the site, so she took on that task, at first on a volunteer basis. By the end of the first year, the site was generating enough revenue to pay Elizabeth a salary, to hire a few part-time programmers for site maintenance, and to pay each of the site founders a small dividend from the profits. Although Elizabeth did most of the day-to-day work of administrating the site and finding advertisers, all five members of the team were active in reviewing and improving the site content. Elizabeth lived a short drive away in the town of Interlochen. She and Ian had become good friends and Ian was thinking it might be time to take the relationship further. Elizabeth had wanted to keep things from going in that direction, but the way Ian described the crime at Beulah Crest and how it impacted him personally, had exposed her to side of Ian that she found attractive.

Ian shared all the information he had about the crime with Elizabeth and his belief that the local police weren't up to the task of solving the crime. Having grown up in a small town in the Upper Peninsula, Elizabeth agreed. "Ian, Babs didn't have any family in the area, and this obviously wasn't a gang or drug related murder, so you know what that means. This is going to difficult to solve. Even a well-equipped and professionally staffed police department would find this one a challenge."

Ian agreed. "You're right, of course. Nick Townsend is a good cop, but the sheriff will step in and screw things up if the case isn't solved in a day or two, which it won't be."

"Ian, does anyone in Benzie County know that you are one of the people who set up the Crime Spartans website?"

"I told my parents the summer we created the site, but no one else. At the time I didn't think it would come to anything."

"That's good. You can provide updates for the site without getting pressure from the police. Take notes about what you see and hear today and let's get together at my place this evening so we can plan how to handle this. In the meantime, I'll get in touch with Roscoe, Megan, and Conner. Roscoe and Megan are social media junkies and Conner is a computer genius who can hack into any system on earth. With their help, we should be able to solve this."

After Ian ended the call with Elizabeth, he felt better. Not only did he feel closer to Elizabeth, he was more hopeful that, with the help of his friends and the Internet, Babs' killer might be identified. Ian's sprits were lifted when Greta came into his office and put her head on his lap, inviting him to pet her.

Albert followed Gretta into the office, with a fresh cup of coffee for Ian. "Come along Greta, you're drooling all over Ian."

"It's alright Albert. Greta is exactly what I need right now. Actually, what I really need is to get back to work. Is Ben still outside? I need to get with him about opening a few of the cottages for the season for the people coming up next week."

After talking with Ben, Ian returned to his office and made copies of the videos and the list of residents for Detective Townsend. He made a second copy of both and e-mailed them to Elizabeth.

While Ian spent the rest of the afternoon catching up on his work, Elizabeth worked on a plan to maximize publicity for the murder and drafted some proposed postings to Crime Spartans. She started by finding whatever she could about Beulah Crest and its owners and residents. As Elizabeth worked through the list from Ian to look for information about the people on it, she was amazed at the interesting mix of people who lived either full time or seasonally at the park.

Nothing that Elizabeth found on the Web pointed to a suspect, but that didn't surprise her. What did surprise her was how quickly the local media picked up on the story. She would include a link to the TV report in the initial posting.

Elizabeth had never actually posted information about a crime or actively posted anything to help solve a crime, but as the site administrator she reviewed all postings made on the site. She had developed an understanding what made a successful posting that would compel Crime Spartan visitors to engage in the discussion.

By the time Ian arrived at her apartment, Elizabeth had drafted the initial posting. She held off on publishing anything to the Web until she could review her plan with Ian. She also forwarded everything she found and her proposed posting to Roscoe, Megan and Connor to get their input.

While Elizabeth was reviewing the draft of the posting with Ian, her computer signaled that she had a call on Skype. It was from Megan. She quickly answered. "Hey, Megan, what up?"

Megan could see from the computer camera that Ian was with Elizabeth. "Hi guys, I just read through what you sent and had an idea. But first, how are you doing Ian? This is pretty close to home."

"A bit shaken up," Ian answered. "At least we're doing something, and that helps. I don't have a lot of faith in our local sheriff. So, what's your idea?" Ian knew that Megan was a wiz at getting active participation on Crime Spartans and on other sites.

"A simple idea, but I need Elizabeth to help set it up."

"You've piqued my interest," Elizabeth commented.

"What if we do a graphic, rather than a text interface for this? Post a map of the park, or even a map of the county that includes the park map. Each trailer..."

Ian interrupted. "We call them cottages."

"Ok, each cottage then. Anyway, each cottage is a hot spot on the map that on-line users can click to provide information about the resident. We can start by putting the names of each resident on their cottage. Users can add relevant information or just gossip. If information comes from elsewhere in the county, we place links to that info on the county map in the appropriate location. The county jail, for example, if someone is being held in custody or the Dairy King, if something related to the murder happens there. What do you think, Elizabeth? Could we do it?"

"I think so, but it'll take time. I'd want to get with a graphic design guy, and if we want to make this interactive, we need to write some code to make it work. We can tell the site users that we're piloting something new until we get all the bugs sorted. What do you think Ian?"

"I like the idea, but my name will be on the map. This is really putting Crime Spartans close to home. We'd also need to include Nigel and Spencer. Probably place the three of us in the Mouse House, where the park office and my apartment is located. The graphic interface could take our site to a new level, but I'm not sure I'm ready for the personal impact to me."

Elizabeth could see that Ian had mixed thoughts, but since she was excited about the map page, she pushed a little harder. "How about if I pull together a few proposed pages incorporating the park map? Nothing goes live until and unless we all agree. We'll need to include Roscoe and Conner in the decision. That will give you some time to think about whether you want to try this approach here, or perhaps wait until later and use it elsewhere."

"I'm OK with that," Ian answered. "I just need some time to take all of this in. Right now, I just want to turn the computer off, have a beer, and think of nothing."

Megan signed off and then Elizabeth opened two beers. She and Ian walked out onto her deck. Rather than sitting in the red folding chairs they usually occupied when Ian visited, they sat close together on the swing and watched the sunset. They didn't say much as they got comfortable, but both soon knew that Ian would spend the night at Elizabeth's apartment.

While Ian and Elizabeth were planning how to use Crime Spartans for the case, the traditional investigation activities progressed back at the park and elsewhere in Benzie County.

Sheriff Van Dyke left the park and drove around the county with a deputy to the different migrant camps and apartments looking for suspects. It was still early in the season, with only asparagus being harvested, so most of the workers were not yet in the fields. Most were getting settled into their accommodations for the summer. By the end of the afternoon, the sheriff identified three migrant workers who didn't have an alibi for the time of the murder and took them into custody for questioning.

At Beulah Crest, Nick Townsend supervised the more appropriate aspects of the investigation. Shortly after Elsie was taken away in an ambulance, he greeted the medical examiner who arrived in his new Ford Mustang. "Good to see you, Dr. Turner. You got here quicker than I expected. I hope you don't plan to take the body down to the morgue in that car."

Charlie Turner laughed as he got his bag out of the car and then shook hands with Nick, who he had known for years. "No need to worry, Nick, the meat wagon is on its way. Sorry it took a while to get here. I was down in Manistee helping out on another case when I got your call. So, what have we got?"

While the medical examiner put on his jumpsuit, booties, and gloves, Nick updated him with some information about the case. Nick knew that Charlie Turner preferred not to hear anything more than the basic background until after he completed his initial examination. "Babs Tucker, a friend of the resident of this cottage, who lives a few doors away, was found dead on the patio at noon today. As far as I can tell, the person who found the body and the dog that alerted her were the only ones to disturb the crime scene."

"OK, let's go see what we have," the medical examiner commented, as they approached the body. As they got close, he stopped and held up his hand. "Nick, please step back a bit while I do my thing."

After a few minutes, Dr. Turner invited Nick to approach the body. "Looks like she was stuck from behind with one strong blow, probably a hammer. I'd say she died within a few minutes. No defensive wounds, that I can see, but I'll know more when I get her on the table. If I'm right, she either knew her assailant, or they struck her from behind by surprise."

"Do you have an estimated time of death?"

"Between 10:00am and 11:30am, would be my best guess. I can be more precise after I do some more tests."

Nick and Dr. Turner were just stepping off the deck when the state police forensics team arrived from Cadillac. They began taking photographs and collecting evidence such as fingerprints and DNA. When they finished on the deck, Nick asked them to check inside Elsie's cottage and also inside the cottage belonging to Babs.

After Nick got the forensics officers started, he saw Dr. Turner off. The medical examiner invited Nick to observe the autopsy, but Nick declined. He wanted to get as much done as possible before the sheriff started to make wholesale arrests of migrant workers. Because of the case in Manistee, Dr. Turner wouldn't be able to do the autopsy until the morning. He promised to call with the results as soon as he finished.

As he watched the Mustang speed off, Nick remembered the park residents who were asked to stay at the Cold Creek until things settled down at the park. He told Spencer to call Nigel and tell them they could return to their homes.

The first to arrive back at the park was Bonnie Campbell. Nick Townsend was walking past her cottage as she approached in her rusted out 1987 Chevy Monte Carlo. Bonnie got out of her car and walked up to Nick and introduced herself. "You must be Nick Townsend, the police detective. You look just like your

son, David. I had him in my English class a few years ago. How's
he doing up at U of M?"

Before Nick answered, he took in the interesting character
that approached. He had to keep himself from laughing as an
old cliché came to mind, "Mutton dressed as lamb." Bonnie
appeared to be about 65 trying to look 30. She still had a trim
figure, augmented with rather large breast implants highlighted
by a tight short dress. Unfortunately, her face, with makeup,
lipstick, and eye shadow liberally applied, couldn't hide the fact
that she was well past her prime. Bonnie's "look" was made
complete by her bright red hair styled in a 1960s beehive, large
gold hoop earrings, countless rings and bracelets, and 4-inch
spiked heels.

"Yes, I'm Detective Townsend. You must be the Mrs.
Campbell who inspired my son to major in English. He finished
last year and is now in graduate school in California. I'm glad
we finally got a chance to meet." The two shook hands and after
Nick mentioned that he had a few questions, Bonnie invited him
in for a cup of coffee.

While Bonnie prepared the coffee and a plate of cheese
and crackers, they talked local small talk. She mentioned the
letters to the editor in the paper about the decline in the village's
maintenance of its beach, parks, and roads and he said something about the new microbrewery in town. While they chatted
amiably, Nick looked around the inside of the cottage. In contrast
to its owner, the home was tastefully furnished with expensive
Scandinavian furniture. Everything was neat and simple, with
no clutter in sight. He was thinking about the contrast between

the person and the house when Bonnie asked, "How about if we sit on my deck? I don't like to smoke in the house." As soon as they settled outside, Bonnie lit a cigarette and continued to have one lit until she saw her guest off.

"So, what can I tell you," Bonnie asked in her raspy voice, as she poured the coffee.

Nick started with his questions. "Were you at the party at the Cold Creek?"

"Yes, I got there a few minutes before noon."

"So, you left home just before the party?"

"No, I left about 10 o'clock. I had a few errands to run. I went over to Mary Lou's farm out on Cinder Road to pick up some eggs and then over to the charity shop in Benzonia to drop off a few things. Let's see… Then I went to the post office in Beulah to mail a package and then to Five Corners to get a little gift for Max. That dammed place has a new name now, but you know what store I mean."

While Bonnie was rattling on about her morning, Nick was trying to come to grips with the woman sitting across the table. He took notes as she talked. He noticed that her manner, voice and accent changed when they walked out onto the deck. "I know what store you mean, Bonnie. Can I call you Bonnie?"

"Of course, you can." Nick was trying to put his finger on what it was about Bonnie that disturbed him as she continued. "I got Max a tie clip with a Petoskey stone. He wears a tie almost every day, even in the summer. Anyway, after they wrapped the gift, I walked over to the Cold Creek. Almost everyone who we expected was there."

Nick continued writing notes and then stopped abruptly. He had to find out what was going on with this woman. "Bonnie, I've got a strange question. I hope it doesn't upset you."

"Detective, I was a high school teacher for over thirty five years. I don't upset easily. Fire away."

Nick paused a minute, deciding how to frame his question. He finally decided a direct approach was best with this woman. "Bonnie, it's like I'm talking to two different women. Inside your home, you had a different accent, different voice, and you seemed to handle yourself differently."

Before she answered, Bonnie placed her hand on top of Nick's hand. "Sorry Detective, it's my fault. Most people only see one of me. I automatically become the other Bonnie when walk into my house. I should have kept her quiet so as not to confuse you."

Nick was wondering if Bonnie was making a move to seduce him. Even with all that makeup, there was something seductive about this Bonnie. He gently pulled his hand back before continuing. "Hold on a minute. You've got me thinking of old Bette Davis and Joan Crawford movies with split personalities and axe murderers."

"Nothing as sinister as that, I can assure you," she answered as she rubbed her ankle against his. "The woman you met inside is the schoolteacher who grew up in Greenwich, Connecticut, who majored in English literature at Wellesley. That was me until I moved to Michigan, the year before I started teaching at Frankfort High School."

Before digging further, Nick discreetly moved his ankle away from Bonnie's. "So, you know about each other? Your personalities, I mean."

"Of course, we do. She used to take over when we were in the classroom. Now that I'm retired, she only takes over when I'm at home. If you had shown up a few minutes later, you would have found me dressed casually, like I was going to a yacht club luncheon, with very little makeup or jewelry, and a without this awesome wig."

"So, are there just the two of you?"

"Yes. Any more would be confusing, don't you think?"

"Two is confusing to me, but it appears you know how to handle two Bonnies."

"It took a few years with a psychiatrist up in Traverse City before I could understand what was going on and how to live two lives at once, but now it seems natural. Trailer Trash Bonnie, that's me, came out while spending the summer with my grandparents at their place up at Torch Lake. It was just after I finished at Wellesley."

"Did your grandparents abuse you?"

No, nothing as gruesome as that. I fell in love with Bud. Actually, it was Wellesley Bonnie. That's what I call her. She initially fell for Bud, but being who she is, she didn't know how to act to keep him. So, I came along to help her. She didn't have a clue of how to deal with a good old boy who lived to hunt, fish, drink and chase women."

"How did you family react to the new personality?"

"They just thought I was being rebellious, and at that point, I hadn't sorted out what was going on. When I moved in with Bud and announced our engagement, my parents and the rest of the family disowned me. I haven't talked to any of them since. The shrink thinks the break with them was a factor in making this personality the more dominant one."

"So, how did things work out with this Bud?"

"Bud Campbell was his name, if you want to check. His name was actually Bud, not something like William or Robert. It was on his birth certificate and our marriage license. Anyway, we were happily married for almost 30 years. He never chased after other women once he had us."

"Us?"

"Wellesley Bonnie and me. I was in charge most of the time, but she popped up now and again to give Bud a little variety. She also went to work and brought home a stable salary and insurance. That insurance paid for my shrink and for Bud's cancer care. Bud never held onto a job more than a few months at a time, so it was good that we had the teaching job."

Nick was fascinated by Bonnie and he could have listened to her talk all day, but he had a case to settle. So, he returned to asking her more relevant questions. "Bonnie, have you got any idea who might want to hurt or kill Babs?"

"No, I don't. Everyone in the park knew Babs and respected her. She helped just about all of us at one time or the other. When I sold our place after Bud died and bought this place, she helped me move in."

"What about Elsie? They found Babs on Elsie's deck?"

"Elsie wouldn't do it. They were like sisters. I don't know what Elsie will do for a bridge partner without Babs."

"No Bonnie, I was wondering if Elsie had any enemies? The murder took place on her deck and from a distance, they look somewhat alike?"

"I see what you mean. Now Elsie is a different story. I don't know of anyone who dislikes her, but I know a few who don't appreciate her tendency to gossip. Reverend Parker doesn't talk with Elsie much. A bit judgmental is that one. A curt hello is about all Elsie gets from her. Not me though. When Elsie starts with 'I'm not one to gossip, but..', I'm all ears. There's usually something juicy in what comes next."

"Anyone else you can think of?"

"I can't imagine him doing anything, but Albert Pankhurst doesn't like it when Elsie lectures him about not keeping Greta on a leash. No one else seems to mind Greta. She's more like the Beulah Crest family dog. We all look after her."

"Anything else?"

That's about it. The rest of us find Elsie amusing and somewhat sad at the same time. I can't imagine that anyone would want to kill her."

Nick was ready to move onto other witnesses when Bonnie mentioned that she had a date who would be arriving soon. He was glad to get away from this woman, who was erotic, in her own bizarre way. As he wrote some final notes while approaching the next cottage, he couldn't decide whether or not Bonnie Campbell was a likely suspect. He'd have to check with the places she visited this morning.

The cottage next door to Bonnie's belonged to Herb and Dorothy Cooper, the retired vets from Cincinnati. As Nick climbed the steps onto the Cooper's deck, he noticed someone on a new Harley-Davidson motorcycle pull into Bonnie's drive.

Before he knocked, Dorothy came from the back of the cottage, accompanied by a golden retriever. "You must be with the police." She shook hands with Nick in a very businesslike manner. "I'm Dorothy Cooper, but please, call me Dot."

"Yes, I'm Detective Nick Townsend, with the Benzie County Sheriff's office. I'd like to ask you a few questions, if I may."

Dot was the opposite of Bonnie. She wore a pair of faded jeans and a checked red and white blouse and flat sandals. She wore no makeup and her hair was cut short. She wasn't unattractive. She just wasn't out to impress anyone.

"Fire away. Anything we can do to help." She motioned for Nick to have a seat at the big round table on her deck. Just as they were sitting down, Herb Cooper came out of the cottage carrying a tray with three glasses of iced tea and a bowl of potato chips. Herb was wearing a pair of faded jeans and a white Ohio State polo shirt. It looked like he had been fit at one time, but as he sat the tray down, it was obvious that he was in pain.

Nick helped with the tray and offered to help Herb with his chair. Herb declined the offer, joking about his health. "I must look worse than I feel, Detective. Don't worry, I just took something. I should be OK in a few minutes."

After everyone sat down, Nick started with the questions. He didn't like the look of Herb, but since Dot didn't seem to be alarmed, he continued. In his usual manner, he started with small talk. "You're from Ohio, aren't you? Are you here for the summer, or are you here all year?"

Herb answered, while Dot fussed with the dog who appeared to have a thistle stuck on her right rear leg. "We meant this to be a summer place for our retirement, but some bad investments pretty much cleaned us out. We've both got some health issues, so, we sold the practice and the house in Cincinnati and moved up here. We were veterinarians. Now we live modestly up here on social security and a small annuity."

Nick wasn't surprised at the detail provided by Herb. Some people wouldn't tell you anything while others would give their life story, given the chance. Nick decided to get more focused with his questions to move things along. "When did you leave for the birthday lunch?"

"We must have left at 11:30 or so. Dot wanted to stop in at the library, and I needed to pick something up at the auto parts store. Is that about right, Dot?"

"Right at 11:30," Dot answered. "The news came on the car radio as we pulled out."

Nick asked, "Did you see anything suspicious this morning here at the park? Any strangers around?"

"Not that I can think of," Herb answered. "Did you see anything, Dot? You're better at noticing what's going on around here than me."

"Hold on a minute while I get this off of Della." Dot paused for a minute as she took a small pair of scissors from her pocket and clipped the fur around the thistle on the dog. "There you go old girl." She took a sip of tea and then continued. "Greta, that's Albert's dog, was barking over by Elsie's cottage. Greta roams around the park pretty freely and gets along with everyone. Della and Greta are friends. Anyway, it's the first time I've ever heard Greta bark. Maybe we should have gone over to see what upset her."

Nick then asked if they knew anyone who might want to hurt Elsie or Babs.

Herb answered first. "We've only been here a year, so we don't know everyone that well. Babs was a saint from all accounts and was good friends with Elsie. She would sometimes bring a stray cat or wounded bird over for me or Dot to look at. We don't practice anymore, but we still have our medical kits."

"What about Elsie?" Nick asked.

Dot answered. "There's an interesting one. Elsie's a bit of a gossip, to put it mildly. We learned everything we would want to know about our neighbors from her when we moved in, and quite a bit more. If there are any secrets in the park, Elsie is the one who knows them."

Herb interrupted. "We knew her husband, Daniel, years ago. He sold medical equipment."

Dot cut in. "Was Big Dan Taylor her husband, Herb?"

"The very one. One day, a few months ago, Elsie was talking about him. How's that for a coincidence?" That guy could sell ice cubes to Eskimos. Remember Dot, he sold us that CT scanner and the MRI."

"The payments nearly bankrupted us, Detective. That was over 10 years ago. We finally sold the equipment 2 years later at a big loss."

When Herb paused to take a sip of tea, Dot furnished more details. "We've gone from one financial mishap to another our whole lives, Haven't we Herb?" Herb nodded in agreement before she continued. "That's why we've had to retire in what amounts to a trailer park. I'm not complaining though. We enjoyed our work and as trailer parks go, this is about as nice as it gets."

Nick didn't like coincidences, but he wasn't sure if there was any motive for the Coopers. He wanted to learn more about Elsie. "Do you think any of the secrets Elsie knows could be dark enough to provide a motive for murder?"

Dot answered. "I can't really say. The gossip includes negative things like who's sleeping with whom or who's in debt over their head, but then she shares nice things, like when Max won $1000 in the lottery or when Della here won a prize at a dog show."

Dot turned her attention back to Della when Herb interrupted. "In response to your question, I don't know if Elsie keeps anything secret. She seems to share whatever she hears or sees around the park. Nothing is a secret once Elsie gets wind of it. I wonder what dirt she has on us. Say Dot, do you remember the parking ticket you got up in Traverse City last month? I'll bet she's got everyone in the park talking about you."

Dot laughed as she patted Della. "It's a good thing she missed Max's party. I'm sure she would have noticed you flirting with Cora, the waitress."

Nick listened while the couple bantered back and forth as he wrote a few notes. After he finished, he quickly excused himself and headed back to the crime scene to see if the forensics lab folks had found anything. It was getting late, and he wanted to head down to the hospital in Frankfort to get a statement from Elsie Taylor.

The forensics people found nothing new at the two cottages or the surrounding area. They took several fingerprint and DNA samples that would be processed later and countless photographs, but they found nothing that might provide a breakthrough. Nick instructed the deputies to remove crime scene tape around Elsie's cottage. Heavy thunderstorms were predicted overnight, so there was no reason to protect the area.

Nick was about to leave when Reverend Parker drove up with Elsie in her car. Although Nick wasn't religious, he had met the minister through his wife, Maggie, who was an active member of the congregation that Hortense Parker led before she retired. He had spoken to the minister a few times when Maggie dragged him to church events. He always thought Reverend Parker was a bit too severe to be a servant of god, but she had a reputation for leading a well-organized and active congregation.

Nick greeted them as they got out of the car. "Reverend Parker, it's good to see you again. And how are you feeling, Mrs. Taylor?"

Elise answered first. "Oh, I'm fine Detective. I don't know what came over me. They poked and prodded me down at the hospital and told me it was the shock of what happened and of losing a close friend. They gave me something to calm my nerves and let me rest for a while. I drifted off and when I woke up, Hortense was sitting in the chair next to my bed."

As they walked up onto Elsie's deck and approached the door to the cottage, the minister was finally able to get a word in. "Hello Detective Townsend. Let's get Elsie into bed so she can rest."

Before Nick could respond, Elsie interrupted. "Nonsense, Hortense. I've been sleeping all afternoon. Now tell me Detective, what's going on? Who killed Babs? Come on in and I'll make some coffee." Hortense was about to disagree but changed her mind when she saw the determination in Elsie's eyes.

Nick was glad of the opportunity to question Elsie and was thankful he didn't need to take the time to drive down to the hospital in Frankfort to see her. "Thank you, Mrs. Taylor. I'd love a cup." He then turned to the minister. "Reverend Parker, I wonder if you could give us some privacy, please. I'll stop by your cottage when I get the chance and talk to you and Mr. Parker."

Hortense didn't like the idea that she was being dismissed so quickly, so she asked, "Elsie, are you sure you're OK? I'll stay if you need me."

"I'll be fine Hortense. Go home and make dinner for Derek. I sure he's wondering what's going on."

After the minister left, Elsie made coffee as she rambled on. Nick didn't interrupt. He often learned a lot by letting people just talk. "Wasn't that nice of Hortense to come down and pick me up? I don't even belong to her church. I go to Trinity Lutheran, down in Frankfort. They're so nice down there. Of course, Babs would have been down in a flash to check on me, but she's gone, isn't she?" Elsie looked at the detective with hopeful eyes as she set out a dish of cookies while thinking, or hoping, that maybe it was all a dream.

"I'm afraid she is, Mrs. Taylor."

"Elsie, please, Detective. I know. I know. Babs really is dead." She took two mugs from the cupboard and poured the coffee before she continued. "So, what can I tell you. I really don't have a clue who could do this."

"Just walk me through your morning Elsie. What did you do? Who did you talk to?"

"It was a normal morning, Detective. I should have been at the hospice down in Manistee, but my car is in the shop getting a new muffler. I puttered around the house and then, after breakfast and doing some laundry, I went for a walk down to the lake."

"When did you leave?"

"Oh, it must have been around 10 o'clock. I put some seed in my bird feeders and then headed down the hill. I stopped and chatted with Arthur for a while and gave him a leftover sandwich. It was such a beautiful morning, I was just daydreaming and enjoying the sun. If only I.."

Nick interrupted. "There was nothing you could have done, Elsie." He was afraid she might become emotional again, so he paused and patted her hand. After she settled and appeared to be ok, he continued with a question. "Elsie, who's Arthur. Does he live in the park?"

Elsie laughed. "I'm sorry, Detective. Arthur is a wild fox. I give him scraps of food and he appears to listen to me ramble on. I know he doesn't care what I have to say and is just waiting for the off chance I have something else for him to eat, but I enjoy sharing my thoughts with him. Much cheaper than a psychiatrist."

"Did you walk into town or did you head the other way toward the boat ramp?"

Elsie refilled the coffee mugs before continuing. "Neither. When I got down to the bottom of the hill, I noticed it was nearly 11:30. I must have been daydreaming and talking to Arthur a long time. Anyway, I picked some lilacs and headed back up the hill. I was going to ride over to the Cold Creek with Babs. I didn't talk to or see anyone on the way down, on the way back, or after I found Babs on my patio. That was a little before noon."

"Elsie, can you think of anyone who might want to hurt you or Babs?"

"I can't imagine why anyone would want to hurt Babs. She was always helping people. A saint if ever there was one. As for me, I'm just a silly old gossip who likes to play bridge." Elsie paused to take a sip of coffee before murmuring something to herself.

"Are you OK, Elsie? Did you think of something?"

"Never mind me, I had a random thought that's just nonsense."

Nick noticed that Elsie was getting agitated and feared that she might have another panic attack, but he pressed her anyway. "Why don't you share what you're thinking with me? It might lead to something that could help, and if not, maybe I can put your mind at ease."

"Oh, it's silly. It wasn't something that happened today, but on Monday over at the bridge club down in Elberta. We get about 10 tables on Mondays, you see. Dot and Herb Cooper, who are very skilled players, also play every week."

"So, what happened?"

"Babs and I were partners and Herb and Dot were at our table for the first round. Herb bid four spades in the first hand and only made three. He realized he would not make his contract after we played the second card and threw his cards down on the table and shouted loudly at Babs about her unorthodox manner of play. Someone at the next table called the director and she gave Herb a warning to behave."

"Was that behavior unusual for Herb, or for that matter, for others at the club? I've never played bridge, so I wouldn't know how people are expected to behave. I always assumed it was a polite game with a strict etiquette for its players."

"Bridge definitely has strict rules of how players should behave when they play the game and almost all of the people at the club follow them. Most of the members are quite nice, but I must say, there are a few who are ill-tempered, like Herb. Occasionally they are downright nasty."

"So, did anything else happen on Monday?"

Babs and I both knew of Herb's temper, so we let it go and continued to play. Then, on the next hand, I bid seven hearts and we made the contract. Herb called the director this time and accused us of cheating. After a heated discussion, the director rejected Herb's complaint and warned him that another such outburst would lead to his expulsion from the game."

"Did anything else happen?"

"No, Herb behaved after that. Dot gave him one of his pills and he settled down. He did have a little tantrum when the final scores for the day were announced though."

"Oh?"

Elsie smiled, for the first time since she started talking. "You see, Babs and I finished the day with the highest score in the room, while Dot and Herb came in fourth."

Nick let Elsie ramble for a while longer hoping that she might share something significant, but no noteworthy clues were uncovered. The rumors of Bonnie's latest affair were shared, along with friendly gossip about most of the people in the park.

After a final cup of coffee with Elsie, Nick decided to call it a day at the park. Tomorrow, he could question the other residents. Meanwhile, he wanted to stop back at the office and find out what the sheriff did that could mess up the investigation.

* * *

It's just as I predicted. I wish I could read lips. Thanks to these binoculars, I can see Elsie and that cop through her kitchen window. I wonder what they're saying.

No matter, I'll stop by Elsie's cottage tomorrow and she'll tell me everything she told the detective and everything he told her. With Babs gone, she'll be looking for a friend she can trust. Now what about Bonnie?

When the killer's thoughts shifted to Bonnie, a warm feeling, and then a calmness, took hold. Something similar happened earlier in the day when plans were finalized for taking care of Elsie, but the feeling was stronger now. It was like there was a voice talking inside the killer's mind.

"Think carefully about how to take care of Bonnie. You did well this morning, but you need to be more careful going forward. Killing the wrong person, especially someone as nice as Babs, is not what you want to do. There's lot to be done if you are going to be successful with Bonnie, isn't there?" The voice was calm and confident.

The killer responded, not by speaking, but with thoughts. *I know, I know. Bonnie is quite unpredictable, isn't she? Since she retired, she hasn't developed a set routine. That tramp is either chasing men or shopping in charity shops for the ridiculous outfits she wears.*

"What about the Mouse House? Doesn't Bonnie go up there almost every afternoon for a cup of coffee? You know she has her eye on Ian."

You're right. She goes up there around 4 o'clock, almost every day. A large coffee with cream and three sugars. I wonder if I could put something in her coffee when she isn't looking.

"Now think this through. You don't want her to die right there in the Mouse House while you're there. You'd immediately become a suspect, along with anyone else who happens to be there at the same time. You'll have to find a poison that acts slowly. It'd be better if she died in her cottage at night, or better yet while in bed with one of her men."

I'll do some research and find something. I know of several poisonous plants that grow in the area. The question is, which one would be best?

CHAPTER 5
Not Really the Calm Before the Storm

A light shower began as Nick left the park and continued through the night. It grew into thundershowers, washing away any evidence that might have been missed at the crime scene by the forensics team. Shortly after dawn, the sky cleared and Wednesday promised to be a bright, but cooler, Northern Michigan spring day.

For the first time in years, Elsie slept in past 9 o'clock. She had trouble falling asleep last night, so she stayed up late reading through old bridge magazines and reviewing hands played by expert players at tournaments. Finally, at 3am, she had two glasses of sherry and fell asleep.

As she was making coffee, she noticed the lilacs on the kitchen table that she picked yesterday. *Perhaps they are bad luck*, she thought, as she put some bread in the toaster. After opening a jar of cherry jam that Babs had made last year, Elsie took the flowers out of the vase and threw them in the trash. As she poured her coffee, she spoke out loud. "Babs, I'll never bring lilacs into the house again. I promise." No one answered.

While Elsie was getting her day started, Nick's day was getting off to a hectic start. He didn't get a chance to stop in at the sheriff's office last night like he'd planned because he got called to a domestic disturbance over in Thompsonville that escalated into a hostage negotiation. By the time the hostage was released, it was nearly midnight. When Nick arrived at the station, he found the place in a state of chaos. The sheriff was trying to question three migrant farm workers he'd taken into custody. All three refused to say anything until the Spanish-speaking lawyer who provided free legal support to the migrant community arrived. The questioning would have been for nothing anyway since two of the suspects didn't speak English and a there wasn't a translator present.

There were also reporters from the local newspapers and television stations, a group of civil rights activists from Grand Rapids, and a diverse group of priests and ministers from around Benzie, Manistee, and Grand Traverse counties. The families of the three men who were being detained were also there, along with about 30 other migrant farm workers. Benzie County had never had such a crowd gather to protest anything before.

The crowds partially resulted from a social media campaign that was launched after the sheriff announced yesterday that he had taken three migrant farm workers into custody for questioning. Katie Wolfe, the sister of part-time park resident Xander Wolfe, who held strong feeling about discrimination and human rights, got the ball rolling by forwarding links for the related news stories to some friends who were social media activists.

Nothing productive was happening at the sheriff's office. Questioning of the three suspects wouldn't begin until the translator and lawyer arrived. The sheriff did nothing but pace back and forth in his office and complain about the delays impacting his case. When Nick tried to talk sense to him, all he could get were comments like, "I know those people can speak English. They only pretend not to when it suits their purpose."

Nick and the other deputies were concerned that the crowd might turn violent, but their concerns turned out to be unfounded. At first the people in front of the sheriff's office were disorganized, milling about and asking each other if anyone was in charge. Realizing there was no leader of the group, Reverend Parker stood on the courthouse steps and called out to the crowd. "Everyone, please, may I have your attention?" She repeated her request several times. Father Dominguez, the Catholic priest from Manistee stood beside her on the top step and repeated her request in Spanish.

Relieved that someone was taking charge, the crowd slowly turned to listen to Hortense Parker.

Once the crowd settled, Hortense continued. "I'm Reverend Hortense Parker and this is Father Dominguez. I hoped we could start with a prayer." The priest continued to translate.

The crowd fell silent and bowed their heads.

"Lord, help us to stand firm for justice when we see injustice, but also give us the strength to do so peacefully. Lord, also provide guidance and enlightenment to the members of our criminal justice system who are charged with making our community safe. Let us all join hands as we ask for the Lord's blessing."

After the priest translated, Reverend Parker asked the clergy members and the leaders of the groups present to join her in an impromptu meeting on the lawn and then asked the crowd to be patient.

Nick watched and understood his wife's opinion that Reverend Parker was very good at organizing. Within an hour, the crowd broke into smaller groups, each with specific tasks. One group shopped for suppliers and made signs for a protest march. Another group wrote a one-page flyer and had copies made at the local print shop. After the flyers were printed, that group broke up into smaller groups to distribute them in the downtown areas of Beulah, Benzonia, and Frankfort. Another group took charge of organizing food and drink for the demonstrators.

Once the groups set off to do their assigned tasks, Reverend Parker approached Nick. "Don't worry Detective. There won't be any trouble. In my younger days, I used to organize protests all the time. We'll make headlines, but we won't do anything illegal or interfere with the sheriff's office."

"So, why are you doing this, if you don't intend to stop the questioning of these three suspects?" Nick asked.

"We're here to put a spotlight on the sheriff's office and in particular on the sheriff. As long as we're here, the press will be here and any injustice that occurs will in the news and on the Web. If Van Dyke steps over the line, the publicity will ensure he won't get re-elected this fall and the property tax initiative for increased funding for his department will go down in flames."

"So, you really think this will help?"

"I do, Detective. Think of it this way. We'll keep the sheriff occupied and out of your way so you can focus on finding whoever really did this. You know he doesn't have any skills in solving crimes."

Nick agreed with Reverend Parker but could not publicly say so. "I won't comment on what you just said, Reverend, but thank you for keeping the crowd peaceful and organized. Meanwhile, while I've got you here, do you mind answering a few questions?"

"Not at all, Detective. As you can see, things are running smoothly. Fire away."

"Ok, for starters, can you tell me about how you spent yesterday morning?"

"Let's see. Derek and I had breakfast around 7:30 and he headed to work a little after 8:30. He only works one or two days a week, at that new dental clinic next to the Dollar Store. My pension is pretty small, and Derek never managed to save much over the years, so the extra income comes in handy."

"What did you do after your husband left for work?"

"I caught up on some e-mails, fussed around the house for a bit, and then walked into town for the birthday lunch for Max. I didn't see anything unusual or any strangers about. I certainly didn't see any migrant workers lurking in the forest or in the park."

"Did you walk into town with anyone else?"

"No, I'm a bird watcher. If I see anything unusual, I stop and make notes in my bird book. I'd rather do my bird watching alone so I can take my time. Oh, did you see the bald eagle that's taken up residence near the end of Lake Street?"

'I saw one recently flying over the lake. Maybe that's him. Anyway, have you seen any strangers in the park recently, or anything unusual."

"Nothing unusual," Detective. But yes, there have been strangers. Bonnie Campbell was picked up at her place by a strange man a few days ago and by another odd-looking character last week. It seems like you never see her with the same man more than once or twice."

"Could you describe these men? At least the recent ones."

"Not really. I didn't get a close look. One drove a big motorcycle and the other drove an old rusted out pickup. A black Chevy, I think."

"Did you see either of them yesterday?"

"No, I don't think so. Bonnie never invites men into her cottage, so one of them wouldn't have spent the night there. They usually pick her up. She goes off with them for a few hours or sometimes for the night. She was at Max's lunch yesterday."

"Did you see her as you walked into town?"

"No, she drove into town in her old Monte Carlo. She could never walk that far in those spiked heels she wears."

Nick and Reverend Parker were interrupted when the protester in charge of food came over to ask whether they should find something to eat for the vegan protestors. After they resolved the food issue, Nick continued. "Reverend, one last question. Do you have any idea who might want to kill Babs or Elsie?"

"Not a clue Detective. Babs was loved and respected be everyone who knew her, and Elsie is just a retired librarian who likes to gossip. Now, if you have any further questions, I'll be home later this afternoon. I still have a few things to do here. Once I get this circus organized, I'll be turning it over to Father Dominguez to run. My husband, Derek, will be home most of the day if you want to ask him anything, but I expect he has nothing to add to what I've told you."

As Nick walked away from Reverend Parker, he had mixed feeling about her. She was passionate about what she was working on and very well organized, but she didn't seem to have the warmth and approachable personality he would expect a minister to have. Also, she seemed to be willing to gossip, at least about Bonnie Campbell.

While Nick was at the station, being distracted by the chaos there, residents of Beulah Crest were starting their day and coming to terms with what had happened to Babs. When Ian walked into the Mouse House to start his workday, he greeted Nigel, Spencer, and Albert who were in the coffee shop. "Good morning all, any news from the sheriff?"

Spencer answered. "Looks like you had a late night. Are you just getting home? Come in and have some coffee. We'll fill you in."

Ian came in and Albert poured him a coffee. As soon as Ian sat down, Greta padded over and put a paw on his lap and barked, playfully. Albert laughed before asking, "Ian, what's up? You're getting the paw and bark treatment from Greta. That usually means good news."

Ian blushed and smiled. "I'm in love, that's all. I hate the idea of being happy with what happened yesterday, but last night my world changed."

"Anyone we know?" Spencer asked.

"I don't think so. She lives up in Interlochen and goes to NMC, up in Traverse. She's not from around here. I've known her for a few years, but last night we both realized we had stronger feelings for each other." Ian didn't want to give too much detail about Elizabeth. He wasn't sure how Nigel and Spencer would react to the Crime Spartans website if they found out that he and Elizabeth were part owners.

Everyone congratulated Ian and then Nigel asked, "When are we going to meet her?"

"Soon, I hope, but she is pretty busy with school, so I can't say when. Meanwhile, what's going on with the investigation? I thought there would be deputies around the park asking questions. I didn't see anybody."

Spencer answered. "The sheriff's arrested three migrant farm workers and I'm guessing he isn't interested questioning any more of the park residents. Nigel and I don't understand your sheriff, or his department. The idea of an elected head of the police force just seems odd to us. It seems like image would be more important than substance with such a system."

Ian sort of agreed. "I don't know how your systems works over in England, but I agree, our sheriff is odd. His top priority is good publicity so he can get re-elected. I'll give Nick Townsend a call to find out what's going on. He's an honest cop."

"Meanwhile, what should we do?" Nigel asked. Do you think they caught Babs' killer?"

As Ian took his phone out of his pocket he answered. "I think it's highly unlikely they've arrested the killer. Whenever anything happens, he pulls in some migrants. They'll be released in a day or two. The county prosecutor is pretty sharp. She won't take a crime of this nature to court without strong evidence."

Nigel refilled his coffee and everyone else's before asking his question again. "So, that still leaves me at a loss as to what we should do,"

Ian answered. "My guess is that once they force the sheriff to release the migrant workers, Detective Townsend will convince him to station a deputy here in the park until they identify the killer. Until then, I'd suggest we have a private security service provide a guard to patrol the park. I'm not sure how much he could do to prevent anything else from happening, but the residents would probably feel safer."

As they sometimes do, Nigel and Spencer both spoke at the same time, saying the same thing. "Let's do it."

Nigel then asked, "Can you organize that, Ian?"

"Sure, I'll make a few calls. Hopefully, we can get someone here by this evening."

Max Silver walked into the coffee shop carrying his birthday cake from yesterday, with the candles removed. No one had eaten any of the cake. Several of the residents liked to bake and often left snacks on the counter. By the end of the day the cake would be gone, and the dishwasher would be full. Albert would turn it on before he left for the day.

Max chatted with other park residents for quite a while before walking back to his cottage to get some lunch. Greta followed him home, knowing she would receive a treat when they got there. As they approached the cottage, Nick drove up. After he got out of his car, he petted Greta and then turned to Max. "Are you Max Silver? I don't think we've met. I'm Detective Nick Townsend, with the sheriff's office."

Max shook hands with the detective and answered. "Yes, I'm Max Silver. Call me Max. Pleased to meet you detective. Have a seat over there on my deck. I'll bring out some iced tea."

"That sounds great. They say it's supposed to be cooler today, but I think it might be a warm one." Nick sat on a chair by the wicker patio table and played with Greta while he waited. A few minutes later, Max came out with a tray containing two glasses of iced tea, a bowl of nuts, and a treat for Greta. As he set down the tray, he commented, "Since you're here, I'm guessing you're still looking for who killed Babs?"

"The sheriff has some people in custody, but until forensics links them to the crime, I'll continue to investigate." That's as much as Nick would say regarding his belief that the sheriff was barking up the wrong tree with the migrants.

"So, what can I tell you? I assume you're here to ask some questions?"

Nick took a sip of tea, and then started with his usual small talk, "Have you lived here long, Max? I don't recall meeting any Silvers living in the county."

"I've only been here for three years. Before that, I taught political science and history at Interlochen and lived up in

Traverse City. We lived in the same house up there for twenty-seven years. My wife's family, may she rest in peace, was from Traverse, you see. I'm the only Silver in Benzie County as far as I know and possibly the only Jew within miles."

"Why did you move down here from Traverse City?"

Max pointed towards the lake. "Look at that view Detective. A place in Traverse with such a view would cost twice as much. A teacher's pension only goes so far." Max paused and took a sip of iced tea before continuing. "Actually, I found out about the park when one of my former students, Xander Wolfe, told me he was buying a place here. He has a cottage just down the street he uses on weekends. Xander's here now because his sister Katie is visiting from Germany. She was also one of my students.

"How do you like living here, Max? It's much more tame than Traverse City."

"It's close to Interlochen so I can go up there to see plays and concerts and also kibitz with friends. Some neighbors here are nice, others are interesting. Babs was one of the nice ones. As for family, I have a son in Israel, one in Brooklyn, where I grew up, and a son in Denver, of all places. When they take a vacation by the lake, they come and stay with me and I get to play with my grandchildren. I go to Tel-Aviv for a few months every winter to escape the snow and visit family. It's a good life."

Nick finished his tea, not surprised by how much information Max was willing to share, then asked a question related to the case. "Did you know Babs Tucker?"

"Who didn't know Babs? This was a special woman. How many mitzvahs she would do in a day, who could count? Always helping people and always a smile. She also enjoyed playing bridge. She and Elsie played several times a week. What Elsie will do now for a bridge partner; I don't know. I'd volunteer, but she's a much better player than me."

"Can you think of anyone who would want to harm her?"

"Such a person would be meshuggeneh, crazy in the head. I don't know who this could be, do you? How about more tea? I have a pitcher in the fridge."

"That would be great. It really hit the spot." Nick was thinking he got too much sun while out with the protesters this morning.

Max came out with a pitcher of iced tea, a plate of sandwiches, and some napkins. When Greta, saw the sandwiches, she got up from where she was lying on the deck and sat down next to Nick. Her intuition told her that Nick was an easy mark. "Eat something Detective, it looks like you haven't had time for lunch. I picked these up this morning at L'Chayim Deli in Beulah."

Nick didn't want to impose, but he had the feeling Max wouldn't let him leave hungry. "Thank you, Max, I also didn't have time for breakfast." After taking a bite of a curry chicken sandwich on an onion bagel, Nick continued with his questions. "Tell me about yesterday morning, Max. What did you do before heading into town for lunch?"

Max took a bite of a chicken salad sandwich and took a sip of iced tea before answering. "Mornings I work, Detective. I write historical novels. I earn very little from them, but I enjoy doing the research. My current work is about the life of the Fisher brothers and Fisher Body. You've heard of them?"

"Of course. Anyone who grew up in Michigan knows of them. I remember the 'Body by Fisher' stamp on my father's old Oldsmobile." Nick thought of prompting Max for more detail but then decided to just let him ramble on. He had the feeling that Max was a great teacher.

"You don't want to hear about the book, I know. You want to know what I did and maybe saw. I'll tell you. I got up around 8 o'clock, made some eggs and toast for breakfast and coffee and then sat down at my computer until about 11:45am. The spare bedroom is my office. It has a window, but I noticed nothing outside or heard nothing unusual. Just before noon I drove into town, supposedly to meet Xander and Katie for lunch, but I knew there was a surprise birthday party. There are no secrets in the park. I saw nothing unusual as I left the park or while I drove into Beulah."

"Have you seen any strangers in the park or notice anyone act differently?"

"I can't say that I have. It's pretty quiet here until the summer residents and visitors come. Elsie is the one to talk with. She knows everyone in the park. You might also talk to Bonnie Campbell. Every now and again she has an interesting character pick her up for a date. As for me, Detective, I have no alibi, if that's your next question. As I've said, I spent the morning in front of my computer screen."

Reluctantly, Nick left Max, after running out of questions. He could sit and talk with the retired teacher all day, but he had a murderer to find. His next stop was the cottage of Max's former student, Xander Wolfe. As he walked down the street to Xander's cottage, Greta followed. *If only she could talk*, Nick thought to himself.

Nick found Xander, and his sister, Katie, to be as welcoming as Max Silver. They were on their deck when Nick approached. Xander got up and approached Nick. While the men were introducing themselves, Greta ran up onto the deck and nuzzled her head against Katie's waist, hoping for a treat, or at least some affection. She got both.

After Xander introduced Nick to Katie, and after Katie brought another glass from the kitchen, they all settled on the deck. Greta sat next to Katie, an easy mark for treats. This time, Nick was offered lemonade to drink.

Again, Nick started with small talk to get to know the Wolfes. "Mr. Wolfe, Max told me you told him about Beulah Crest when you bought a place here. How did you come across this place?"

"Xander, please, and Katie. We're not formal around here. To answer your question, we both know Nigel and Spencer, the owners of the park. We met them on board The United States 21. Did you hear about the murders on board the ship a few years ago? We were all seated at the same table in the dining room."

"Yes, it was in the news for days," Nick answered. "It must have been a terrible experience."

"It was," Xander replied. I still have nightmares about what happened, and what almost happened to all of us."

"The bishop and judge who were murdered during the crossing sat at our table," Katie added. "On the positive side, all the rest of us at the table became close friends and see each other as often as we can. When Xander was doing his post-doc work at Oxford, he frequently spent weekends at Nigel and Spencer's home in Dorset."

Xander continued. "I bought this place soon after I took the job at Northwestern in Chicago. I'm on the physics faculty there. I come up on weekends in the summer and during breaks during the school year. Katie and other family members and friends use the cottage whenever they get the chance. We both went to Interlochen for high school, so we have quite a few friends in the area."

Nick continued with his standard questions. "Can I ask what each of you did yesterday morning before lunch at the Cold Creek?"

Xander answered. "Katie headed off early to see some friends at Interlochen."

"I took Xander's car," Katie added. "I visited one of my dance instructors and sat in on one of her classes. I can give you her contact information if you're looking for an alibi for me."

"Are you a professional dancer?" Nick asked.

"No. I'm also interested in science, so I went to medical school. I do medical research. Much more work in that line than for dancers, especially once you're over 30."

Katie refilled everyone's glass with lemonade as Nick asked another question. "You two are much younger than most of the people who live here. How do you get along with the neighbors?"

Xander answered. "Katie and I were both home-schooled until we went to Interlochen, where we boarded, so we grew up comfortable with people older than ourselves. It took us years to figure out how to interact with people our own age. I'm the youngest of the tenured faculty in my department at Northwestern and get along well with the older faculty members."

"And I'm the youngest in my lab," Katie added.

Xander continued. "As for the neighbors, I know more of the seasonal people than the full-time residents. I don't come up that often in the winter. Most of the seasonal people aren't here yet. I do know some of the year round residents though. Max, you know about, since he told you about me. He was my favorite teacher at Interlochen. He taught me how to think and ask questions."

"Mine too," Katie added.

Xander continued. "Babs was the mother hen of the park, taking care of everyone, Elsie's a bit of a gossip, but harmless, and Bonnie is a hoot. Her trailer trash act is awesome. She actually went to Wellesley and is from an old Boston family. I didn't realize it at the time, but we met her parents when we were on the ship.

"Don't forget the Parkers," Katie added.

"Yes, the Parkers," Xander continued. "Derek pulled a wisdom tooth last summer that I should have had pulled years ago. Good dentist, but not a happy man. Talks about money, or I should say the lack of it, all the time. Hortense runs the show at that house. Very efficient from what I've seen, but not the warm and friendly person I would want my minister to be, if I were religious."

What did you do yesterday morning?" Nick asked Xander.

"Not much. After Katie left, I worked for an hour or so on a presentation I'll be making at a conference next month and then I walked over to the Mouse House for a cup of coffee. Ian and Albert were there, and Ben was outside planting flowers. I asked Ian about a trail up near Empire that Katie and I plan to hike tomorrow. After two coffees, I walked down the steps to the lake. I saw Elsie talking to the fox we see around here now and then. Elsie calls him Arthur. I waved to her but didn't stop to talk."

"Did you see anyone else?"

"I don't think so. No, wait a minute?" Zander paused and took a sip of lemonade before continuing. "After I left the Mouse House, I thought I saw Elsie on her deck, but it must have been Babs. I was surprised a few minutes later when I saw Elsie feeding the fox. She couldn't have made it to the meadow before me."

"What time did you see someone on Elsie's deck?"

"I'd say a little after 10 o'clock. I continued down the hill and then took my kayak out onto the lake. I leave it down on the shore. I paddled to the other side of the lake and then into town. By the time I got there, it was almost lunchtime, so I went over to the Cold Creek. Katie arrived a short while later."

"Think back about any details of who you saw on Elsie's deck. You may have seen Babs, but you might also have seen her killer."

"It was just a glance, Detective. I saw some movement on Elsie's deck and assumed it was her. I saw the back of a woman about Elsie's height who had grey hair, like Elsie. I couldn't tell you more. If I remember anything later, I'll let you know."

After Nick learned what he could from the Wolfes, he walked over to the Parker's cottage. It was in the least desirable spot in the park, near the front gate, with a deck looking out onto the Frankfort Fighway. If Nick were to guess, this was the least expensive cottage in the park because of its location. Greta followed Nick about halfway to the Parker home, then changed directions and headed back to the Mouse House.

Nick knew Derek by sight from church events, but the two men had never met. When Derek opened the door, he was polite, but formal. He asked to see Nick's badge before inviting him into the cottage. He offered no iced tea or lemonade. After closing the door, Derek commented. "I suppose you have some questions about Babs, Detective."

Nick tried the small talk, but he didn't get much in response. "How long have you lived here in the park, Dr. Parker?"

"About three years," was the response, with no further elaboration.

Nick tried again with a more open question. "How do you like it here?"

"It's inexpensive, and it's close to work, Detective. Now, save the small talk for Hortense and get on with it. I'm meeting my wife for coffee in a few minutes."

"Ok, Dr. Parker. I'll be brief. Tell me about your activities yesterday morning." The detective and the dentist stood in the kitchen as they talked.

"I had breakfast with my wife and then left for the office around 8:30. I only had one patient yesterday morning, at 9 o'clock. I left the clinic an hour or so later and went to the post office and then the hardware store, before driving up to Beulah for Max's lunch at the Cold Creek. I didn't stop back here, so didn't see anything."

"Can you think of anyone who might want to cause harm to Babs or to Elsie?"

"I keep to myself as much as possible, Detective, so I didn't know Babs well and I avoid Elsie, and her gossip. I did some business with her husband years ago that led to a financial disaster, so I give her a wide berth. The money I lost helped pay for her cottage. As for the other residents of this dump, I don't socialize with them much. I went to Max's lunch as a favor to Hortense. Even though she's retired, she still sees it as her duty to minister to these people."

"Can you tell me more about this business venture, Doctor?"

"I can, but I won't. It has nothing to do with Babs. Now, if there isn't anything else, I should be going. I'm meeting my wife."

Nick left, learning no more from the dentist. He made a note in his notebook to dig deeper into the finances of Dr. Parker and Dr. Cooper. The next interview he wanted to conduct was with Nigel Piddlemarsh, the co-owner of the park.

Before walking over to the Mouse House, where he hoped to find Nigel, Nick made a call to Deputy Kathy McGregor to check on her progress. He had asked her to contact the employers of the park residents who Ian had told him were at work yesterday morning. The deputy had worked through most of the list and confirmed alibis from all the employers she had contacted. She still had two more employers to contact. Before hanging up with Kathy, Nick asked about how things were going at the sheriff's office.

"It's settled down a bit," Kathy responded. "Reverend Parker left after lunch and Father Dominguez took over. It's all very organized and calm, but the sheriff is fuming. He can't do anything though. If he tries to break this up and it turns violent, his chances of getting re-elected would evaporate."

"So, he's still trying to question the three migrants?"

"Trying is the key word, Nick. About an hour ago, the legal aid lawyer arrived, accompanied by a high-power criminal defense lawyer from Lansing. Rumor has it the criminal lawyer has offered to represent the defendants for free. He's talking to the three suspects now."

"Ok, Kathy, thanks. I'll come back to the office after I talk to the other owner of the park, the one with the funny name, Piddle something. Meanwhile, finish working that list of the people who were at work. Also, do some digging into the finances of the dentist, Dr. Derek Parker and also the retired veterinarian, Herb Cooper. Also, see what you can find out about the business affairs of Elsie Taylor's late husband. He died a short time before she moved here. I think he sold medical equipment."

"The sheriff will be upset if he finds out what I'm doing, Nick."

"I know, but he's unlikely to notice with that circus that going on outside the station. If he gives you any trouble, let me know. I'll take responsibility for assigning you the work. Meanwhile, any word from forensics or the coroner?"

"Both called and said they would have a report to you by the end of the day, tomorrow. They both said not to expect any surprises though."

"Ok, thanks. I'll see you in a little while."

CHAPTER 6
Poison

B onnie walked over to the Mouse House for a coffee a little later than usual. When she arrived, she found the coffee shop to be quite busy. In addition to everyone who was at Max's birthday lunch, Ian, Albert, Ben, Spencer, and Elsie were there. As Bonnie made her way across the room, someone had already poured a cup for her in her unique Harley-Davidson mug. Bonnie assumed that Albert had filled the cup because he usually did that for her.

Each of the regular coffee shop visitors had their own cup or mug that they kept on a rack near the coffee machine. There were several other mugs on the rack featuring various Michigan tourist sites for guests to use. Everyone knew the mug with the picture of a big motorcycle belonged to Bonnie.

As Bonnie was about to take a sip of coffee, she noticed Detective Nick Townsend enter the room. She smiled at him and waved. He waved back before approaching Nigel and Spencer, who had just finished talking with Elsie. "Mr. Piddlemarsh, we haven't had a chance to talk. Do you have a few minutes?"

"Of course, Detective," Nigel answered. "Let's go out onto the porch. It's a bit quieter out there. Would you like a cup of coffee?"

"No, I'm fine. Everyone has been giving me something to eat or drink all day."

When they got outside, they took seats at a small table at the end of the porch. Greta followed them out, took a drink from bowl at the side of the porch, and then sat down next to the detective. After they got settled, Nigel told the detective, "Call me Nigel please. Now, how can I help?"

Nick was a bit put off by Nigel's accent, which seemed to be more upper class than Spencer's, but he felt nothing else to suggest that Nigel would be unwilling to help. He started with an open statement to see how open Nigel was about his background. "Spencer told me you and he own several parks like this back in England."

"We do Detective. First, let me tell you that nothing like this has ever happened at any of our parks. The worst we ever get is a fight when people have too much to drink. You see, most of our parks have a pub on site."

"Bar fights I understand, Nigel. Go ahead."

"OK. My family owns quite a few houses around England and Wales, each with quite a bit of land. Most of the estates go back hundreds of years. After my father died, I learned that we were nearly bankrupt and at risk of losing everything. The way they regulate land use in the UK means we can't build houses or do anything industrial on the land, but we can build residential parks like this one. Holiday parks, as we call them, are considered recreational use of the land and are therefore exempt from many of the restrictions."

Bonnie Campbell interrupted Nigel and Nick when she walked onto the front porch and stumbled while going down the step. She caught her balance as both men jumped up to help her. "I'm sorry to interrupt, gentlemen. I don't know what's come over me. I feel a bit dizzy."

"Can we help?" Nick offered. "We can walk you back to your cottage, if you'd like."

"No, I'm fine. You two get back to finding out what happened yesterday. Once I eat, I'll feel better. I was stupid enough to drink a few Bloody Marys at the Corner Bar on an empty stomach."

Nick and Nigel watched as Bonnie stumbled toward her cottage. It wasn't far, just across the lawn from the Mouse House. Greta followed her and waited until she went inside before returning to her spot next to Nick.

After they sat down again, Nigel continued. "Spencer came up with the idea for the parks and I used my family connections to get financing for the first one. It was so successful, the cash it generated financed the next park and we just kept repeating the process. Most of the parks are much bigger than Beulah Crest, with about 100 cottages. We call them lodges over there."

"Impressive," Nick commented.

"What's impressive is how Greta has taken a liking to you, Detective. I've heard she's been following you around all afternoon and now she's next to you. I wish she could talk."

"Me to," Nick answered, before asking another question. "Could you walk me through yesterday morning? What did you do, and where did you go?"

"Spencer and I have a house across the lake from here. It's the big yellow one, just outside the village. We left there just before 10 o'clock. I dropped Spencer off here and I headed into Beulah. I parked by the restaurant and walked up to the bank. I then walked over to the East Shore Market to pick up some wine, then back to the Cold Creek to get things organized for Max's lunch. I had a beer there while waiting for everyone to arrive."

"Did you notice anything unusual at the park when you dropped off Spencer?"

"No. I didn't talk to anyone at the park yesterday morning. Spencer got out of the car at the Mouse House and then I drove off. Ben was out front planting some flowers, and I saw Greta on the front porch with Albert. I didn't notice anyone else. No, hold on. I saw Xander Wolfe walking toward the stairs that lead down to the lake. Did Ian or Spencer mention to you that we have a camera by the gate? Ian can give you a copy of the video of everyone who entered and left the park."

"Yes, I've already got it. Thanks. Now Nigel, can you think of anyone who might want to harm Babs or Elsie?"

"I can't. Spencer and I are only here a few times a year, so we don't know all the residents as well as we would like. Elsie and Ian are the two that know everyone, and to a lesser extent Ben, and of course Albert. I know it's not nice to say it, but Elsie is the collector and distributor of park gossip. As for Ian, he lives at the Mouse House and manages the park. Ben knows people because he does maintenance work for many of them and also opens and closes the cottages for the seasonal people. Albert is in the coffee shop most days."

Nick learned about all he could expect to from Nigel, so he thanked him for his time and ended the interview. As he got up to leave, he noticed Greta sleeping soundly on the porch next to where he had been sitting. When he reached down to pet her, she barely responded.

Nick headed back to the station to find out how the sheriff was doing with his questioning and to see if Deputy McGregor had finished following up on the alibis of the residents who were at work yesterday. The protestors were still out front, but the group was smaller. Nick talked to Father Dominguez and learned that the protestors split into groups, each taking four-hour shifts so they could maintain a candle lit vigil throughout the night. Nothing new emerged from the questioning of the migrants and Kathy had cleared all the people who had been at work yesterday morning.

Nick was about to leave for the day when the deputy at the front desk called and told him that Ned Swanson was looking for him. Ned was a small-town lawyer who had a tiny office above the jewelry store in Frankfort. He was in his late 70s, but still handled simple matters like wills, probate, and minor civil cases for established clients. He hadn't taken on a new client in several years. Ned grew up in Elberta, went to law school in Lansing, and opened his one-man law practice in Frankfort almost 50 years ago.

Nick had the deputy send Ned back to his office. When Ned poked his head through the door, Nick got up and greeted him warmly, with a handshake. "It's been a while, Ned. How are things down at the gun club?"

Ned was an expert marksman who could still shoot better than anyone in the county. "Oh, these cataracts are playing hell with my aim. I'm finally getting them fixed next week. How's Maggie doing?"

"Busy as ever, but fine. How about a cup of coffee?"

"No, I just have a few minutes. I'm meeting the grandkids over at the Hungry Tummy for dinner."

"OK. What can I do for you? You look a bit frazzled.

"I've been practicing law in this county for fifty years, and I've never had a client murdered until now. I suppose that's why I'm in a bit of a state."

"I assume you're talking about Babs Tucker."

"Have there been any other murders lately? Of course, that's who I came to talk to you about." Ned paused and took a deep breath before continuing. "I'm sorry for snapping, Nick. It's just that Babs was one of a kind."

"Totally understandable, Ned. She'll be missed. Now, what do you want to tell me?"

"She changed her will about six months ago. I don't think it has any bearing on your case, but I thought you should know."

"Was the change significant? Who are the beneficiaries?"

"Yes, it was. In the previous will, which she signed about a year after her husband died, Babs left everything to her niece down in Ohio, the one who bought Babs' house and then quickly flipped it for a sizeable profit. The niece is Babs' only living relative."

"So, what changes did Babs make?"

"She left her cottage, everything in it, and $50,000 cash to Ian De Vries. She left $50,000 and her bridge trophies to Elsie Taylor, $50,000 to her church, and rest, about $250,000 in stocks and bonds, to Alexander Wolfe. I believe he calls himself Xander."

"What about the niece in Ohio?"

"She gets nothing. There's a comment that she got her share when she flipped the house down on Crystal Avenue."

"Anything else?"

"There's stipulation for Ian that he takes care of her two old cats, Chocolate and Fudge, for as long as they live. After they're gone, he's free to sell the cottage. Also, there's a policy and some money to cover the funeral costs and a short explanation of why she made the bequests."

"Anything interesting?"

"I'll let you judge if it's interesting. She said the bequest to Elsie was obvious since she was her bridge partner and because she was like a sister. The money for Ian is so he can afford to pay the land lease and taxes on the cottage and perhaps start a business. She doesn't say why she left Ian the cottage other than it being a home for her cats. As for Xander, it's her hope that he uses the money to fund his research and to help students at the university where he works. Although Babs expressed her desires of how the bequests were spent, she stated that those requests were not binding. Ian and Xander can spend the money as they wish. Finally, she asked if I'd sort out the funeral details if the niece doesn't want to make the arrangements."

"Does Ian, Xander, or the niece know about the changes to the will?"

"I don't think anyone knows of the recent change, but I can't be sure. If anyone does, I would guess it's Elsie. She seems to know everything that goes on at that park."

"I'll talk to Elsie, Ian, and Xander tomorrow. Meanwhile, let's keep this quiet for a while."

Back at the Mouse House, after everyone had left the coffee shop, Spencer and Ian joined Nigel on the front porch. The owners wanted to talk to Ian about the maintenance budget for the summer and the plans for the 4th of July parade. Ian suggested they have a pizza delivered and watch the sunset from the porch while they talked.

As they were finishing their pizza, a red Ford F-250 pickup drove up to Bonnie's cottage. "Looks like Bonnie's got a date," Ian commented. "That's Will Preston's truck. He and his brother dig most of the wells around here. I haven't seen him visiting Bonnie for a few months."

"I hope she's feeling better," Nigel commented. "It looked like she had a few too many when she left here a couple of hours ago."

The three on the porch returned to park business and talked for a while until they were interrupted by Will Preston. "Hey Ian. Sorry to interrupt, but do you know if Bonnie Campbell is around? Her car is in her drive, but she doesn't answer her door or her phone. We have plans for tonight."

Before Ian could answer, Nigel spoke up. "I saw her walk over to her cottage about two hours ago. We've been on the porch here all that time and haven't seen here leave." Nigel turned to Ian and told him to get the key to Bonnie's cottage. Keys to each cottage we kept in the park office safe.

While Ian ran into the office Will asked, "You must be the British guys who own the park? I'm Will Preston."

Nigel responded as they shook hands. "I'm Nigel Piddlemarsh and this is Spencer Butcher. Pleased to meet you. Yes, we're the owners, but Ian manages the place."

Spencer and Will were shaking hands when Ian returned with the key. He told Will, "I can't give you the key, but we can all walk over and take a look."

"That's great," Will answered back. "I wouldn't normally worry, but with what happened here yesterday, everyone is talking. I'm wondering if the sheriff caught the real killer. The protesters in front of the sheriff's office don't seem to think so."

"My guess is that Bonnie fell asleep," Nigel commented. "She looked pretty tired when she left the coffee shop a while ago."

When they approached Bonnie's cottage, everything was quiet. There were no lights on, but that wasn't surprising because it wasn't dark yet. Ian rang the doorbell and knocked. "Mrs. Campbell, it's me, Ian. Is everything OK?" He knocked a few more times and rang the doorbell again.

"Go on and open the door," Nigel instructed. "Something isn't right here."

The door wasn't locked, so it turned out Ian didn't need the key. After opening the door, he shouted. "Mrs. Campbell, are you here? Are you OK? It's Ian. I'm here with Will, Nigel, and Spencer." There was no response, but they could hear the sound of water running in the kitchen sink.

As soon as Nigel turned the lights on, they saw Bonnie. She was lying on the kitchen floor. It appeared that she was getting a glass of water from the tap when she fell. There was a small bloodstain on the granite countertop and on the floor near Bonnie's head. A shattered water glass was on the floor next to her.

Will, who was a medic when he was in the army, checked Bonnie's pulse. "She's dead. I'd say for at least an hour or two."

At this point, Spencer took charge. "Right, let's all get out of here. Turn off the lights and don't touch anything." As they turned to leave, he continued. "Ian, call Detective Townsend and tell him about Bonnie. I expect he'll be more useful than that damn sheriff. Let's all go up to the Mouse House and wait for the detective to arrive."

* * *

What a day it's been. I was up at dawn. What was it, 5am? No wonder I'm so tired. It was well worth it though, don't you think?

The voice in the killer's mind returned for the first time since shortly after the murder of Elsie. *"Yes. You did well, but let's go through everything to be sure you've made no mistakes."*

That's a good idea. Ok, I got up before anyone else in the park and carried my bike down the stairs to the trail by the lake.

It was barely light, and I almost tripped, but I didn't. I took my bike because I didn't want the camera at the gate take a picture of me as I left or when I returned.

"Are you sure no one saw you leave the park? What about Greta? Did she bark?"

I don't think anyone saw me, and no, Greta didn't bark. She was sleeping on the porch of the Mouse House. When Albert forgets to let Greta in at night, she sleeps there.

"Ok, what did you do next?"

I biked on the trail to that swampy area about halfway to Frankfort and picked some water hemlock. I wore rubber gloves and put what I picked in a plastic bag. I didn't see anyone on the trail. I wore a big hat and an old loose-fitting jacket that I got at a charity shop in Manistee. I've never worn either before. I threw them both away at a trash can at the Dairy King this afternoon.

"Now think, did anyone see you when you returned to your cottage?"

Elsie waved to me as I approached my cottage. She's usually up pretty early. I'd already taken off the jacket and hat and put them in the trunk of my car by then, so I think I'm OK with her.

"Nevertheless, we may need to reconsider Elsie's position on the list. I know we agreed to take care of her later so she can share gossip with you, but I now think she needs to be next. You know how she talks. If there's any chance she saw you taking off the jacket and hat, everyone in the park and the police will hear about it from her."

You're right. Let's keep going through the rest of my day and see who else might pose a risk.

"Ok, go on. What did you do next.?"

I put the hemlock in a small pot of water and boiled it until most of the water had evaporated so I had a concentrate of the poison. I put the liquid into a small medicine bottle, and I put it in my pocket. I then washed everything thoroughly and put the wet hemlock back into the plastic bag. I threw the plastic bag, along with the rubber gloves in the kitchen trash can.

"Are you sure that's wise? If for some reason they search your home and find it,…"

You're right. I'll take it out of here and dispose of it in town somewhere. I'd burn it in the fireplace, but it might leave a residue.

"Before you do that, let's just go through the rest of the day."

OK. After I cleaned up, I made breakfast as usual, read and fired off a bunch of texts and e-mails, then headed over to the sheriff's office to join the demonstrators. I talked to many people at the demonstration, including Nick Townsend and the sheriff. I don't think either knows who the killer is, especially not the sheriff who is obsessed by migrants. There were several other park residents at the demonstration who talked to the sheriff or the detective.

"Now, think about what happened at the Mouse House. Are there any loose ends there?"

I don't think so. I was one of the first there. Before I went inside to give Bonnie the poison, I put ground up sleeping tablets in the water bowl that Ian keeps on the porch of the Mouse House for Greta and any other of the park dogs. If something went wrong, I didn't want that damned dog to start barking.

When I went inside, I saw that someone had already taken Bonnie's mug from the rack and filled it with coffee. They must have noticed her approaching the coffee shop. I hoped whoever poured the coffee had added a lot of sugar so Bonnie wouldn't notice the taste of the hemlock, but I couldn't see how I could add the poison. Then, I was lucky when a few seconds later, Nick Townsend came in and everyone turned toward him, expecting him announce something about the murder. I took the opportunity and quickly poured the contents of the medicine bottle into her coffee. A few seconds later, Bonnie came up thanked me for filling her cup. She thought I had filled it with coffee.

"Sounds good, so far."

Albert then came over and asked if I wanted a refill. I acted as upset about Babs' murder as everyone else appeared to be. I left about the same time as many of the others. I watched from my kitchen window when I got home, hoping Bonnie would leave before the poison took effect. Of course, she was the last to leave. She appeared to be drunk as she left, so maybe the poison had already started to work. The detective and Nigel helped her down the step when she almost fell.

"Think now, did the detective or Nigel seem alarmed by Bonnie's behavior?"

No, they watched Bonnie walk over to her cottage, then sat down and talked for a while. Nether looked towards my cottage or Bonnie's, while they were talking.

"What about Bonnie's coffee cup?"

Oh my God, the coffee cup! Albert or Ian usually run the dishwasher at the end of the day. If they did, I'm fine, but what if they didn't. The mug with the poison might still there, and every-one knows which mug belongs to Bonnie. They lock the Mouse House up for the night. Ian's studio apartment is around the back and has a separate entrance. I can't just knock on his door and ask him if someone ran the dishwasher. I'll have to get over there first thing in the morning and check.

"That's unfortunate, but there is nothing you can do about the coffee mug now. You do need to take the plastic bag with the hemlock and the gloves somewhere and get rid of it. In the morning, be sure to be up early and verify that Bonnie's mug was washed. Also, start thinking about how you're going to take care of Elsie Taylor. If she's a potential witness, she's your next priority."

The killer did as the voice instructed and immediately left the park to dispose of the evidence. Rather than go into Beulah, the killer headed over to the McDonald's in Benzonia and put the plastic bag in a trash trash bin near the door. Fortunately, they were open late. Before heading back to the park, the killer ordered some fries to eat on the way home.

CHAPTER 7
Fear

When the killer pulled through the park gate after returning from McDonald's, there were several police cars in front of Bonnie's cottage. Many of the park residents were milling around in small groups talking among themselves. They had already placed crime scene tape around the perimeter of the cottage and several deputies were preventing people from coming close.

The killer parked the car in its usual spot and walked over to join the crowd. Almost everyone who was in the coffee shop earlier, along with Will Preston, formed a small group near Elsie's cottage.

The killer joined them just in time to overhear Will telling the group what happened. "I had a date with Bonnie. We've known each other for years. When she's between boyfriends, we get together."

"So, what happened to Bonnie?" Elsie asked Will. "Did you see her?"

"When Bonnie didn't answer her door, I asked Ian to help me check if she was OK. Ian has keys to all the cottages. It turns out we didn't need a key, but anyway, when we went in, we found Bonnie lying on the kitchen floor." This news visibly shook Elsie, so Reverend Parker walked over to her and put an arm around her shoulders to comfort her.

Before Will could continue, Ian interrupted. "Sorry Will, I just thought of something. I'll be right back." Ian turned and ran toward the Mouse House.

Will continued with his story. "I'm sorry to say that Bonnie wasn't breathing, and I couldn't find a pulse. It looked like she'd been dead for a while."

"Do you think she was murdered?" Xander asked.

"There's a small bump on her head, but not big enough to cause much harm. I think it was from when she fell. Whether she had a heart attack or some other natural reason for her to lose consciousness suddenly, I couldn't say. Given what happened to Babs, we called Nick Townsend right away. He's in Bonnie's cottage right now."

Elsie began to cry, and Katie joined Reverend Parker in trying to comfort her. Elsie settled down a bit and was about to ask Will a question when Albert ran over from the Mouse House in a panic. "Herb, Dot, could one of you help? I can't get Greta to move. She's on the porch of the Mouse House. It's like she's been drugged."

Dot answered. "I'll come. She started to walk off with Albert and then paused and turned around before calling out to her husband. "Herb, go check on Della. We took her up to the Mouse House this afternoon when we went over for coffee. She could have eaten whatever Greta had."

Elsie cried out. "Two people dead, and now the dogs. What's going on here?" Reverend Parker and Katie tried to get

Elsie to go back to her cottage to rest, but she refused. "I'm not going anywhere. I want to know what's happening and it's probably safer here in a group."

"Are you sure you'll be OK?" Katie asked.

"Don't worry, I'm not going to have another one of those panic attacks. I took one of the tablets the doctor gave me when I saw the police cars arrive."

Everyone turned when Ian ran past the group toward the crimescene barrier, carrying something in a plastic bag. He talked briefly with a deputy and handed the package to him before returning to the group.

"What was all of that about?" Derek asked. "What did you give to that deputy?"

Ian paused for a moment to catch his breath before answering. "I had a crazy thought, probably nothing. If Bonnie was poisoned, maybe they put the poison in her coffee. I forgot to run the dishwasher before I left the Mouse House today and wasn't sure if Albert did, so I ran back to check."

"I saw Albert turn on the dishwasher before I left," Elsie commented. "So, there's no way to know if someone put poison in Bonnie's coffee."

Ian responded to Elsie. "That's true, Albert ran the dishwasher, but the dishwasher was so full, a few dirty cups and dishes were left in the sink. I found Bonnie's coffee mug there and gave it to the police. There was still some coffee in it, so they should be able to test for poison."

"If they find poison in her coffee," Xander exclaimed, "One of us is the killer. We were all in the Mouse House when Bonnie was there."

Derek interrupted. "Don't forget Dot and Herb. They were also there, along with Albert and Nigel and Spencer. Albert usually pours the coffee for Bonnie. He likes it when she flirts with him."

Ian commented. "I don't think it was him. I was talking to Albert when Bonnie came in."

"That's right," Derek agreed. We ran out of coffee cream. You were talking to Albert while you were getting more from the refrigerator."

Katie interrupted. "Ben, the guy who does maintenance around here, was also there. I overheard him asking Ian a question about one of the summer residents."

"Stop it. Stop it right now," Elsie shouted in a firm and decisive tone that no one had ever heard her use before. This was not the soft-spoken Elsie everyone knew.

"What is it?" Katie asked.

"I'll admit it."

Everyone fell silent, when they heard what Elsie said. Surely, she wasn't the killer.

The sudden silence surprised Elsie, but she soon continued, not realizing why people had fallen silent. "Yes, I'll admit I'm frightened, but you know what, I'm more angry than frightened. Two of my close friends are dead. I'm angry and sad about that, but I'm even more angry that one of my other close friends is possibly the murderer. We're a family here at Beulah Crest and someone is tearing our family apart."

Reverend Parker tried to comfort Elsie. "It's all right, dear, we'll get this sorted out."

Elsie removed the minister's hand from her shoulder and gently pushed her back, before speaking. "It's not all right Hortense and it won't be until whoever is doing this is brought to justice. Until they resolve this, and perhaps even after, the Elsie everyone knows is no more."

"What do you mean?" Reverend Parker asked. "Let's take a moment to say a prayer for the strength to get through this?"

Elsie responded in a very firm and unemotional tone. "I'll tell you what I mean, Hortense. The Elsie whose cottage was always open to her neighbors will now keep her doors locked. Don't knock on my door, unless you're accompanied by the police. The Elsie who frequently visited her neighbors and yes, I'll admit it, the Elsie who liked to gossip, will keep to herself while in the park. One of my neighbors is a murderer and I don't intend to be the next victim. Now, if you will all excuse me, I'm going home where I'll be locking my door. The rest of you can pray for whatever you like."

The shocked group watched as Elsie turned and walked toward her cottage. They didn't realize it at the time, but by tomorrow, most of the park residents would begin to act in the same way. They would lock their doors and even though it was turning out to be a beautiful spring, people would no longer sit out on their decks.

Albert continued to run the coffee shop at the Mouse House, but not many would come, other than Ian, Nigel, or Spencer. When they did come, to learn of how the investigation was going, they brought their own coffee.

Even the dogs in the park found life different. For the first time in her life, Greta's movements were restricted. Albert bought a leash and Greta could no longer roam freely. Della and the other dogs in the park were also kept inside and only taken outside when on a leash.

After Elsie left, the group split up. Ian, Will, Spencer, and Nigel went back to the Mouse House to wait for Nick Townsend to finish at Bonnie's place. They left word that Nick could find them there. Everyone else followed Elsie's example and headed home and locked their doors.

Back at the Mouse House, the men who found Bonnie's body met Albert on the front porch, petting Greta. "Any news?" Albert asked. "Dot said that it looked like someone gave Greta sleeping tablets. It appears it was a mild dose though, and Greta should be OK by tomorrow." Greta briefly looked up when she heard her name, but then fell back to sleep.

Ian answered Albert's question. "Nothing new, so far. Detective Townsend is still over at Bonnie's place with the medical examiner and the forensics people. I called Herb Cooper on the way over. It looks like Della was also drugged."

"Is she OK?"

"Just sleepy, like Greta. I'll have the detective check the water in Greta's bowl here on the porch. Maybe the killer was afraid Greta might see something or recognize the killer and bark."

"Greta's wandering days are over," Albert commented, while gently petting the sleeping dog. I won't let her out of my sight until the killer is behind bars. I don't know what I'd do without her."

"She's been here for all of us," Nigel added. "She's part of what makes this place special."

Spencer was about to agree when the small group was interrupted by Detective Townsend. Everyone was so focused on Greta that none of them noticed Nick come up onto the porch, accompanied by one of the forensics officers. "How are you doing? I understand that all of you found Mrs. Campbell."

Will answered. "Yes, detective. I assumed Bonnie's cottage was locked, so I asked these folks if they had a key. It turns out we didn't need it, because the cottage wasn't locked." Will paused to take a breath and wipe a tear from his face. Ian and Nick, who both knew Will, were surprised that the 6'5" man who was once the state wrestling champion, was on the brink of falling apart.

"Take you time," Nick told Will.

Will regained his composure and continued. "Anyway, we opened the door and found Bonnie on the kitchen floor. I checked for a pulse and when I couldn't find one, Spencer told Ian to call you. It was pretty clear that she'd been dead for a while."

Albert interrupted. "Detective, did Ian tell you that Greta was drugged? So was Della, the Cooper's dog. He thinks the killer might have put something in her water bowl here on the porch." Albert turned and pointed to the water bowl at the far edge of the porch.

"Are the dogs OK?" Nick asked.

"They'll be fine," Albert answered. "The Coopers, who are retired vets, checked them over. They said they'll sleep soundly until morning but will be OK."

Ian then asked, "Detective, any word on how Mrs. Campbell died?"

Nick bent down to pet Greta before turning to address the men. "Not yet. The medical examiner has some suspicions, but he needs to do the autopsy to be sure. We should know more in the morning. Meanwhile, I'd like all of you who were at the coffee shop the same time as Bonnie to come down to the station tomorrow morning to answer some questions. I assume that's all of you, except Will."

Ian answered. "That's correct. Will arrived here about two hours after Bonnie and everyone else left the coffee shop."

"Ok, then. Could the rest of you meet me at my office at 10 o'clock?"

Nigel and Spencer looked at each other and then Nigel spoke. "Detective, we're not familiar with how your police system works here in America, but we hear stories of corruption and people being abused while in custody. Look at those migrants the sheriff's been holding. It's obvious by what happened here this evening that they're innocent. Should we be calling a lawyer or the British Consulate? We've heard what the sheriff thinks of foreigners."

"You're free to do so, but I just want to meet somewhere where we can talk. I need to close the Mouse House for a while so the forensics people can go over the place. Sargent Tyson and I will be sealing the place off until his people can examine it for evidence. Ian, can you stay at your parent's house tonight?"

"I'll give my girlfriend up in Interlochen a call. I was planning to go there anyway but got delayed by all of this. If my office is closed tomorrow morning, 10 o'clock works for me."

While Nigel and Ian made phone calls, Nick and Sargent Tyson placed crime scene tape around the Mouse House. When Ian got off the phone, Nick asked him to lock the Mouse House and give a key to Sargent Tyson.

As everyone was about to leave, Spencer asked Nick a question. "Detective, are you going to post any officers here at the park this evening, and for that matter, until they solve this? If not, we've made tentative arrangements for some private security guards starting tomorrow."

"I'll have two deputies patrol here tonight and tomorrow. If the sheriff doesn't agree, I'll let you know so you can bring in private security."

By the time everyone left, and the medical examiner had taken Bonnie's body away, it was nearly 11pm and people at the park were tired. One deputy was stationed at the gate and another was tasked to walk around the park. Every hour they switched positions. There was little need for the police patrols though, because everyone in the park had securely locked themselves in their cottages.

Elsie was angry that she felt it necessary to lock herself in her cottage, but she found comfort in having Babs' cats around to keep her company. Earlier in the day she had gone over to Babs' cottage and brought Chocolate and Fudge home, along with their litter box, food, and toys. She had never had pets, but now began to realize why people like having them.

As midnight approached, Elsie was in bed tossing and turning, unable to sleep. She was thinking about what she would do tomorrow. She needed to find a new bridge partner. That would be difficult because few people in the county could play as well as Babs. Perhaps she would volunteer to help run the tournaments or teach some bridge classes. She would also stop over at the Maples down in Frankfort and the hospice in Manistee to let them know that she could volunteer an extra day a week at each place. Anything to keep her busy and away from the park.

Albert wasn't going to leave Greta alone on the porch of the Mouse House. He could lift her but carrying her all the way home was more than he could handle, so he borrowed Ben's wheelbarrow and used it to take the sleeping dog home. Greta slept on the floor next to Albert's bed.

Ian left the park and drove to Interlochen. It was past midnight when he pulled up to Elizabeth's apartment. He didn't tell her about the second murder when he phoned, so his appearance shocked her when she opened the door. She had been thinking about him all day and planning what to say to him when he arrived. Besides sharing what she and the team had done in developing the webpage for the Crime Spartans site, she wanted to talk about last night and about how their relationship might be going. When she saw him outside her door, all the planning of what to say was forgotten when she greeted him. "Ian, you look terrible!"

Ian hadn't thought about how the events of the day had affected him personally or physically. He felt exhausted, so his response was equally unplanned. "I love you too."

Elizabeth wasn't sure how to respond. She was hoping to hear those words, but she wanted to hear them spoken in a more serious manner. "Come in and tell me what's going on."

After Ian sat down and after Elizabeth poured them both a drink, Ian told her about what happened at the park, including finding Bonnie's body, and his fear that Bonnie may have been poisoned while having coffee at the Mouse House.

After each had two shots of tequila, they felt more relaxed. Elizabeth wasn't sure about Ian's feelings for her, so she kept the conversation focused on what happened at the Beulah Crest. "We've finished a draft of the Crime Spartan page for the park. Would you like to see it now, or wait till tomorrow?"

Yesterday, Ian wasn't sure about putting Beulah Crest on the website, but after today, he was ready to do anything. He loved the place, and like Elsie, he was angry and frightened. "Bring your laptop over and show me what you've done." Ian was glad that when she sat down, she sat close to him and placed the computer partly on her lap and partly on his.

Elizabeth gave him a tour of the page. "As you can see, there is a satellite image of the park and a map. The map contains links. If you click on a cottage, a screen pops up with information about the owners or residents. Here, I'll show you Elsie's."

Elizabeth clicked on Elsie's cottage and a screen popped up with information about Elsie Taylor.

Ian scanned through the page on Elsie. It contained data about her mortgage, her taxes, what she and her husband did for a living before retiring, a list of her bridge awards, her hobbies, her church, and photos of her at various events. There was a button with a link for site users to add general information, a second button for users to add motives, and a third to add other information about Elsie related to the crime.

"Oh my God, Elizabeth, where did you get all this stuff? It says here that Elsie was arrested in 1980 for marijuana possession in Ann Arbor and in 1977 for disturbing the peace in Brooklyn. It says her husband was convicted of fraud and was awaiting sentencing when he died. Who would've guessed any of this? Do you have this much on everyone in the park?"

"We have quite a bit on almost everyone, including you, Nigel, and Spencer. All of us have been at it all day. Everything we found is available to anyone who knows how to look on the Web. Nothing has yet been added to the motives section or to the section for specific murder related information linked the residents. Users can identify any of the residents as being a suspect and describe why. They can also add additional suspects and include similar information on them."

Ian was afraid to look, but his curiosity got the better of him. Perhaps it was the 3rd shot of tequila that got him to spend the next few minutes scanning what Elizabeth and the others found out about the other residents of the park.

On Nigel, Spencer, and Xander's pages there was quite a bit about murders that took place on an ocean liner a few years ago. Ian knew about the British titles the park owners had and that they had money, but he was surprised to find out how wealthy Nigel and Spencer actually were. In contrast he was surprised to find that the Coopers and Parkers had declared bankruptcy a few years before moving to Beulah Crest and both couples were living on very limited incomes.

He then learned that Xander pleaded guilty to disturbing the peace and was put on probation while a senior at Interlochen. He led a protest about animal rights after which he threw a can of red paint at a woman wearing a mink coat to a student recital. Max Silver was also charged for a similar offense related to the protest, but that case was dismissed for lack of evidence.

Even though Katie Wolfe didn't live in the park, there was information about her linked to Xander's cottage. She had been detained and questioned after one of the faculty members in her medical school was murdered. His body had been found in a janitor's closet on her floor in the student residence. She was the only resident on the floor without an alibi, so she was held and indicted for the crime. After a week, she was released for lack of evidence. The crime was still unsolved.

Ian paused before clicking on his name, one of the three listed on the Mouse House. He took Elizabeth's hand before commenting. "I'm afraid to ask what dirt you have on me."

Elizabeth laughed and kissed Ian on the cheek. "You're pretty tame, except for reckless snowboarding that got you banned from Crystal Mountain. We learned you're a licensed real estate agent, you were a star in theatre productions in high school, you've had too many speeding tickets, and you're as poor as me. Is there anything else I should know?"

"Nothing I can think of, but if you ask my mom, I'm sure she can provide some embarrassing photos from my childhood. Seriously though, I have to think about this. The site could be explosive, especially if people in the park and around Beulah start adding real dirt on the residents. If we do this, my name can't be publicly associated with the site, at least not until the crimes are solved."

Elizabeth could see that Ian needed some more time to take everything in and felt if she pushed any further at this point, she might lose his support. "Ok, let's talk about it in the morning. It looks like you could use some rest. I know I'm exhausted."

Ian was about to agree and go to bed, but the drinks gave Ian more courage; enough to say what he was thinking. "What I said earlier, it's true, you know."

"What, about Bonnie being poisoned?"

"No, about loving you."

The killer finally made it to bed a little after 2am. As soon as the light was turned off, the voice returned. *"Things didn't go quite as planned, did they?"*

No, they didn't. I should have thought about the coffee mug and made sure it was either washed or destroyed. That trouble-some Ian gave the cup to the police. They're sure to find a residue of the poison. Once they verify the cause of Bonnie's death and link it to the poison in her coffee, all hell is going to break loose around here.

"Yes, it sure will. The question is, should you continue with your work of clearing the people from the park that need to go or should you pause for a few days and let the dust settle?"

I don't have an answer. I'm still trying to sort out how I made such a mistake with the coffee mug. Perhaps it's because I haven't planned properly. Usually, I write out a detailed plan before I begin any project, but because of the risk involved, I haven't done so here.

"The risk of creating a written plan is too great, so don't even think of writing anything down. Take your time and let the dust settle. There is no set timetable. At least now, Bonnie won't be speaking at Babs' funeral. You may need to, if Elsie is unable."

I'd rather not, but it might be unavoidable. What if they have both Babs' and Bonnie's funeral at the same time? That would be horrible, wouldn't it? Neither has family in the area, so it could happen. Hopefully, Bonnie's relatives in Boston will want to have her funeral back there. Until everything is decided, I'll just have to act upset and frightened like everyone else in the park and carefully plan how to take care of Elsie. Do you still think she should be next?

"Unless you can think of anyone else who poses a bigger risk, Elsie should be next. It might be a good idea if you take care of her outside of the park."

I can't think of anyone else right now, but over the next few days I'll watch and listen to see if anyone else says something that leads me to believe they've seen something. As for Elsie, I agree.

Away from the park will be best. The problem is, how to find a way to get her to go to some remote spot. Like you said, I need to take time to plan this one properly. I'll do that.

"*Ok, Dear, that sounds good. Now get some rest and focus on remaining calm. Think of how people expect you to act and then act that way. If you need me, just think of me and I'll be here for you.*"

* * *

When Ben arrived for work on Thursday morning, he headed to the Mouse House for a cup of coffee, like he usually did before starting his day. He typically met with Ian over coffee to review any new maintenance requests that came in. He knew he had a busy day ahead because he needed to open two cottages for summer residents who would be arriving on Saturday. Since he hadn't heard back from the pool service company that was tentatively scheduled to fill the pool next week and check the operation of pump and filter system, he wanted to check if Ian had talked to them.

As he approached the Mouse House, Ben noticed the crime scene tape surrounding the building. He was wondering what was going on when he was greeted by Deputy Jake Summerlin. "Morning Ben. How you doing this morning? Nasty goings on around here, don't you think?"

"Morning Jake. What's going on with the Mouse House? Something to do with Babs' murder? Have you seen Ian?"

"Haven't you heard? Bonnie Campbell dropped dead yesterday evening in her cottage. They're thinking someone put something in her coffee, right here in the Mouse House. Won't know for sure until later today when the results are in from the forensics lab and the medical examiner."

"You don't say! Bonnie wasn't a saint, like Babs, but I'll miss her. She added a bit of color around here. Any suspects so far? It can't be those migrant workers the sheriff has locked up." Ben didn't share the fact with Jake that he had a fling with Bonnie a few years ago. Jake mistook Ben's look of concern for what was actually Ben's fear that the short affair might be uncovered as part of the murder investigation.

"Can't tell you much more Ben. Not while they're still looking into things. I can tell you the sheriff released the migrants this morning. The prosecuting attorney said there wasn't enough evidence to hold them. Not sure if that's true or it's because they had those high-powered lawyers, but they're free and no other suspects are being held."

"Have you seen Albert or Ian?"

"Ian and Albert are meeting Detective Townsend at the sheriff's office later this morning along with the owners of the park."

"How's Albert taking it? He acts as if he owns that coffee shop. If Bonnie was poisoned there, he'll take it hard."

"He was pretty upset when I talked to him a few minutes ago. He's headed over to L'Chayim for a coffee before he goes to the station. You can catch him there, if you want to talk to him."

"That's OK. I'll see him when he gets back. I still have some more flowers to plant out by the gate and some cottages to open today. I'll stop over by Elsie's for a quick coffee. If she's home, she always has some to share, along with news about what's going on around here."

Ben unloaded the flats of flowers and the garden tools he had in his truck by the front gate then drove over to Elsie's cottage where he parked. He saw her car in the drive, so he walked onto her deck and knocked on her kitchen door. Usually Elsie would respond by saying something like, "come on in Ben," or "take a seat on the deck, and I'll bring out some coffee."

This morning, her response to his knock was quite different than her usual. "What do you want, Ben?" she asked curtly.

"Thought I'd pop over for a coffee and a chat. Is everything alright?"

"No, everything is not alright. There've been two murders in two days in this park. Now, go away and leave me alone. I don't want to talk to anyone who lives or works here until they solve this."

Ben was surprised by Elsie's behavior, but he could tell by her voice that she was frightened. "Ok, Elsie," he shouted back to her through the kitchen door. "I'm leaving. If you need anything, let me know."

Ben drove his truck to his parking space near the Mouse House and then walked over to the front gate to begin planting the marigolds and petunias in the new flower beds he'd put in after the gate was installed. As he walked through the park, he didn't see anyone other than the police standing in front of

Bonnie's cottage and Jake guarding of the Mouse House. Even though cars were in many of the driveways, none of the residents were outside on the sunny spring morning. The only movement he saw all morning was the arrival of the forensics team when they came to finish their work.

Ian didn't have time to stop back at the park before heading to the sheriff's office to meet Nick. By the time he left Elizabeth's apartment in Interlochen, it was after 9 o'clock. They didn't get to bed until after 2am, and he didn't sleep well, so he had a difficult time getting up. Elizabeth said he woke up twice during the night in a panic, screaming something about Bonnie and Babs. Over coffee, before he left, he told Elizabeth to go ahead and make the Beulah Crest pages live on the website. "Even if it eventually costs me my job, it's more important to catch the killer."

When Ian arrived at the sheriff's office, he found Nigel, Spencer, and Albert talking in the parking lot. There were no protesters out front; only a few volunteers led by Reverend Parker cleaning up the litter from yesterday's protests. Ian joined the other three men and they all walked into the station together. The sergeant at the front desk had them take a seat in the lobby and called back to Nick to announce their arrival.

A few minutes later, Nick came out to the lobby and invited Nigel and Spencer to come back. As they started to go, Nick called back to the desk sergeant and told him to get some coffee for Ian and Albert. Nick took them to a small conference room, where coffee and doughnuts were laid out on a table at the front of the room.

After everyone got some coffee and was seated, Nick started the conversation. "Nigel, I overheard part of your conversation on the phone yesterday with what I assume was the British consulate or embassy. It sounded like you thought you might be arrested or detained today. That's not my intention. Right now, we don't have enough evidence to hold anyone."

"That's all well and good, Detective, but tell that to those poor farm workers your sheriff held in custody for the last two nights. I heard they were finally released this morning."

"They were, fortunately. I don't think the sheriff will be doing anything like that again, at least not on this case. There's too much negative press coverage about his harassment of migrant workers and the county prosecutor is watching this case very closely. Some of the county commissioners have even threatened to withhold funding for the department if any lawsuits arise out of this investigation."

"I'm glad to hear it," Spencer commented. "Now, how can we help?"

"I understand that you were both in the coffee shop at the Mouse House yesterday at the same time as Bonnie. Tell me what you did and saw while there."

Nigel answered. "We arrived shortly before you came in, Detective. What was it, about 4:30 or so?"

"Closer to 5 o'clock, I'd say," Spencer commented.

"I think you're right," Nigel responded, before continuing. "We talked briefly to Ian and decided to meet later to talk about some park business and then Elsie approached us to ask if we would be attending Babs' funeral."

"Then you came in, Detective," Spencer added. "I remember Ian talking to Albert when Bonnie interrupted and asked Ian to get some more coffee cream, since he was standing in front of the refrigerator. She commented that whoever poured her coffee must have run out of cream because there was barely any in her coffee."

"We didn't know Bonnie that well," Nigel added, "but we do know that she's very particular about her coffee. Three sugars and lots of cream. We only use milk in our coffee back in England."

"Speaking of England," Nick asked. "What's with the lord and sir stuff? I overheard you talking on the phone last night when you referred to yourselves and Lord Piddlemarsh and Sir Spencer."

Nigel answered. "Those are the titles we have at home, Detective, but we use them sparingly and never here in America. They're useful when talking to government officials, like the one I talked to yesterday at the consulate or when booking a table at a restaurant. I inherited my title when my father died and took his seat in the House of Lords. Spencer was granted his for setting up and running a successful charitable foundation."

"Interesting, I suppose," answered the detective, "but I guess British titles aren't related to the investigation. So, what happened next in the coffee shop?"

Spencer replied. "You and Nigel went out onto the front porch to talk. I stayed and talked to residents until Albert started clearing up and people began to leave. I didn't notice or hear anything out of the ordinary other than the coffee shop being more crowded than normal. Albert was a bit frazzled, probably because he's not used to so many people there at once. Everyone was talking about Babs and speculating about who the killer might be. Hold on, I just thought of something."

"Go ahead," the detective commented. "Any detail could be important."

"I overheard Bonnie ask Albert if he was using a flavored blend of coffee. She wasn't sure if she liked the taste." Albert told her it was the same coffee he'd been using for the last year. He speculated that maybe the cream had turned."

"Did you notice if she drank more than just a sip of her coffee?"

"I think she drank most of it. I saw her take a sip or two while talking to Reverend Parker and as she was leaving, I saw her put a nearly empty cup in the sink. Albert had already filled and turned on the dishwasher. That was just before he left, which was just before I did."

"Can either of you think of anything else out of the ordinary?"

"Bonnie was just being Bonnie," Nigel answered. "I saw her flirting with Ian. I was distracted for a second when I saw Katie walk over to talk with Elsie and Dot Cooper. I then noticed Xander alone with Bonnie for a minute. Being who she is, she flirted with him. He didn't seem to mind, but I think he was relieved when Katie called for him to join her and the others to answer a question."

Spencer added a comment. "What's strange, now that I think of it, is that Bonnie didn't appear to be drunk until we saw her leave a little later. One would think the coffee would make her more alert, not less, if she had a few drinks at the Corner Bar earlier. If something was put into her coffee, that would explain why."

Nick ran out of questions. He had learned a few more details, but nothing he heard from Nigel and Spencer conflicted with what he observed himself while at the Mouse House. After the park owners left, Nick asked Ian to come back to the conference room.

As Ian entered the room, he headed straight to the table with the doughnuts and coffee. "May I, Detective? I missed breakfast and could use something about now."

"Help yourself and then come over and have a seat. How are you holding up with all that's going on at the park?"

Ian took the two remaining chocolate cake doughnuts with chocolate and coconut frosting and brought them to the table with a coffee. As he sat down, he answered. "I don't know. I haven't slept well the last two nights. Babs was like a grand-mother to me and I talked to Bonnie just before she walked back to her cottage and died. She was my English teacher in high school. Did you know that?"

"I did. My son tells me she was the best teacher he ever had."

"I agree with that. Now what can I do to help?"

"I was at the coffee shop yesterday, so I probably saw what you did, but tell me about yesterday afternoon anyway."

Ian finished his first doughnut and took a sip of coffee before he went on to explain what he did and saw that afternoon.

He didn't add anything new to what Nigel and Spencer had said. By the time he was finished going over everything he remembered, he had finished the other chocolate doughnut and his coffee. "I wish I could tell you more," he commented, as he got up to refill his coffee cup and Nick's.

"I wish you could too, Ian, but everything you've said is consistent with what I've seen and heard. Tell me. How do you like living over at Beulah Crest? Have you ever wanted to buy a place over there? That studio apartment of yours at the Mouse House is pretty small, isn't it?"

It's tiny, that's for sure, and it would be nice to live in one of those cottages, but I'd never qualify for a mortgage and the rent on one is too expensive for me. I don't really care though because I enjoy working for Nigel and Spencer. I just don't earn that much and probably won't for the foreseeable future. Although I manage the place, I only work half time at the park for little more than minimum wage and free rent."

"I thought you had other things going, like real estate."

"I got my license when I was up at Ferris State because I was bored there, but I only sell one or two cottages a year and maybe a house or two elsewhere in the county, mostly when asked for help by friends. It's easy work for someone like me who grew up here and knows everybody, but it's not my passion. I just don't devote a lot of time to it."

"What about your band?"

"It's fun, but we're not in it for the money. We make a few bucks, get free drinks from the clubs, and meet girls. Like everything else around here, it's a seasonal thing. We get very few gigs once the summer is over. Now that Elizabeth and I are getting on so well, I'm not sure how much longer I'll keep playing with the guys."

"So, what is your passion. What do you really want to do?"

"Beer, Detective. I want to learn everything there is about brewing beer. I work a shift or two a week at the new micro-brewery in Beulah, but that's mostly serving. I'm trying to get them, or the people who own the brewery in Frankfort to take me on as an apprentice so I can learn the trade of brewing."

Ian and Nick talked for a while longer and then Ian left. As Nick walked Ian to the lobby, he thought about what Ian told him. Money didn't appear to motivate the guy. Even if he knew about Babs' will, he wouldn't want or need the money enough to kill her.

Nick didn't see Albert in the lobby. He was about to ask the desk sergeant if was still in the station when he saw Albert in the parking lot smoking. Nick went outside and asked Albert for a cigarette. "Don't tell my wife," he commented when Albert give him an unfiltered Camel.

Albert didn't add anything new, other than some details about Greta begin given something to make her sleep and the fact that he had better get home soon to take her outside. "She's never been kept inside, Detective. She's not going to like it one bit."

When Nick went back inside to his office, he couldn't help wondering who filled Bonnie's cup with coffee. No one remembered filling the cup and no one saw anyone else fill it. If there was poison, was it added when the cup was filled, or later?

Nick started to make a call to the medical examiner when the sheriff barged into his office, screaming. "Have you seen that website? What the hell is going on here? We've already had enough bad publicity on those damned murders."

"What website?" Nick asked.

"It's called Crime Spartans. It's filled with all kinds of crap about the murders. What kind of nonsense is this? They're even inviting the public to help solve the crime."

"I'll take look," Nick responded. "Maybe it'll provide some leads."

"Find out who's running it, and shut it down. They've got videos from the protests and interviews from the lawyers who got those migrants released."

"I'll look into it, Sheriff, but I don't know if we have the resources to track down who runs the site or if we can legally get it shut down."

"You find out who runs that damned site, and I'll shut them down, personally. Do you hear me?"

"Ok, Sheriff. I'll look into it." As the sheriff stormed out of his office and down the hall, Nick laughed to himself, knowing that recent events meant the sheriff had little chance of being re-elected. This morning over breakfast, he learned from his wife that the Benzonia Township Supervisor was going to run for sheriff in November. The popular and respected supervisor had family and business connections throughout the county and would easily defeat Sheriff Van Dyke, especially given the circus this murder investigation had become.

After the sheriff left, Nick called the medical examiner to find out if he had any results yet. After exchanging pleasantries, Charlie Turner, the medical examiner, got right to the point. "Nick, she was poisoned. It looks like a concentrated distillation of hemlock was added to her coffee."

"Hemlock, like the stuff Socrates drank?"

"The very same. I sent a sample to a lab down at Michigan State in East Lansing to determine the exact variety of hemlock, but that's what killed her. I talked to the forensics folks. They found it in her coffee cup and a small amount in the sink at the coffee shop at Beulah Crest."

"Dr. Turner, where do you get Hemlock? I can't imagine you find it on the shelf at Shop-N-Save."

"You're right, but there are varieties that grow in this part of Michigan. The native species, Cicuta maculate, or water hemlock, grows near streams and wetlands. There's another poisonous variety, Conium maculatum, that is not native. I'm not sure how or when it took root here, but you can find it growing in a number of places. Once we determine the exact species, we'll be able to tell you where the plant came from. I know someone over at the Forest Service who'll know where it grows, once I get the exact type of hemlock identified."

"What else do you have, Doc? I can tell from your voice that there is more."

"You're right, there is. Mrs. Campbell was a heavy smoker which probably contributed to her having lung cancer. It was somewhat advanced, perhaps still treatable, but probably not. I didn't see any evidence of treatment for the cancer though, like drugs, radiation, or surgery. So, I can't say if she knew. If she did, I couldn't rule out suicide."

After Nick got off the phone with Dr. Turner, he noticed the time. It was almost 2 o'clock, and he realized that he hadn't had lunch yet. He decided to head over to McDonald's for a quick hamburger, before heading back to Beulah Crest to talk with Xander and a few others. On his way out he asked Deputy McGregor to join him. She'd been on the computer and phone all morning and had also lost track of time, so she joined Nick. The deputy seemed excited, so Nick was hopeful that she'd found something. During the short drive through Benzonia, Nick asked, "What have you found? You look like you stumbled onto something by the way you're fidgeting?"

"I'm not fidgeting, but something is going on. Before I get to that, all the people who weren't at the Cold Creek for Max's lunch were cleared by their employers or whoever else they were with. Of course, Spencer, Ian, Ben, Elsie, and Albert were all still at the park, so maybe they are all in on it, but I don't think so."

"As they pulled into McDonald's Nick asked, "Drive thru or eat in?"

"Let's do drive through and then go over to the park and talk. I came across something on the Web I want to show you. I don't want to talk about it in the restaurant."

When they placed their orders, Kathy ordered her hamburger without cheese, which meant they had to park for a few minutes while the special order was made. Nick was about to ask what Kathy had found on the Web, when a young guy with a McDonald's uniform approached carrying the food order. Both

Kathy and Nick recognized him as Josh McKenna, the quarterback for the past two years at Frankfort High School. Nick greeted Josh and then asked, "Shouldn't you be in school, Joshua?"

"There no school today," he answered as he handed the officers their food. "A teacher catch-up day or something. Anyway, I told Amy at the drive thru to have you park here because I wanted to show you something. After seeing that webpage about the Beulah Crest murders, I thought you might be interested."

"The webpage?" Nick asked.

Kathy interrupted. "I'll tell you about it while we're eating. What did you find, Josh?"

Josh took something out of another paper bag he was carrying. "I found this behind the trash bins near the front door. You know the ones, where people put their trays on the counter above the large bins. Someone spilled something, so I took the bins out to mop the area and found this on the floor." Joshua handed the plastic bag containing the hemlock the murderer had placed there yesterday evening. The bag contained the leaves and roots that had been boiled and a few others that hadn't fit in the small pot used to brew the poison. Those were still relatively fresh.

Nick asked, "Do you know what this is, Josh?"

"It's water hemlock, Detective. We had a chapter on poisonous plants in natural science last year. It grows in a swampy area near Elberta and in a few other places not too far from here. Do you think this is what killed Mrs. Campbell? My older sister had her for English a few years ago and really liked her."

"I don't know," Nick answered, "but we'll take it, and have it examined by the lab. Do you have cameras here?"

"Just by the drive thru. There's usually one inside by the registers, but it broke a few days ago. A new one should be installed later today." Nick and Joshua talked for a few minutes while Kathy went inside and got a copy of the drive thru video from the manager. They didn't expect to find anything, but it was worth the chance.

When Kathy retuned to the car with a copy of the video on a thumb drive, Joshua had already gone back inside the restaurant. "Nick, I've got the video from yesterday and today. It's good quality, but it only shows cars going through the drive thru and who's in them. Nothing of the parking area or entrances."

"Did you learn anything else while talking to the manager?"

"I asked him, and the cashiers, if they saw anyone throw anything strange away or if they saw any residents from the park here today or yesterday. Nothing on the trash, but the manager saw Reverend Parker yesterday evening. He belongs to her church. Usually she does the drive thru, but yesterday evening she came inside and placed a take-out order. Her husband came in this morning for breakfast with someone the manager didn't recognize, but from the description, it sounds like Herb Cooper."

"Ok," Nick commented. "Let's go over to the park and eat. Everything's cold by now, but I'm starved." Nick drove the car over to the township park and they found a table in the shade overlooking the baseball fields. When they sat down, and started to eat their cold burgers and fries, Kathy took out her iPad and pulled up the Crime Spartans webpage for Beulah Crest. "So, is that the webpage they're talking about?"

"It is, and it's got more stuff than when I looked at it before we left the station. It looks like Josh, or someone from McDonald's posted. There's a picture of the hemlock found in the trash with a comment describing what it is and speculating it may have been used to poison Bonnie Campbell."

"Let me see." Nick moved next to Kathy at the picnic table to get a better view of the screen. After exploring the page and clicking on the various links to pages with information on the residents, suspects, and comments, he realized why the sheriff was upset. "This is explosive, Kathy. I wonder how much of this stuff is accurate. We'll have to check all these leads out. Reverend Parker, her husband, and Dr. Cooper are listed by people on the site as suspects because they were seen in McDonald's, where the hemlock was found. Someone else commented that Herb Cooper has a motive related to a grudge over bridge"

"They're not the only suspects listed on the site. Someone is pointing to Xander Wolfe and Ian De Vries because of what was in Babs' will. Apparently, she left her cottage to Ian and some money to Xander. There's another post suggesting that Derek Parker, and Herb and Dot Cooper have motives for killing Babs, assuming they mistook her for Elsie, because her husband sold medical equipment. The Coopers and Dr. Parker went bankrupt after buying expensive equipment from him."

"Look, another just popped up. It says that Albert Pankhurst may have killed Bonnie because he was jealous of her and Will Preston."

"There's another one that's even more crazy. It's suggests that Ben Weldon killed them both because he's anxious to start his new job as sexton at the township cemetery. It asks if he gets paid for each burial or whether the township pays him a flat salary for the job. This is ridiculous. How do we handle all this, Nick? Can't we shut this thing down?"

"I really don't know. This is new territory for me. Can we find out who's posting this stuff, and can we find out who runs the website?"

"I'm not sure. My guess is that we won't be able find out who the site visitors are and who's posting things, unless they use their real names. This morning I was able to access the site and create a username for myself without providing any personal information."

"What about the people who run the site? Can we track them down?"

"We might be able to, but I'm not sure. There's a process for setting up and registering a site, but if it's done through set of holding companies or is registered in another country, it might be difficult. I can start digging when we get back to the station, but I'm no expert. We might need to call in the state police cyber-crimes unit, but I'm not sure if they'll help. They're more focused on crimes like fraud committed via the Internet."

"Start digging when we get back. Whatever you find, let me know first before you tell the sheriff. I don't want him going off and doing something that will make the situation worse. One more thing. See if you can find out who Bonnie's doctor was. Call Elsie Taylor. She'll probably know. She seems to know a lot about everyone in the park."

"What are we looking for?"

"According to Doc Turner, Bonnie had fairly advanced lung cancer. If the hemlock at McDonald's is a hoax and doesn't match the hemlock in Bonnie's stomach, suicide could be a possibility."

"I'll get right on it." Kathy was about to close her iPad when she saw another post appear on the Crime Spartan page. "Nick, there's another post and this one isn't anonymous. It's from Elsie Taylor. She's says Babs left her $50,000 in her will and she's offering all of it as a reward to whoever who can provide information leading to the arrest and conviction of the Beulah Crest killer."

"That's just what we need. A big reward just brings out the loonies with leads that waste our time. As if we don't have enough of those in this investigation. The phones will be ringing off the hook by the time we get back to the station."

CHAPTER 8
So Many Clues

B ack at Beulah Crest, the residents were quickly learning about the Crime Spartans site. Elsewhere, Helen Rhodes, the director of the Elberta bridge club, found out about the site from her son, who was a social media junkie. After looking through the site and anonymously adding a few comments suggesting Herb Cooper was the most likely suspect because of his temper when playing bridge, she sent a text to everyone on her bridge club list containing a link to Crime Spartans. Bridge players Elise Taylor and Dot and Herb Cooper were on the list as was Reverend Parker because the club had used her church meeting room for a district tournament. Max Silver and Xander Wolfe were also on the list because they occasionally partnered and played bridge at the club when Xander was in town.

Elsie mentioned the site to Ben when he stopped back at her cottage to check if she was OK. He was worried because of the way she acted. She still wouldn't let him in, but she did tell him about the website. Ben then spread the word to everyone he ran into throughout the day, including Albert, who re-opened the coffee shop after the forensics specialists took down the crime scene tape.

The coffee shop was pretty quiet, but by late afternoon, people started to stop by, not for coffee, but to talk to each other about the website. Most continued to bring their own coffee or iced tea from home. Ian was told about the webpage by Ben who greeted him as he got out of his car. "Did you see that website, Ian? It's got something about everyone in the park, even me. Lots think Herb Cooper did it, but I can't see it. Anyone who loves dogs like he and Dot couldn't be a killer. My money's on Derek, the reverend's husband. A cold fish, is he, make no mistake about it."

Ian let Ben ramble about the Web while he pulled his thoughts together. He knew he would eventually hear about the website from residents, but he was surprised that of all people, Ben would be the first to bring the subject up. When he felt ready to talk without betraying himself, he responded. "I heard about the site, Ben. Is there really that much on it about the park?"

Ian helped Ben put some tools away as Ben answered. "I ain't read through all of it, on account of me being pretty busy today, and I've only seen it on my phone, which is too small to see some of the text, but there's quite a bit there." Ben paused to take a sip of coffee from his thermos before continuing. "Nigel and Spencer should be paying you more by the way, and can you believe that Xander Wolfe threw paint at a woman wearing a fur coat up at Interlochen? And his sister, there's a dark horse. Accused of killing her professor at medical school."

Ian tried to appear surprised and then asked Ben not to talk about the residents of the park. "Ben, things are tense enough around here without spreading more gossip. Do you think you could keep from talking about the website with the residents? I'd appreciate it, and I think Nigel and Spencer would as well." Ben reluctantly agreed and left Ian to get back to work.

When Ian entered the Mouse House, he saw Albert and Greta in the coffee shop. Albert looked up from his laptop computer and greeted Ian. "Morning Ian. Well, I suppose it's afternoon by now. How'd it go at the sheriff's office?"

Ian poured himself a cup of coffee and sat down across from Albert, hoping Albert wasn't looking at the webpage. "I stopped in at the East Shore and picked up a couple of sand-wiches. Care for one?" Ian handed Albert one of the sandwiches before he could answer.

"Sure, thanks." Albert unwrapped the sandwich before asking again about the meeting with Nick at the sheriff's office. "Is everything OK? You look upset. Did something happen with Detective Townsend?"

"No, not really. He asked some weird questions about how much money I make and what I wanted to do with my life?"

"Cops are always nosy. Don't think anything of it." Albert turned his computer around so Ian could see the screen. "Have you seen this?"

Ian nodded. "I have. I looked at it earlier."

"There's a lot of personal information on it, Ian, about park residents, including you and me. Someone thinks I killed Bonnie because I was jealous of Will Preston. Can you believe that?"

"No, I don't think you're a killer, Albert." Ian got up and refilled both of their coffee cups. "I can't imagine that it's actually someone who lives in the park."

"Folks seem to think Herb Cooper or Derek Parker are the most likely suspects, but did you see the comment about Dot? She was arrested for assault down in Ohio, years ago. Sounds like they had a row, and she punched Herb. Broke his jaw, she did."

"Do you really think that's true, Albert?"

"Who's to say? Anyone can put anything on the Internet. Greta likes them both, and she a better judge of character than most. So, probably not." Greta heard her name and padded over for some attention and hopefully some scraps from the sandwiches. Ian, always the easy mark, was happy to provide both.

Ian told Albert he had some paperwork to catch up on and walked over to his office. Greta followed while Albert checked the front door to be sure it was closed so Greta couldn't wander off. Ian didn't have much paperwork. He just wanted an excuse to go to his office and check the website and his email.

The first thing he looked at was the metrics page that tracked how many people visited the site and also how many clicked on the embedded links to advertisers. Each click to an advertiser generated revenue to the site owners. He was surprised how many visited the site and then clicked links to advertisers. There were ten times more visitors than the previous record day, and visitors were from around the country, not just Benzie County, and there were even quite a few from outside the country.

At first, Ian was thrilled the site was drawing in so many new users and therefore generating record revenue, but then he realized he would be making money because two people had been murdered. Making money from the murders of friends just didn't seem right. He was about to call Elizabeth, but then decided that he would need to talk to her in person. He didn't want Albert or anyone else in the park to overhear his conversation. He'd go up and see her this evening.

After checking the site metrics, Ian read through everything that was posted on the site. He was surprised to see someone suggested that he and Xander were named as suspects because of what was in Babs' will. The person who accused Ian and Xander didn't disclose the details of the will. As he continued to read, he was amazed to find that all of the other year-round residents of the park had been accused, as were Ben, Nigel and Spencer.

The clues and accusations were not only pointed at park residents. Someone accused the sheriff because they felt the publicity would help him get re-elected; Babs' niece because of the inheritance; Will Preston, because he didn't approve of Bonnie's other men; and some of Bonnie's former students, because she had failed them in English.

After reading through every post, Ian found no real evidence had been posted, other than the hemlock that had been turned over to the police at McDonald's. It was all rumor and accusation.

At the Cooper's cottage, Herb and Dot both got the text from Helen Rhodes at the same time, while they were having breakfast. As usual, Herb ignored the ping sound phone made to indicate a text, as was his practice since retiring. Dot, who couldn't understand how anyone could ignore a text or call, promptly looked at her phone. When she clicked on the link in the text and saw what was on the Crime Spartans website, she dropped her phone.

"What is it, Dot?" Herb asked. "Did someone else get killed in the park?"

"No, but you should see this site. Helen over at the bridge club sent the link. It's all about the murders. Someone put hemlock in Bonnie's coffee yesterday."

"Nothing like the tried and true methods," Herb joked.

"Stop that right now," Dot snapped. She paged through the site before continuing. "Oh, my God, Herb. There's a bunch of people who think you killed her and Babs."

"Really, why would I do that. Well, maybe Babs. I still think she was cheating last week, but seriously, why would I kill either of them?"

"I don't know. Of course, you didn't." Dot was still paging through the site as she was talking. "Good God in heaven, Herb. Someone says I killed them. Where would I find Hemlock?"

"You do have a temper, Love. You don't lose control often, but when you do...."

Although most of the residents stopped by the Mouse House sometime during the afternoon to see if there was any news, the Parkers did not. Hortense spent the morning helping to clean up after the protesters and Derek saw two patients; one for a root canal and the other to fit a crown. They both got home around one o'clock and Hortense warmed up some leftovers for lunch.

Derek didn't set the table, like he usually did while Hortense was cooking. He took his computer out and logged into the Internet.

"What are you doing?" Hortense asked. "Would you set the table, please?"

"In a minute, dear. Ruth Tanner, my 10 o'clock root canal told me about this website with a bunch of stuff about the murders here in the park. I was just taking a look."

"Let me know if it has anything interesting," Hortense commented as she took the leftover sweet & sour pork and fried rice out of the microwave. "Helen from the bridge club sent me a text about it, but I didn't get a chance to look at the site while I was at the sheriff's office."

"It's got more gossip than Elsie could spread in a year. Quite a few people think Herb is the murderer because of his temper. Some think I'm the murderer because I'm distant and cold. How's that for a laugh."

"I never thought you were distant and cold, love. At least they're not accusing me."

"Oh, but they are, my pet."

Hortense almost dropped the fried rice but managed to catch it in time. "I'm a minister for heaven's sake, and besides, when would I find the time to murder two people?" Hortense set the table and poured iced tea while Derek answered.

"Someone with the user-name Avenger says you have no alibi for Tuesday morning, and he says you don't approve of Elsie's gossip."

"I don't approve of her gossip, but what's that got to do with Babs' murder."

"Babs was killed on Elsie's deck. Avenger thinks you mistook Babs for Elsie. It's not like you're an experienced killer. Perhaps you made a mistake."

"What utter nonsense."

"Of course, it is. I was just teasing, but someone who calls himself 'Cherry Picker' agreed with Avenger. He says you're a sociopath whose career with the church was a farce. He goes on to say that you're cold and calculating."

"Sounds like we're made for each other then, doesn't it? Turn that thing off so we can eat. I'm starving."

"Yes, dear, but be careful when you go out. I know you aren't the murderer, and I know you think the same about me, but there are people who think one of us is. Such crazy people can do anything. Then there's the person who actually killed Babs and Bonnie. We have to watch out for him."

Xander and Max didn't read the text because it was sent while they were on their way, with Katie, to an alumni luncheon and concert at Interlochen Arts Academy. Max was focused on their conversation while they were in the car and Xander, as usual, had left his phone back in the cottage.

When they arrived at the school, they took a walk around the campus before heading over to the buffet picnic in front of Kresge Theatre. Katie was the first to notice something was amiss. Rather than being greeted by old friends and collogues, she noticed that people were whispering and pointing as they approached. When Katie saw her 11th grade roommate, who was now with a ballet company in Los Angeles, she approached her to ask what was going on. Xander and Max followed.

Stella, the former roommate, tried to act casual as the three approached. She gave Katie a brief hug and said with a nervous laugh, "Hi Katie, Xander, oh… and hi Mr. Silver. It's good to see you."

Katie responded for all three. "Ok, Stella, what's going on. You and everyone else we know are staring at us."

"I didn't know, and I don't think anyone else did," Stella answered.

"Didn't know what?"

"About the Beulah Crest murders and that you were indicted for murder when you were in medical school. They haven't solved the murders at Beulah Crest or the murder of your college professor and you and Xander were both on that ship where those people were killed."

"So, you think I'm a murderer," Katie snapped.

"No, well, I don't know," Stella answered with a nervous laugh. "More people think it was the veterinary doctor or the dentist, but you often seem to be in the wrong place at the wrong time, don't you?"

Max stepped between the two women to help calm what was becoming an emotion filled discussion before asking Stella a question. "Where did you learn about what you just told us?"

"From the Crime Spartans website, of course. It started this morning. Someone looking at the new fountain Googled the name of the woman it was named after, Babs Tucker. The Crime Spartans webpage came up as the first result, with information about the Tucker woman's murder and Beulah Crest. Within an hour, almost everyone had gotten a text with a link." Stella reached into her purse and pulled out her phone. "Here, I'll show you."

Katie was visibly shaken by what she saw on the site. Her arrest for the murder of her favorite professor was the most frightening event in her life and she still had nightmares about the murders on the ocean liner. Xander tried to comfort her and Max suggested that they quietly leave.

Katie responded to Max's suggestion the way Xander knew she would. "We're not leaving, Max. I'm not a murderer and neither are you or Xander. Let's have lunch and tell anyone who thinks we are what's what." Katie led Max and Xander to the buffet line, leaving a speechless Stella behind.

* * *

Since there was nothing on the killer's calendar for the afternoon the troubled Beulah Crest resident decided to get some fresh air away from the park and take a walk along the shore of Lake Michigan. As soon as the car left the park and turned right on the Frankfort Highway, the voiced returned. "*I know the website has upset you, but you needn't to be?*"

The killer responded without actually speaking. *How can you say that?*

"*Sure, you're accused of being the murderer, but so is everyone else in the park, plus some others who don't even live there.*"

Yes, but the site has everyone stirred up and talking about Babs and Bonnie, and the murders. Everyone will be watching and looking for clues. It will be more difficult to take care of the others in the park who need to go and it's more likely that someone will stumble on evidence that will link me to the murders.

The voice remained silent until the killer parked the car in the lot above Elberta Beach and had walked to the shore. Since it was still May, and the tourist season hadn't started, the beach was deserted. It was a sunny warm day, but the water in the lake was cold. The was no breeze, so the lake was calm and crystal clear. As the killer started to walk south along the water's edge, the voice returned. *"What you say about the website is true. Perhaps someone will post something that will link you to the crimes, but you can also post to the site."*

I hadn't thought of that, but what would I say?

"You could accuse some of the people that need to be removed from the park of murder."

I suppose I could, but who?

"How about Herb Cooper. A lot of people already think he's the killer. We could even take this a bit further."

What do you mean?

"You still have the hammer you used to kill Babs, don't you? You were going to dispose of it, but I don't think you did."

No, it's still in the trunk of my car. I know it's stupid, but I forgot all about it once I decided to take care of Bonnie.

"Of course, you did, but now you can use it to take care of Herb."

Oh, I couldn't. I wouldn't want to risk a fight with him. He has quite the temper.

"No, don't you see. You could put the hammer somewhere in or near his cottage. Perhaps in his car. Then, you post on the website that you saw him hiding the hammer."

I couldn't leave it out in the open or in his car. Della, their dog would find it and alert him or Dot, about the hammer.

"What about a toolbox or someplace where the dog can't go?"

Herb keeps a toolbox in the shed behind his cottage. I don't think the shed is ever locked.

"Well, there you are. Put the hammer in the toolbox and then post on the website that you saw Herb put it there Tuesday afternoon. Be sure to wipe your fingerprints from the handle."

I suppose I could, but couldn't they trace the posting back to me.

"Not if you post from a public computer. They have one or two at the library."

He's on my list and it doesn't matter to me if I kill him or if I send him to Jackson Prison for the rest of his life. Either way, he'll be gone from the park. You're right, as usual. I'll hide the hammer this evening and then go to the big library up in Traverse City or one of the cafes tomorrow to post to the website. I won't be recognized there.

* * *

When Nick and Kathy got back to the station after lunch in the park, the phone calls had already started coming in. There were six messages from callers on Nick's desk, and the desk sergeant had another five from calls he had just taken. Nick knew all of the calls would need to be followed up, just in case one provided a valuable lead, but he didn't look forward to the time he and others in the department would waste.

Before Nick looked at the messages, he had several things he needed to do. First, he called Dr. Turner to tell him about the hemlock found at McDonald's. The medical examiner said he would send a courier over to pick up the evidence and take it to the lab in Lansing. They would be able to verify if this sample matched the poison in the coffee cup found at the Mouse House and in Bonnie Campbell's stomach. If there was a match, he would have to rule out suicide.

Next, Nick planned to head over to Beulah Crest to talk Ian and Xander about their inheritance and to learn if they knew about Babs' will. Before he left the station, he handed the phone message slips to Kathy and asked her to make a start on them.

On his way out of the door, he ran into Ned Swanson, who was coming in. He greeted the lawyer from Frankfort. "Hey, Ned, don't tell me you've got another will to talk about?"

"It's a sad business, Nick, but unfortunately, I do."

Nick turned around and escorted the lawyer back to his office. Once they were settled and Nick poured himself and Ned a cup of coffee, they got down to the matter at hand. "So, let me guess. You did Bonnie Campbell's will."

"You're right, of course. I did both of Bonnie's wills. The first, just after she married Bud Campbell over 30 years ago and then an updated one a few weeks ago. I prompted her to create the latest one."

"Why was that? Did something significant happen to change her circumstances?"

"I should have insisted she change her will back when Bud died, but Bonnie was in such a state at the time, she wouldn't do anything. In her previous will, everything was left to Bud. He, by the way, left everything he had, to her. It wasn't much."

"So why did you encourage her to draft a new will after all that time?"

"She came to me for advice on how to handle a large inheritance. Her 105-year-old grandmother from Boston recently died and left everything to her."

"I'd heard that Bonnie came from a wealthy family, but I'd also heard they disowned her when she married Bud."

"They did, but apparently the grandmother didn't fully go along with the harsh treatment from the rest of the family. The grandmother we're talking about is the one who had a cottage up at Torch Lake that Bonnie visited as a child. I'm still sorting through everything, but let's just say that Bonnie Campbell was the wealthiest person in the county when she died."

"Ned, are you going to tell me who was in the will or are you going to make me guess?"

"Before I do, let me tell you that you're going to be amazed by how similar Bonnie's will is to the one Babs made. I wouldn't be surprised if the two women talked before Bonnie drafted her will. Bonnie didn't care about the money and didn't want the hassle of managing so much wealth. She was content with the simple life her teacher's pension provided and her home at Beulah Crest. She left everything to someone who she felt could use it wisely to help others, Max Silver."

"So, Max is now the wealthiest man in the county. Did he know about the will? Did she say why he gets the money or anything about restrictions on how it's used?"

"No, I don't think he knew, and she didn't tell anyone else about her inheritance, except perhaps Babs. She was afraid people would treat her differently if they knew she was wealthy."

"What about restrictions on how Max can use the money?"

"It's just like what Babs did with Xander. There are no legal restrictions. She left a note to Max in which she apologizes for placing the burden on him and then asks him to use the money wisely to help students and other young people in need. Since he was a respected teacher, she hoped he would understand and take up the challenge. The way she had me write the will, there's nothing legally binding on how he can use the money."

"Did she mention anything about cancer? The medical examiner found it in her lungs."

"Yes, she did, Detective. She was scheduled to start therapy next week and was optimistic about her survival."

After Ned Swanson left, Nick finally headed over to Beulah Crest to talk about the inheritances with Ian and Xander. Now he would add Max to the list. It was early evening as he pulled his car up to the Mouse House. It was locked up for the night, so Nick headed around the back to the entrance to Ian's studio apartment. Ian was opening the door to leave to spend the night at Elizabeth's place when Nick was about to knock.

"Hi Detective. I everything OK?"

"No new developments, Ian, but I wanted to ask you a few more questions. It shouldn't take long."

"Sure, I'm in no hurry," Ian answered. "Let's go around to the coffee shop and talk. There's a lot more room there than in my little apartment." Ian escorted Nick around to the front of the Mouse House and opened the front door with his key.

After they were settled, Nick opened the conversation. "Ian, are you aware that you were in Babs' will?"

"I saw on the Crime Spartans website that she left me something, but the person who posted didn't say what it was. The same person accused me of killing Babs, for whatever she left me."

"You'll find out soon enough, so I'm going to tell you. I'd like to get your reaction."

"Sure, my old Subaru could use new brakes, so a little money would come in handy."

"It's a bit more than that. She's leaving you her cottage and $50,000. She wants you to take care of Chocolate and Fudge."

"Elsie Taylor has the cats right now, but I could look after them. They're both pretty old. Fifty thousand will pay for a lot of cat food and vet bills."

"I'm sure it will."

"Wait a minute, Detective. Did you also say Babs left me her cottage? What about her niece down in Ohio?"

"Nothing for the niece. Apparently, Babs thought the profit she made flipping the house she sold her was enough. There is a restriction though. You need to keep the cottage as long as the cats live."

"No problem there. I'm not planning on going anywhere. So, this is for real, Detective? Babs really left me her cottage?" Ian was close to tears.

"It looks like it. Talk to Ned Swanson to learn about the details. You know him?"

It took a few second for Ian to answer, while he got a hold of his emotions. "Of course, Ned's a legend down at Dad's gun club. Sorry for being so emotional. It's just that Babs…" Ian couldn't continue, so he got up and walked over to the coffee machine and made two cups of coffee and then brought them back to the table.

"Are you ok, Ian? I know it's probably a bit of a surprise."

"It's not that, Detective. It's Babs. I can't believe she's gone, and now to hear about this. She helped so many people over the years who really needed it, and now she leaves me so much when I'm already so fortunate. I don't know if I can accept it. I'll take care of Chocolate and Fudge, if Mrs. Taylor doesn't want them, but I'm not sure about the cottage and all that money."

"Talk to Ned. He can give you more insight into what Babs was thinking and why she did what she did. Also, talk to that new girlfriend of yours. Then, decide what to do."

Nick left Ian in the Mouse House and walked over to Xander's cottage. On the way across the park, he thought about his conversation with Ian. The young man seemed to be genuine, but then again, he was considered to be a good actor back in high school when he starred in a number of plays.

When Nick arrived at Xander's cottage, Xander and Katie were in the kitchen making a light dinner. After the upsetting day at Interlocken, neither were very hungry, but they fussed in the kitchen for something to do rather than think about the day and recent events. The knock on the door was a welcome interruption.

Xander was surprised to see the detective when he greeted him. "Come in Detective. I hope there's no more bad news. I think we've had enough for a while. On top of it all, that website has everyone stirred up."

Nick came into the kitchen and Katie invited him to sit at the table. "Care for some salad, Detective. Xander and I were just about to eat."

"No, I'm fine. I had two cold hamburgers and cold fries for lunch today that didn't settle well. I just had a few questions"

"Our lunch up at Interlochen wasn't all that great either," Xander commented. "Everyone was talking about the Crime Spartans website and pointing to us as potential suspects."

All three sat at the table and Nick asked his first question. "That website is stirring up a lot of trouble. Now, on another subject, Xander, I have a question. Did you know that Babs left you some money in her will?"

"No. Why would she do that? She was a nice woman, but I didn't know her all that well, and I don't really need anything. I'm paid pretty well by the university."

"You'll need to talk to her lawyer, a guy named Ned Swanson down in Frankfort to get the details, but from what I understand, she wants you to use the money to help poor students. It's almost $250,000."

"Wow," Katie exclaimed. "You could set up a scholarship fund with the money or maybe hire some students for your lab."

"I suppose I could. But I wonder why she chose me?"

Nick and the Wolfes talked about the will and then the website for a while. Xander filled him in on the details of the murders on the ocean liner and Katie give him the details about the murder charge she faced in medical school. Nick could tell that both events were still upsetting for the brother and sister to talk about, but when he left the cottage, he had no indication or feeling that either of them was the killer.

After leaving the Wolfe's cottage, Nick walked over to the cottage of the wealthiest man in the county. Max got up from his computer, where he was working on his book, to answer the door. He greeted Nick with a question. "Ah, Detective, you have some news? It's good I hope."

"I don't think it's the news you're hoping for, but I think it's good."

"So, come in then and tell me. The mosquitoes are out for blood tonight."

"Thanks, Max." Once he and Nick were settled in Max's comfortable living room, Nick started. "Max, did you know anything about Bonnie Campbell's financial situation or anything about her will?"

"No, I can't say that I did, or do. From all appearances, I wouldn't be surprised to learn that she was financially embarrassed. Of course, that's just an assumption based on the old car she drove, and the charity shop clothes she wore. For all I know, she was a wealthy, but eccentric millionaire. I didn't know her all that well, other than to chat now and again in the coffee shop at the Mouse House. We usually talked about our schoolteacher days."

"Funny you should say that she might have been a millionaire, Max. She was probably the wealthiest woman in the county."

Max fiddled with his beard while responding. "I always wondered what the truth was about her. She was much more intelligent than most people assumed. They were distracted by her clothes and flirting, but if you talked with her and really listened, you could tell there was a brain there. What a waste?"

"Max, she left that fortune to you."

"Why would she do that. Will Preston was her closest friend, although I'm not sure how strong their relationship was."

"From what I gather, she wants you to use the money to help young people. You'll need to talk to her lawyer, Ned Swanson to get the details."

"She was a schoolteacher who cared about her students. Perhaps that was it. Caring about our students is something we both had in common. I now wish I had gotten to know her better. Now, on another subject Detective, have you seen that awful website?"

"Yes, Max, I have, if you're talking about Crime Spartans. You can't imagine how much work it's creating for us."

After discussing the website for a few minutes, Nick left. He enjoyed talking with Max, but it was getting late and he wanted to get home. He'd been neglecting his wife and wanted to spend some time with her. As he drove away from Beulah Crest, the detective felt no closer to solving the crime. He couldn't see where any of the three who gained the most from the deaths was the murderer.

As Nick was leaving the park, Ian decided to close up the Mouse House and head up to Elizabeth's apartment in Interlochen. He wanted to talk with her about the website, which was getting frightening with all the speculation and gossip shared there. He also planned to tell Elizabeth about Babs' will.

When he arrived, Ian found Elizabeth on a conference call with their website partners, Conner, Roscoe, and Megan. They were discussing the success of the Beulah Crest pages and potential changes. Ian walked in and kissed Elizabeth before joining the call. He mostly listened, feeling too close to what was happening to be objective.

* * *

The killer got to bed late. Once settled and comfortable, thoughts about the long day came to mind. *Well, I've done it. I snuck into Herb's tool shed and put the hammer in his toolbox.*

The voice in the killer's head asked, *"Did you wipe off the fingerprints?"*

Yes, I wiped the handle clean, but I didn't wipe the head. It is covered with dried blood from Babs' wound. I'm hoping that when Herb sees the posting I make on the website tomorrow; he'll look in his toolbox and pick up the hammer and leave fingerprints.

"Even if he doesn't touch the hammer, the police will assume he wiped the handle of prints. If he does pick it up, it will be an added bonus."

I agree.

"The tricky part will be making sure the police find the hammer in Herb's possession before he has the chance to hide it or throw it away."

I've thought about that. After I post on the Web tomorrow morning, I'll head home and keep a watch on Herb's cottage.

"Then what?

I have a cheap pre-paid cell phone I bought in England last year to use while I was there. It still has a few dollars of un-used time. When I get home, I'll text Herb and Dot with a link to the website and a comment about the evidence in Herb's toolbox. Then, I'll text the sheriff and Detective Townsend and tell them that the murderer hid the murder weapon in the Cooper's toolbox, and I'm afraid he's about to use it again soon.

"It might just work. Be careful that no one sees you watching the Cooper's cottage. Maybe it would be best to stay away from the park until after the police arrest Herb."

CHAPTER 9
More Arrests

Nick left for the station early Friday morning. He stopped off, on the way, at the Ursa Major coffee shop in Beulah and picked up coffee and some pastries for himself and the other deputies. When he arrived at the station, he was surprised to find Kathy and the sheriff were already there. Kathy often started work early, but the sheriff rarely showed up before 10am.

Kathy was working her way through the clues that were left on the website and the other deputies were working through all of the phone messages left about the murders. Kathy brought Nick up to date on what she and the others had learned from the calls and Web, but there was nothing substantial. Nick took a stack of phone message slips and started to return calls himself.

Nick was on his 15th phone call when the sheriff burst into his office and screamed. "Townsend, have you seen this?" The sheriff showed Nick the screen on his phone.

"What's that, Sheriff, something else on the Web?"

"I just got a text. It says where the hammer used to kill Babs Tucker is hidden. It's in Herb Cooper's toolbox." While the sheriff was shouting, Nick's phone pinged, announcing the receipt of the same text.

Back at Beulah Crest, Dot Cooper was drinking a cup of coffee and reading the morning paper by herself when she received the text from the killer. Herb wasn't home because he was at the nursery down in Frankfort picking up some flowers for their deck. He didn't receive the text or the call his wife had made to him because the nursery was in one of the dark spots not covered by his cell phone provider.

Dot wasn't sure what to do. First, she looked at the Crime Spartans website and quickly found the post about the hammer. She was about to call Nick and tell him about the text and the website posting and then thought it might be a good idea to check the toolbox herself. *It's probably just a prank,* she thought to herself. *If there's nothing unusual in Herb's toolbox, I won't bother the detective with a phone call.*

It was windy outside, so Dot put on a jacket. The shed was never locked, so she didn't need a key. As soon she put on her Jacket, Della jumped up and down expecting a walk. The active dog wasn't allowed outside unsupervised since she was drugged, so she was excited at the prospect of a walk.

"All right Della, hold on. Let me get your leash. After I check the toolbox, we can go for a walk down by the lake." Dot didn't notice the police car coming through the front gate of the park as she opened the garden shed door and turned on the light. As she opened the toolbox, she didn't hear the car carrying the sheriff and Detective Townsend pull up and park on the street in front of her cottage.

When Dot picked up the hammer with the blood-stained head, Della barked. Dot thought Della was barking because she smelled the blood on the hammer when in fact, the dog was announcing the approach of the two men who had their weapons drawn. Dot was startled when Della pulled on her leash, forcing her to turn around and see the approaching officers.

The sheriff pointed his gun at Dot and shouted. "Drop the hammer and put your hands in the air! Right now!"

Startled, Dot dropped the hammer and tried to calm Della. Nick stepped forward and took Della's leash before Dot could say anything. The sheriff pushed Dot against the wall of the shed and handcuffed her while Della's frantic barking alerted nearby neighbors.

Elsie walked over from her cottage and Ian, Ben, and Albert ran over from the Mouse House. Not wanting to leave Greta alone, Albert brought his dog.

Everyone started talking at once. Elsie shouted, "It can't be Dot, can it? Is that the hammer she used to kill Babs?"

Albert took Della's leash from the detective as he spoke to Dot. "Don't worry. I'll take care of Della until this is sorted out. Is Herb around?"

The sheriff, who wasn't accustomed to having such an active audience when he was arresting a suspect finally yelled to everyone, "Everyone, be quiet and step back. There may be more evidence here."

As soon as Albert took Della's leash, Nick nudged everyone back across the street. "Please stay off the Coopers lot. We'll be roping it off for the forensics folks to inspect."

After everyone was away from the scene, Nick returned to where the sheriff and Dot were standing near the shed. Dot was in a state of shock, crying softly, not quite understanding what was going on. She was about to say something when the sheriff interrupted. "Nick, please read Mrs. Cooper her rights while I put this hammer in an evidence bag." The sheriff then put on a pair of pair of latex gloves and picked up the hammer and put it into the plastic evidence bag he had just pulled out of his pocket. He then returned his attention to Dot, who had just verified that she understood her rights.

Before the sheriff could say anything, Dot told him, "I have nothing to say until I talk to a lawyer. I'll call Ned Swanson as soon as you'll let me and ask him to find a criminal defense lawyer. I'm sure he'll know of someone. Until then, I won't answer any questions."

"If that's the way you want it, Mrs. Cooper, that's OK with me," the sheriff answered. "If you want to lawyer up, fine. We'll play this by the book. Just don't expect any favors from me." Just then two more police cars pulled up. Jake Summerlin, Kathy McGregor, and two other deputies got out of the cars.

The sheriff then started issuing orders. "Deputy McGregor, please take Mrs. Cooper to the station and book her for the first-degree murder of Babs Tucker. Jake, get this lot marked off with crime scene tape. You other two, put out an all points for Herb Cooper. I don't know if he's the killer or if she is, but I don't want him running loose until we get to the bottom of this."

The sheriff then turned to Nick. "Get that hammer down to the crime lab and get it checked for fingerprints, DNA, and whatever the hell they can find and get the lab folks here to go through this cottage and shed with a fine-tooth comb."

Nick was going to do all of those things anyway, so he just agreed. If Dot, Herb, or both of them turned out to be the murderers, the sheriff would surely take credit for the arrest. Nick was surprised that he hadn't called the press on the drive over to Beulah Crest. Since the sheriff personally ordered the arrest, he would also have to take the blame if it led to nothing.

Out across the street, the group watching the arrest grew. Hortense and Derek Parker joined the group and a short while later the Wolfes and Max Silver walked over. Della finally stopped barking after Dot was put into a police cruiser and taken away.

A few minutes later, Herb Cooper came through the front gate and pulled up to his cottage. He wasn't able to pull into the driveway because Jake had already blocked it crime scene tape. When he saw the police cars in his drive he jumped out of the car and shouted to the sheriff and Nick. "What's happened? Is Dot OK.? Where is she?"

The sheriff pulled out his gun and pointed it at Herb, who immediately froze, like a deer in the headlights. Nick thought pulling the gun was a bit over the top, but there wasn't much he could do. He walked over to Herb and handcuffed him. The sheriff put his gun away and approached Herb. "Mr. Cooper, we found your wife holding the hammer that appears to be the one used to kill Babs Tucker. She was seen removing it from the toolbox in your shed."

"What are you talking about?" Herb shouted. His temper was beginning to boil. "Where's Dot? Is she OK?"

Nick answered. He was afraid the sheriff would inflame the situation further. As he spoke, he lifted the evidence bag so

Herb could see its contents. "Herb, we found this in your shed. It appears to be covered in dried blood." Herb was about to interrupt, but Nick put his hand on his shoulder a looked directly at him before he continued. "Herb, this is what's going to happen. I'm going to read you your rights and then we're going to take you down to the station where you can see Dot. You can call a lawyer, if you want. Do you understand?"

Herb nodded. His temper subsided and slumped over in submission. Nick somehow had the ability to calm agitated suspects.

Nick read to Herb his rights from the card in his pocket. Nick had long ago memorized what was on the card, but it was department policy to read them from the card to be sure there was no variation. He had done the same with Dot.

After Herb indicated that he understood, Nick asked, "What can you tell me about the hammer Herb?"

"I've never seen it before, Detective. I haven't been in the shed or toolbox since last week. It wasn't there then. I'm guessing Dot told you the same thing."

The sheriff interrupted. "She refused to say anything until she talks to a lawyer. We were hoping you would be more cooperative, Mr. Cooper."

The veterinarian gave the sheriff a cold stare before answering. "It's Dr. Cooper, Sheriff. I think I'll go along with Dot and wait until we talk to a lawyer. I'm invoking my right to see a lawyer and to remain silent."

"As you wish, Dr. Cooper." I'll have one of my officers take you down to the station, where you'll be booked." As the sheriff spoke, Jennifer Reynolds, the reporter from the *Benzie County Record-Patriot* pulled up. As soon as the sheriff saw the reporter, he told Nick to go talk to the other residents who were gathered across the road and that he would take Dr. Cooper to the station.

As the sheriff escorted the handcuffed suspect to his car, the reporter took photos and videos. When the sheriff reached the car, the reporter asked, "Any comments sheriff?"

The sheriff waited until the reporter began to video record his statement on her phone before he answered. "Jennifer, we've taken Dr. Herb Cooper and his wife Dorothy into custody. They are suspects in the murder of Babs Tucker here at Beulah Crest in Beulah. A hammer that appears to be the murder weapon was found in their possession. That's all I can share now."

"Thank you, Sheriff. Do you have anything to say, Dr. Cooper? Did you kill Babs and Bonnie?"

Herb covered his face as he ducked into the back seat of the police car, not saying a word to the reporter. After allowing Jennifer to take a few more pictures, the sheriff got in the car and drove off with his suspect.

The crowd across the street from the Cooper's cottage had grown as events unfolded. Someone sent a text to Nigel and Spencer about the arrests, so they drove over to the park from their home across the lake and joined the crowd. As they arrived, one of the deputies was marking off the Cooper's lot with crime scene tape.

"I'm getting tired of seeing that yellow tape around here," Elsie commented to no one in particular. As the crowed watched the officers, she continued voicing her thoughts aloud. "I can't believe either of the Coopers did it. Yes, he cheats at bridge, but other than that, he's all talk. As for Dot, well the way she dotes on Della, her dog, it's just not possible. People who are kind to dogs don't go around killing people."

"I tend to agree," Albert added as he continued to pet Della behind her ears. "I can't see either of them as killers."

"Well, if not one of them, then who?" Reverend Parker asked. "I agree, it doesn't seem likely either of the Coopers killed Babs or Bonnie, but if they aren't the murderers, who is, and how did that hammer get in their shed?"

Before anyone could answer, Jennifer approached the group and tried to ask questions. By unspoken agreement, no one said a word to her. After repeated attempts, Spencer finally told her to leave. "Ms. Reynolds, this is private property. Please go. If you wish to come past our gate again, please call either myself or Ian, the park manager, and ask for permission to enter." Ian joined Spencer and escorted the reporter to her car while the group watched.

After Jennifer drove past the gate, Elsie commented. "I don't like that woman. We have enough going on here without her stirring the pot."

Albert was the first to respond to Elsie's comment. "I agree, Elsie. She seems to know what the sheriff is up to and it's almost as if he calls her to the crime scene to get publicity."

"I wouldn't be surprised," Max added. "Then again, perhaps that reporter has one of those radios that can track police calls. I would if I were in her business. I'm just glad we have that detective, Nick Townsend, on the case. He seems to be more of a professional law officer than our sheriff."

The group started to break up after a short while. Albert took Della and Greta with him back to the Mouse House and re-opened the coffee shop. Max decided to join him. As the broke away from the others, Albert asked, "Max, any idea what's going on? I don't think either of the Coopers did it, do you?"

While the killer was still within hearing distance to the two men, Max replied. "I agree. I saw someone rooting around in their shed last night. Perhaps they planted the hammer there." Before Max could continue, a squirrel ran past, causing Della and Greta to start barking.

Albert interrupted Max as he bent down to pet the dogs. "Settle down girls, you've seen squirrels before. Now lets go get some coffee. I'm not letting either of you out of my sight until I know they've really caught the killer."

Max continued telling Albert about what he saw last night after they reached the Mouse House, where Ian joined them for a coffee. "I wish I saw more, but it was dark. Someone did go into Herb and Dot's shed late last night and then walked away. Whoever it was, he didn't go into the Cooper's cottage."

Ian asked, "Did you see who it was?"

"No, it was dark, and I had my reading glasses on. I can't see far with them, especially at night. Even if I had my other glasses on, I wouldn't have seen much. My night vision is for nothing."

"Did they drive away in a car?" Ian asked.

"No, I don't think so," Max replied. "I didn't see or hear another car for at least 20 minutes when I saw the Wolfes pull into their driveway. I wish there was more we could do."

"There is," Ian answered as Albert refilled everyone's coffee mugs. "You should call Detective Townsend and let him know what you saw. Even if you don't know who you saw, maybe someone else did. The detective can ask the other people in the park if they saw anyone. As for me, I'm going to get some more motion activated cameras and place them around the park and also put one by the stairs down to the lake."

Spencer and Nigel came in while Ian was talking. Albert got them each a coffee as they sat down. Spencer took a sip of coffee before commenting. "Great idea about the cameras, Ian."

Nigel interrupted. "Do you think you can get them installed today? I think we'd all feel better if they were."

"I think so," Ian responded. "I'll head up to Traverse City and buy all of the equipment we need. I have a friend at NMC who's a hardware nerd who can help me get the right stuff. We can set it up so I can get a feed of all the cameras in my office. Ben's already said he would help installing the cameras."

While the discussion about the cameras was going on in the Mouse House, the person who put the hammer in the Cooper's shed was beginning to panic. The killer only overheard Max say that he saw someone in the garden shed, but not that he didn't know who the intruder was. Not knowing what to do, the murderer decided to take a walk along the lakeside trail and sort out what to do.

While walking down the stairs to the lake, the voice returned. *"I'm here. Take a few deep breaths and take control of your emotions. You need to be calm and think this through."*

The killer stopped about halfway down the steep stairway and took several deep breaths before continuing down tp the lake.

I'll try, but how can I be calm? You heard what Max said. He saw me in the shed.

"He saw someone. He didn't say that he saw you."

Shouldn't I put Max at the top of my list and think of a way to eliminate the risk of his going to the police? I never liked him anyway. He's not from around here.

At the bottom of the stairs the killer paused to decide which way to turn. After a few minutes, a decision was made to turn right and walk into Beulah for an ice cream. It was still early in the season, so there weren't any people on the trail. In a few weeks, that would change.

"You really need to think this through. If someone else from the park is killed or even dies of natural causes before the Coopers go to trial, the investigation will continue, and the Coopers will probably be released. Do you want that to happen?"

No, I suppose not. Especially not Herb. He was on my list and now, hopefully, he'll go to prison. Dot has issues too, so it's just as well if she also goes, but if Max saw me, then what?

"We'll cross that bridge when and if we come to it. Meanwhile, now is the time to let the dust settle for a while. Once the Coopers are gone for good, we can think about what to do next. Work on

your plan to take care of Elsie, but don't take any action on it for now. That will give you something to keep your mind occupied."

I suppose. It's just, well, I don't like loose ends.

"I know, but don't worry. I'm here with you. When it's time to act, I'll let you know. We have a number of troublesome people who need to go, but we need to be more careful and plan better than we did with Babs and Bonnie. Holding off until Herb and Dot are convicted will give us time to do that."

While the killer walked into town and was thinking about what the voice had to say, Ian left the Mouse House and headed up to Traverse City to buy the cameras and related equipment. On the way, he called Stephen, the programmer who helps Elizabeth with the Crime Spartans site and arranged to meet him at Best Buy to help with the purchases. Stephen said he could come down to Beulah afterwards to help set things up.

Since Stephen would be in class at NMC for the next two hours, Ian decided to stop at Elizabeth's apartment on the way to fill her in on what happened. It turned out that Elizabeth knew more about the arrests than Ian did. When Ian knocked on her door, Elizabeth quickly answered and then asked, "Are you OK?" Before he could answer, she pulled him into the apartment and hugged him in a tight embrace.

The events of the morning finally caught up with Ian and he broke down and started sobbing. Elizabeth led him to the sofa, where they sat together while she held him close until he settled down. Finally, he began to talk. "Did you hear they arrested the Coopers? I can't believe it. I sold them their cottage and… Well, I just can't believe it was them."

Elizabeth wiped a tear from Ian's eye and gently pulled his hair off of his face before responding. "It's already on the website, Ian. Someone posted the video taken by that reporter of your sheriff arresting Herb Cooper and there is a lot of detail about the arrest of Dot, including the sheriff pulling his gun, and someone named Albert taking care of the Cooper's dog, Della. It says the sheriff caught Dot trying to hide the hammer she, or Herb, used to kill Babs."

"Why hide the hammer in their own garden shed? They could have thrown in into the lake or into a swamp where it would never be found."

Elizabeth got up and headed over to the kitchen. "I'll make us a cup of herbal tea. While I'm doing that, take a look at the website. My laptop is on the table next to the sofa."

Glad for something to do, Ian picked up the computer and looked at the screen. There were several more postings since Elizabeth had looked at it a few minutes ago. "Someone just posted that Herb had a fling with Bonnie Campbell last year and there's a photo of them together taken at the Corner Bar in Beulah."

"Any idea who posted that one?"

"No, their user-name is 'Trailer Trash', with nothing in their bio. Hold on…"

"What?"

"Someone's posted a video of Dot being escorted from the police car into the county jail for booking. Wow!"

"Wow, what?" Elizabeth ran into the living room to see what was going on. When she got there, Ian restarted the video.

It showed Deputy McGregor helping Dot get out of the car. As she was getting up, Dot swung her handcuffed wrists into the deputy's face hitting her just below the left eye. Two other officers quickly grabbed Dot and rushed her to the ground as she tried to run away.

"Poor Dot," Ian sighed. "Even if she's not the killer, and I don't think she is, they'll nail her for assaulting a police officer and who knows what else. It looks like Albert will be keeping Della for quite a while."

"I think you're right. Oh look, the same person posted a video of Herb Cooper being escorted into the jail. He looks more resigned to his fate." After the video ended, Elizabeth kissed Ian on the forehead and headed back to the kitchen, to pour the tea.

"Put some lemon in mine, if you have any."

"You don't put lemon in herbal tea!"

"I do. I put lemon in and on everything."

"Whatever," Elizabeth's responded as she squeezed some lemon juice into Ian's mug. "Take a look at the site metrics and see how many people have viewed it today."

Ian loaded the metrics page for Crime Spartans. "Oh, my God, Elizabeth! There are nearly a thousand hits today, just in Benzie and Manistee counties, and over two hundred thousand hits from across the U.S. and almost as many international hits. This is ridiculous."

Elizabeth carried the mugs into the living room and set them on the coffee table. "You better get some security guards for the park, Ian."

"You think there'll be another murder?"

"I hope not, but there'll be crowds. This is going viral and lookie-loos will be out in droves. I'd hire several guards, if I were you, especially on weekends, and if this goes on, probably for the summer when all the fudgies are up. I love the summer, but I hate the tourists." "Fudgies" are what northern Michiganders call tourists from "downstate" or southern Michigan.

"I suppose you're right. I'll stop off at the security company while I'm up in Traverse and get them to come on-site today. We'll have the most secure park in the country."

"I'm glad. I don't want the Beulah Crest Slayer to get you. Are you coming over tonight?"

"I thought you'd never ask. Of course, I am. It's becoming a habit that I intend to keep. If I haven't said it, thanks for being there for me. This has been a tough week and I really do appreciate all you've done to help."

Not sure how to respond to Ian, Elizabeth turned the conversation back to the website. "Before we break out the wine tonight, I want to do a conference call with Conner, Roscoe, and Megan. You saw how many hits we're getting because of Beulah Crest. What if we have pages covering a dozen similar crimes going at the same time. We could be talking millions of hits a day, which is big time."

"You're right, of course, but can we hold off for a few days? I'm up for using how we handled what's going on at Beulah Crest and doing the same for other crimes, but this one is too close to home for me to be rational on the things we need to be rational about."

Elizabeth was excited and wanted to move forward quickly with expanding the site, but she could see Ian's point and also see the emotional impact it was having on him. "How about if we keep doing what we're doing until we're sure they caught the guy who killed Babs and Bonnie and then step back and draft a revised business plan using what we learn from all of this."

"Ok, I can do that. I also want to keep the focus on Beulah Crest, to keep the pressure on the sheriff and others to be sure this is solved properly. You know our sheriff; for him justice is secondary to his re-election."

"You're right of course. Identifying the killer is the most important thing. After it's over though, how about we invite Conner, Roscoe, and Megan up for a long working weekend to do a proper plan for the website that includes everything we've learned."

"OK. We could all stay in Babs' cottage. I wouldn't feel as guilty about her giving it to me if we could do something useful there."

Elizabeth playfully pulled Ian up from the sofa and then pushed him toward the door. "Now go! Get those cameras set up and the guards hired. The sooner you get that finished, the sooner you can get back here for that glass of wine."

Ian playfully saluted and answered as he allowed himself to be pushed "Yes ma'am, whatever you say."

On the way up to the electronics store in Traverse City, Ian called Nigel to ask for approval to hire the added security guards. Nigel answered his phone from the Mouse House, where he and Spencer were talking with Albert and some of the other residents. Nigel readily agreed. "Great idea. I was just about to call you and suggest the same thing. The sheriff has deputies at the front gate and at the stairway to the lake, but he said he'll stop providing deputies once the crime scene folks are done with their work at the Cooper's cottage."

"Is everything else OK at the park?"

"It's a circus Ian. Albert thinks it's because of that website. Cars are parked along the highway from Lake Street all the way to the farmer's market. Everyone wants to see the crime scene. We even had a group of Boy Scouts walking around the park asking the police questions. They said they were working on a crime prevention merit badge."

Ian realized that Nigel's phone was on speaker mode when Spencer interrupted. "The condo complex next door has volunteers taking turns at their entrance to stop the tourists from parking there. Oh, and there's a group protesting in front of the sheriff's office about how they handled Dot's arrest. Elsie drove past and saw Reverend Parker and some other ministers among the protesters. She said there was also a group there from the bridge club carrying signs."

Nigel added a comment. "Xander said that one of the food trucks was across the road from the sheriff's office selling tacos to the protesters."

Ian interrupted. "I'll get back as soon as I can and get the extra security guards at the park tonight. Is there anything else I can do?"

Nigel answered. "Not that I can think of. I think the extra guards and the cameras will be a big help. Oh, did I mention the reporters from the Traverse City TV stations and from several newspapers are at the gate. We're not letting any of them in the park. Make sure the security folks know to keep them out."

"I will. I've got to go now. I just arrived at the electronics store and I can see Stephen's car." Ian hung up and met up with Stephen in the store.

By early evening things at the park settled down a bit. Word had spread about the security guards and that access to the park was restricted to residents and invited guests. Ben stayed late and helped Ian and Stephen install the cameras. By nightfall, everything was set up. Ian could monitor all the video feeds from his office. Ian, Nigel, and Spencer could also access the video feed and history from their phones.

CHAPTER 10
Murder Charges

After Dot was booked, she called Ned Swanson. As Ned arrived at the jail, Herb was being led to the booking officer by the sheriff. Jennifer Reynolds was there with her camera recording when Ned asked the sheriff, "Are you also arresting Herb?"

"Yes, Mr. Swanson. Both are being charged with the murder of Babs Tucker. You can see your clients after I've booked them into the jail."

Ned shouted to Herb as he was taken inside, "Don't say a word until we talk. I told Dot the same thing when she called."

An hour later, Ned met with his clients in a small conference room adjacent to the holding cells. One of the deputies stood outside the locked door. Inside, Ned asked his clients, "Have either of you said anything to the sheriff or anyone on his staff since you were taken into custody?"

Dot, who had a large scrape on her left forearm and a bandage on her forehead answered first. "Not a word, other than to answer a few medical questions to the nurse who bandaged me."

"Nothing from me either," Herb added. "So, what's next, Ned?"

"First off, continue to refuse to answer any questions and don't talk about the case to anyone else. Second, you need a criminal defense attorney. That's not me. I do wills and trusts for a living. This is way out of my league."

"I know," responded. So, who do you suggest?

"I called Joe Quandaro up in Traverse while driving here. He's the best criminal lawyer in the area and the firm where he's a partner has the resources to back him up. He'll be here in about an hour to talk with you."

"This Joe is from Traverse City," Dot commented. "Wouldn't we be better off with one of the best criminal lawyers in the state, although God only knows how we'd pay for such representation?"

"You could go with a high-power law firm from Detroit or Grand Rapids," Ned answered, "but I don't think you would do better than Joe. Not only is he a great defense attorney, he's local. He grew up in Elberta and he knows everyone in the court system in Benzie and how things work around here. A big city lawyer would alienate a jury, if it comes to that, and all the other players, including the judge and courts clerks."

Herb responded. "Ok, let's at least talk to this Joe Quandaro. We're still outsiders here. Maybe it would be a good idea to use a local guy to represent us. What do you think, Dot?"

"I suppose. It can't hurt to talk with him. This whole mess is still going to cost us a fortune. Ned, what about a public defender?"

"You could go that route, Dot, but I wouldn't advise you to make that decision. I'm a pragmatist. Forget about what you learned in high school civics class. The justice system is fair, but only if you spend a lot of money to protect your rights. If you can't put up a strong and competent defense, which is expensive, you go to jail. It's that simple."

Herb agreed. "You're right, of course, Ned." Turning to his wife and taking her hand, he continued. "Dot, we have two choices. Bankruptcy and hopefully freedom, or we spend the rest of our lives in prison. We've been bankrupt before and survived, but I don't think either of us would survive prison."

Dot agreed with her husband. "I know I wouldn't and with your health issues, you wouldn't either. Ok, Ned, let's talk to this local guy you like."

While waiting for Joe to arrive, Ned reviewed the basic procedures of the court and what the Coopers could expect to happen over the next few days. The next thing they could expect would be an arraignment before a judge. Ned thought it unlikely that bail would be granted, but he acknowledged that Joe could provide better information on that subject.

They had just finished talking about bail when the deputy knocked on the door and let the lawyer from Traverse City enter. After introductions were made, Joe told the Coopers about his background. "I grew up in Elberta and went to Frankfort High School. I worked at the firm, where I'm now a partner, summers while I did my undergraduate degree at Michigan State and during law school at Michigan. Ned will get you summaries of cases I've tried over the past few years, and you can judge for yourself if you want to retain me for the duration. Meanwhile, let's get prepared for the arraignment and bail hearings."

Dot liked Joe's no nonsense style and wanted to hire him, but she had to ask about costs. "Joe, I'm glad Ned pulled you in, and I think Herb and I would like you to represent us but let's review the costs. What are we talking here?"

Herb nodded in agreement before Joe answered Dot. "It's hard to estimate costs at this stage, Dot. Can I call you Dot?"

"Of course. Go ahead with what you were saying."

"It depends how far this goes through the courts. Once I read through the evidence and we talk about the details of the case, I'll have a better idea of where we stand. If this goes to trial, it could easily go over $100,000. If we can get the case dropped fairly quickly, a small fraction of that. I'll need a $20,000 retainer once we get things started. If we're successful at getting the charges dropped quickly, most of that will be refunded."

The Coopers both agreed to go ahead and hire Joe. Ned then excused himself and left his clients in the capable hands of his colleague. After he left, Joe had the Coopers walk him through the events of the past few days and then he asked them to tell him about anything in their past that could be brought up by the prosecution.

Dot shared information about her conviction for assault when she punched Herb and Herb told Joe about the various business failures and the dealings they had with Elsie's husband. "On the Web they say I killed Babs because I mistook her for Elsie and I held a grudge against her husband, who died years ago. It's nonsense, but there you are."

Joe then asked, "What's with the Web? Are you telling me this is getting a lot of play on the Internet already?"

Dot answered. "Go to the Crime Spartans website. You won't believe all of the nonsense there. Some of it is accurate, but a lot of it is just gossip. Someone posted that we hid the hammer we used to kill Babs in our garden shed. I went out to check if it was out there just as the sheriff pulled up. I think the killer is using the site to frame us."

"Do you have any enemies who would take such drastic steps?"

"We get along with everyone at the park," Dot answered. "Now, there are some at the bridge club who don't approve of Herb's temper and aggressive style of play…"

Herb interrupted. "Now really Dot, do you actually think someone at the bridge club has it in for us? As for my style of play, what do you mean aggressive. I just don't tolerate people who cheat."

"I've never seen anyone cheating at the club, and that includes Babs and Elsie. They just bid and played those hands better than we did. That said, Elsie is a sly one. Can you trust anyone who gossips as much as her? She's a state champion bridge player, so she's smart. Perhaps she is trying to frame you for killing Babs. After all, Babs was her best friend and bridge partner."

"Even if she is trying to frame us," Herb responded, "I don't see Elsie killing Babs. They were like sisters. That still leaves the question of who killed Babs, and for that matter, Bonnie."

Joe let the couple banter back and forth for a while longer and then asked them to stop, so he could summarize what he had heard. "I heard several things. First, neither of you killed

Babs Tucker. Second, you have no idea how the hammer ended up in your toolbox. Third, you think this Elise at the park didn't kill Babs, but she may want to frame you, and finally, you are not popular at the bridge club."

"Correct," Dot answered. "Now, when can you get us out of here?"

"I can't say right now. The sheriff has arrested you and will be forwarding his evidence to the prosecuting attorney. She'll review the evidence and decide if there's enough there to issue a warrant. If she issues a warrant, you'll be held in custody until you are arraigned in District Court. That's a hearing before a judge where the formal charges are read, and the question of bail is raised. I'll try, but this is a murder charge, so if I get bail, it will be set very high, probably over a million dollars."

Dot gasped while Herb calmly asked a question. "So, how long will we be stuck here while the prosecutor decides whether to charge us?"

"Unfortunately, this is Friday evening. You'll probably be here for the weekend. Now, before we go further, I have a few questions."

"What do you need to know," Herb calmly answered.

"At this stage I have one question for both of you. What did you tell the sheriff or his deputies?"

Dot answered first. "I said nothing, Joe. As soon as they read me my rights, I told the sheriff that I would invoke my right to be silent and that I wanted to call Ned and ask him to find a criminal lawyer. I learned to keep my mouth shut when I was arrested back in Ohio."

"How about you, Herb?"

"I invoked my right to remain silent, but after I answered a question or two from Nick Townsend. When the sheriff got nasty, I shut up."

"What exactly did you say, Herb?"

"I told the detective I'd never seen the hammer before and that I hadn't been in the shed or toolbox since last week and the hammer wasn't there then."

"What's next?" Dot asked.

"I'll talk to the prosecuting attorney to see if she has a strong case and to try to convince her to drop the charges. If she intends to go forward, I'll talk to some contacts in the sheriff's office and then I'll get our investigator to start talking to potential witnesses. We have a social media guru at the office. I'll have him go through everything on that Crime Spartan website to see if there is anything we can use."

Before Joe left the Coopers, he gave them some instructions. "Before I leave, I want to make something perfectly clear. Don't talk about the case or anything that could possibly be related to it, with anyone. Consider every person other than myself or my associates as working for the police or the prosecutor. Don't speak about the case with anyone and if you two are together, don't talk about the case if there is a chance anyone can hear you. Is that clear?"

The Coopers both agreed to remain silent.

It was early evening when Joe left the jail and the Coopers were taken back to their cells. He called the prosecuting attorney, Angela Berg, on her cell and set up a meeting on Monday morning. Joe knew Angela from law school, and they were on good working terms with each other. She was a strong adversary but was fair in the courtroom and the political arena. Angela agreed to call the sheriff over the weekend and review his evidence before they met on Monday.

The first night in the holding cells was more difficult for Dot than it was for Herb. Joe said that he would check with Albert to be sure Della was cared for, but Dot still worried. When she wasn't thinking about Della, money was the focus of her thoughts. It hadn't sunk in that she and Herb could spend the rest of their lives in jail, so she didn't dwell on that. Money though, was another thing. She's been poor as a child and had gone through bankruptcy with Herb. It wasn't a pleasant process and she was afraid, that given his health issues, Herb wouldn't be able to handle the stress of everything.

Surprisingly, Herb remained calm. His main concern was that he received his medications, but it turned out he didn't need to worry. After he gave his medical history to the booking officer, arrangements were quickly made to have a doctor visit and have his prescriptions delivered from the pharmacy. The sheriff, fearing bad publicity and a lawsuit, quickly authorized the medical expenditures when the booking officers told him about Herb' s medical problems.

After a light supper, Herb spent a few hours writing down the most difficult bridge hands he could remember playing. He often did this when faced with a difficult situation. Afterward, he went to sleep. He was the only man held in the men's section of the holding cells, so it was a quiet night.

* * *

Back at the park, the person who put the hammer in the Coopers' toolbox and who killed Babs and Bonnie had the best night of sleep in days. Herb, who was on the list, and Dot, were no longer in the park and were destined to spend the rest of their lives in prison. That was two fewer people to have to plan how to remove from Beulah Crest.

There was no need to call on the voice, at least for the time being. The excitement of seeing the Coopers taken away was followed by a calm that was a reward for doing God's work. Thoughts moved on what to do once the trial was over. *The voice suggested creating a plan to take care of Elsie, but I think I need to focus on Max. Max saw someone in the Coopers shed, so he's a bigger risk. On the one hand, I can take care of Elsie at any time. She gossips so much that I don't know that anyone really listens to her anyway. On the other hand, there's Max. He's a respected teacher. If he talks or even worse, files a complaint, he'll be taken seriously.* After turning the lights off and climbing into bed, the killer developed several scenarios in which Max was killed or, at the least, forced to move away.

After thinking about options for Max, thoughts shifted to the Crime Spartans website. *I used the site effectively to get Dot to put her fingerprints on the hammer handle and to get her and Herb arrested for Babs murder. What about Bonnie's murder? If the Coopers aren't suspected of killing her, will the charges stick for the murder of Babs? I don't think so. Perhaps some evidence needs to be planted to incriminate them. I could then use the website to spread some rumors to force another police search after I plant some evidence, of course. I could also use the site to lay the foundation for how I take care of Max. I'll think more about that once I sort out how to incriminate the Coopers for Bonnie's murder.* After thinking through some ideas about using Crime Spartans, the killer fell into a deep dreamless sleep and didn't wake until morning.

* * *

The morning after the Coopers were arrested was quiet at the park. Curious tourists and amateur crime sleuths began to lose interest in visiting when they realized the security guards would turn them away and the cameras would photograph them or take videos if they tried to trespass on the property.

Over the weekend, life at the park slowly moved back towards something resembling normality. Summer residents started to return for the season and Albert found himself busy again at the Mouse House coffee shop. Not convinced that Dot or Herb were the murderers, he still wouldn't let Greta or Della out of his sight. The dogs weren't upset, since they became the center of attention for the coffee shop visitors.

On Saturday morning, Ian scanned through the video clips from the previous night. There wasn't much to see. The cameras only recorded when they sensed something or someone moving. There was a short clip of the Wolfes arriving home after seeing a movie at the theater in Frankfort and a few other clips of residents returning home for the evening after attending a concert at

Interlochen. There was nothing after midnight except for some clips of Arthur, the fox, running through the park and two deer nibbling wild strawberries near the top of the stairway.

On Sunday, Nate Santiago, who lived with his mother in the cottage next door to Albert, set up a small business. A junior at Benzie Central with plans to major in finance at Kalamazoo College, Nate was not one to let an opportunity to make money pass. He discreetly brought three guests (customers) at time through the gate and took them on a walking tour of the park, with stops for pictures at the Cooper's garden shed, Bonnie's and Babs' cottages, and the coffee shop where Bonnie drank the poisoned coffee. He conducted one tour a day after school and two a day on weekends. His customers paid $20 each for the opportunity to be a part of what Nate called "Benzie County crime history in the making."

After the 2nd day of the tours, Ian realized what Nate was doing, but decided to let him continue after warning him to avoid disturbing park residents and to keep his activities low key. In return, Nate agreed to let Ian know if he or his "guests" saw anything suspicious.

Reverend Parker spent Saturday morning at the sheriff's office helping to organize the protestors, but there was little work to do there. Many of protestors from the previous protests were there and well-developed processes for obtaining publicity were being used. Most of those marching outside the sheriff's office weren't sure of the innocence or guilt of Dot and Herb, but they were confident of their objections to the tactics used by the sheriff.

Hortense returned home and prepared lunch for Derek, who had spent the morning online reading through all the new postings on Crime Spartans and other social media and news sites. When Derek brought his laptop computer to the kitchen table, he got a cold stare from his wife. "Hortense dear, don't give me that look. You're just as interested in what's on that site as I am."

"I won't deny it, but I just don't like you bringing your computer to the table."

"I thought you'd want to see the video of your protests. They already have some up from this morning."

Hortense took a bite of her sandwich and tried to appear upset, but finally gave in. Alright Derek, show me the latest. I'm sure Elsie is tied to her screen soaking in all the gossip the Crime Spartan site can offer. I'd rather see it online than lister to her."

Derek turned the computer so they could both see the screen. He clicked through various pages and added his commentary. "This is a good shot of you at the protest. I like the way the sunlight reflected off the cross you were wearing. Maybe God was sending you a message."

"Don't be silly, Derek. If God has a message for me, it won't be in a video on a trash website. Is there anything else interesting? Does it look like Dot and Herb are really the murderers?"

"There's a lot on Dot. She was actually convicted of aggravated assault on Herb, even though he refused to testify."

"How did they get a conviction?"

"There were several witnesses who saw her break Herb's jaw. It happened in their front yard, years ago down in Ohio.

She got probation and had to take anger management classes. There were also several police calls to their house over the years for domestic disturbances, but no additional charges. Some of the people commenting think she must have lost her temper, although I can't see how Babs could cause anyone to get that angry."

"So, our Dot has a temper. What about Herb? What do our neighbors have to say about him."

"No criminal record and most of the comments about him are positive. The veterinary community thinks highly of him. No one here can see a motive. There doesn't appear to be a motive for Dot either, for that matter. Anyway, the only dirt on Herb is from bridge players. He was almost banned from the club in Elberta, and there are comments about incidents at clubs in Ohio."

"Has he ever been violent?"

"No, he just shouts a lot. There's a consensus from the bridge community that he's disruptive. I can't believe how many of them posted. Anyway, when his opponents make an unconventional bid and then win the hand, he complains loudly and accuses them of cheating. He did it at the bridge club last week and accused Babs and Elsie. Apparently, there's a tournament director who acts like a referee. She dismissed Herb's complaint and warned him to behave or she would eject him from the game."

"I suppose that could be a motive, for either, or both of them."

"I don't see it, Hortense. Herb and Dot have been playing bridge for what is it, thirty years, and all of a sudden, he bashes in the head of a little old lady who beats him at a card game. I know those bridge players can be a testy lot, but no, I can't see it."

"Anything else of interest?"

"There's some dirt on Ben. A small group think he's the killer. I don't see how it's related, but apparently his wife has a gambling problem. A few think Albert is the killer. He rarely leaves the park because of an anxiety disorder. There's a whole list of things that upset him, according to one post. Things like noise, crowds, and cats. Babs had two cats, and you know how Bonnie liked to play loud music."

"No good motive, so far. Anyone with a good motive?"

"Ian, Max, and Xander have the best motive."

"What's that?"

"Money. There's lots of speculation about what Bonnie and Babs left them. I'm surprised they haven't been questioned more by the police."

"Any dirt on you or me?"

"On me, not too much. Someone asked if you should trust a dentist who goes bankrupt, and there's a comment about Elsie's husband selling me the equipment that led to our financial ruin. Other than that, it appears I'm technically a good dentist who's main shortcoming is lack of empathy for my patients."

"Anything new on me?"

"One nasty posting. Someone commented that you were very high strung in high school and they weren't surprised when you had a breakdown the summer after graduation. They say you've been unstable ever since. The rest of the new comments are about your activism and your roles in the church. There's a petition asking you to do the eulogies at both funerals."

"I expect they'll ship Bonnie back to Boston, or wherever she came from. As for Babs, I would be honored."

After lunch the couple decided to take a walk along the lake into Beulah. There was no real reason to go into town other than to drop a few letters off at the post office. It was just a nice spring day. On the way back they stopped off at the Mouse House to get a cup of coffee. Albert was there, along with Katie, Xander, and Max. Della and Greta were there as well, but were sleeping in the corner by the fireplace. Hortense was the first to greet the small group. "Hello all. We're glad to see things getting back to normal. It's been frightening having a killer around."

Albert took the Parker's mugs from the rack and Hortense filled her cup and Derek's before refilling everyone else's. While Hortense was pouring the coffee, Albert asked, "Do you really think they caught the killer, Reverend? I would never guess it of Dot, or Herb for that matter."

"I don't know," was her response, "and if I did have an opinion, I wouldn't want to share it at this point. The police and the courts will sort through everything and get to the truth. All I can do is pray for Herb and Dot and publicize whenever that sheriff steps over the line."

Katie then asked, "What do you think, Dr. Parker? We've all been talking and none of it makes sense."

"Of course, it doesn't make sense. I'll go along with my wife and not say anything more until the courts render a verdict."

After answering Katie's question, the Parkers went out onto the front porch to drink their coffee.

"That's an odd couple," Katie commented to the others after the Parkers left. "I'm just a visitor here, but I think she's a bit hard to be a minister and as for him, there's no way I'd have him fill a cavity. I think he might enjoy watching people squirm when they're in his chair."

"She comes across as a bit unyielding," Albert commented, "but she has done a lot for this community over the years." As Albert was talking, Greta and Della woke up and joined the group. Greta placed her head on Xander's lap and Della placed her head on Katie's. The dogs created a sense of calm in the room that had been disrupted by the Parkers.

A few minutes later the dogs rushed to the door to greet Elsie. Knowing she often carried treats in her pockets, the dogs followed Elsie as she filled her coffee cup and joined the others.

Albert greeted Elsie. "Good to see you out and about again Elsie. Is everything all right?"

"I suppose so," Elise sighed as she poured some cream into her coffee. "I took a drive up to Northport to clear my head and come to grips with what's happened. I had lunch there and then sat on the beach for an hour or two and just let my mind wander."

"Did you come to any conclusions?" Max asked.

"Two. First, I'm not going to be afraid anymore. Maybe Dot and Herb are the killers and maybe not, but I'm not going to lock myself up in my cottage and be frightened. There are too many things I could be doing. By the way, I don't think the

Coopers are the killers. Herb's all bark with no bite and Dot's, well, Dot's Dot."

"What's the second conclusion? Katie asked.

"My gossiping days are over. I read what people said about me on that website and it's not good. I'm surprised the killer didn't go after me. Maybe he did and mistook Babs for me. Anyway, I haven't decided how to redefine myself, but things are going to change. Maybe I'll learn how to play poker or ride a horse. I don't know. I think I'll stop playing bridge for a while to give me time to think of something new." The dogs hadn't left Elsie's side while she talked. Noticing them again, Elsie gave them each a treat. "There you go girls."

On Sunday, the Wolfes left the park and drove to Chicago. Xander dropped Katie at O'Hare airport for her flight to Germany and then returned to his apartment in Lincoln Park to prepare for the week ahead. He didn't have any classes to teach this semester and his lab was pretty much shut down for the next few weeks while new equipment was being installed, so he only had a few things to wrap on Monday and Tuesday before returning to Beulah. He hadn't planned to spend the summer in Michigan, but once he and Max learned about the inheritances from Bonnie and Babs, they decided to use the summer to plan how to set up scholarships and foundations to carry out the wishes of the two women who left the money for them to manage.

While Dot and Herb spent the weekend in their cells at the jail, their lawyer, a junior associate named Pearl Jones, and Calvin Cutler, a paralegal, worked on the case.

Pearl started digging into the backgrounds of the Coopers and her neighbors at the park. Joe asked her to coordinate these tasks with a private detective the firm used in such cases. Pearl also pulled together a summary of what was posted on the Crime Spartans website related to the murders and started to research case law of social media involvement in criminal cases.

Calvin contacted Nick and also some contacts at the crime lab to find out as much as possible about the evidence collected in the case. Calvin grew up in Benzonia and had a few friends and cousins in the sheriff's office and at the crime lab.

Joe spent some time researching case law related to evidence, prepared some initial arguments to use with the prosecuting attorney and at the district court arraignment, and he met with an analyst in the firm's IT department who occasionally did research related to the Internet. Joe wanted to know if he could learn the identities of people posting on the website, where they posted from, and who the owners of the site were. He didn't know how much the Crime Spartans site would play in the case, but intuition told him it would play a part.

Because Joe was a senior partner at the firm, he had a private conference room adjacent to his office. When he took on a major case, the conference room was converted to a war room. Calvin, who had worked on several big cases with Joe before, was in charge of setting up and managing the war room. As the case progressed, the walls would be covered with information.

On Sunday evening, Joe and his team met in the war room to review what was learned over the weekend and to plan next steps. Joe reviewed his plan with the team for his meeting with the prosecuting attorney, Angela Berg, and revised it based on input from Pearl and Calvin.

On Monday morning, Joe woke with a clear head and was ready to do battle with Angela. At law school, Joe and Angela enjoyed arguing about fine points of the law. If Angela wasn't already married when they were in law school, Joe could have fallen for her. During the 30-minute drive from his home on Lake Ann, Joe went through what he would say to Angela.

Angela was in her office before 6am. Her staff did most of the work on smaller cases, but Angela took the lead on major cases, especially the more difficult ones. Her relationship with the sheriff was tenuous at best because of his frequent arrests of migrant workers and other minorities without cause or admissible evidence. She had refused to issue a warrant for the last people arrested for this crime.

When Joe walked into her office at 9am, Angela was prepared. After pleasantries and questions about each other's families, Joe got to the point. "So Angela, where are you going with this?"

"I've got good news and bad news for you Joe. On the positive side, I'm not going to issue a warrant for Herb Cooper at this time. There's no direct evidence to link him to the crime. Now, if the lab finds his DNA on the hammer or if the sheriff can find evidence of his participation in a conspiracy to commit murder with Dot, I'll charge him. Unfortunately, I can't hold him until next week with what we have. As you know, we won't have the DNA results on the hammer until next week."

"That's a good start," was Joe's response. "Now what about Dot?"

"I'm going with first degree murder. Her fingerprints were on the hammer, it was in her possession, and the dried blood on the hammer is AB negative, which is the same type as Babs Tucker. As you know, that's a pretty rare blood type. Of course, if the DNA tests show the blood is not from the victim, I'll need to reconsider. Given the rare blood type, I feel that I have enough to hold her."

"What's with the 1st degree charge? A hammer is used to kill someone in a fit of rage or on the spur of the moment. It's not the weapon of choice for a premeditated murder."

"Normally, I'd agree, but come on Joe, did you read the report from the forensics folks and the medical examiner? It's pretty clear that Mrs. Tucker was surprised by the attacker and was struck from behind. The killer snuck up on Babs Tucker and smashed her head in with the hammer. There's also her conviction for assault and her history of domestic violence. She's got a temper, but in this case, I believe she planned the murder.

"The hammer could have been Elsie's, or it may have belonged to the victim herself. Perhaps she was returning it to Elsie. There's no proof that Dot Cooper owned the hammer," Joe rejoined.

"Perhaps not, but according to two witnesses, the hammer didn't belong to the victim, or Elsie, the owner of the cottage where the murder took place."

"What two witnesses? I didn't see these witnesses in the preliminary police reports we saw."

"There aren't any yet, but there are two comments on that website saying that neither Babs nor Elsie owned a hammer," Angela replied.

"So, you're using gossip on a website to issue a warrant for 1st degree murder?"

"Usually, I wouldn't, but the two people who posted used their real names. I asked Nick Townsend to follow up with both. One is Ben Weldon, the grounds keeper who does odd jobs for people around the park and the other is from Babs' best friend Elsie, who said the victim had arthritis in her hands and couldn't grip a hammer. Babs couldn't even hold her cards when she played bridge. She used a device to hold them while playing."

"Where's the motive, Angela? Without a clear motive, do you really expect to get a conviction on first degree homicide?"

"The Coopers thought Babs and Elsie were cheating at bridge?"

"Seriously?"

"I'm still going through all the crap on that website and there is also a long way to go in the investigation. I'm sure more on the motive will emerge. It's early, Joe, but I already have enough to issue a warrant and to hold her. Then there's the charge for assaulting a police officer."

"What about bail?"

"It's first degree, Joe. I'll be asking for no bail."

The two attorneys argued back and forth, but the Cooper's lawyer didn't expect to change the prosecutor's mind. His main goal in meeting with her was to learn how strong of a case the state felt it had. Near the end of the meeting, both were interrupted when their phones beeped, indicating receipt of texts from the court clerk. The district court arraignment would be this afternoon in front of Judge Murphy.

After Joe left the prosecutor's office, he walked over the jail to meet with his clients. After sharing the good news about Herb's pending release, Joe told them about the charges against Dot and the likelihood she wouldn't be granted bail. He then went on to explain that the bail hearing in district court later in the afternoon was only the beginning of a long process. He would make motions to dismiss the case and for bail, but he told the Cooper's that neither was likely to be granted.

Herb was more visibly upset than Dot, but he settled down once Dot asked him to focus on helping their attorney to get the charges dropped. She also gave him a list of household tasks to do, including picking up Della from Albert and taking her home.

Herb didn't get released until just before Dot's district court arraignment. The sheriff delayed the release, hoping he could convince the prosecuting attorney to issue a warrant for Herb. After two attempts to convince her, the sheriff ordered his deputies to release Herb.

Herb sat in the visitor's gallery of the courtroom, just behind Dot and her legal team. Since Calvin, the paralegal and Pearl, the associate in the firm, were already in Benzie County working different aspects of the case, Joe had them join him at the defense table. Having them there sent a message to Dot and to the prosecutor that the full resources of the firm would be used to win the case.

Dot and Herb were both surprised at how brief the arraignment was. The charges were read, and the judge advised Dot of her rights and reviewed a number of related legal issues. Although Joe had told her earlier about the arraignment process, Dot was surprised that she wasn't asked to plead guilty or not guilty. The formal pleading would happen later in the process.

Joe made well written and effectively presented motions for dismissal and bail that were both denied. Judge Murphy commented that Dot's attempted escape and assault of Deputy McGregor weighed heavily in his decisions.

A preliminary examination hearing was scheduled for two weeks later. Before they took Dot back to her cell, Joe explained what was next. "Dot, at the preliminary hearing, the prosecuting attorney will present evidence and witnesses to convince the judge that there is at least probable cause to believe the charged crimes were committed and that you committed them. I, of course, will present evidence and witnesses to counter the charge.

"Is there a jury?" Dot asked.

"No, that's a long way off Dot, if ever. At the preliminary hearing, Judge Murphy will decide whether the charges will be dropped or whether you will be bound over to circuit court for trial on the charges made by the prosecutor. He may also modify or reduce the charges. I'll have a pre-exam conference with the prosecutor a few days before the court appearance. Hopefully, we'll have enough evidence by then to convince her to drop the charges and it can end there."

"In the meantime, what do I do, other than sit in a jail cell?"

"Calvin, Pearl, or I will be asking you, and Herb, a lot of questions over the next few days. We'll need you to be open and truthful in your answers. We'll also be investigating your background, as well as the background of your neighbors. I don't think we'll get this resolved until we find out about the other murder at Beulah Crest."

"I'll tell you all I can, and I'm sure Herb will as well."

"There's one more thing to remember. Not a word about the case, or anything remotely relate to it, to anyone other than me or my associates. Is that clear?"

"Perfectly. Everyone else is working for the prosecutor or sheriff. I remember what you told me on Friday."

When the guards took Dot back to the jail, Joe looked for Herb, who was waiting for him in the lobby of the courthouse. "Let's go Herb, I'll drop you at home. I want to take a look at your cottage and where the two murders took place."

On the way back to the park, Joe asked Herb to repeat what he had told him earlier. Herb gave the answer that Joe wanted. "I'll tell anyone who asks anything that I've been instructed by our lawyer not to talk about the case and we are optimistic this will be resolved soon."

"Perfect, Herb. The neighbors will all be asking you questions, so stick to the line. I don't want to see anything on that website that came from you."

When they approached the gate to the park, the security guard let them through after Herb identified himself as a resident and showed the guard his ID. As they drove up to Herb and Dot's cottage, Herb commented, "The security guard is new, and I spotted some new cameras. You'd think they wouldn't bother once we were arrested."

"Pearl mentioned them in a text she sent earlier today. The park owners are more concerned with the nosy tourists who are poking around. I expect the dust will settle soon. Now, give me a quick tour of the place. Our investigator will be here later this week, but I want to have a look so when he reports his findings, I can see how things fit in here."

Herb gave Joe a tour of his cottage and showed him the shed where the hammer was found. He then took him past Elsie's cottage and then over the Mouse House. No one was in the coffee shop, but Ian was in his office, so the front door was open. Herb took the lawyer into the house and showed him the coffee shop where Bonnie drank the poison.

When he heard the front door open, Ian came out of his office and greeted Herb with a handshake. "Herb, welcome back. I know you couldn't have done it." Ian then shook the lawyer's hand. "Hello Mr. Quandaro. It's good to see you again. Herb, Mr. Quandaro got me off a bogus minor in possession of alcohol charge a few years ago. You're in good hands." Ian then noticed that Dot wasn't there. "Where's Dot? They're not still holding her, are they?"

Joe answered. "They're still holding her, Ian. I'm not going to say more about it, and neither will Herb. You can understand why. That said, it's good to see you. It's been awhile. How are your parents?" Joe and Ian, who were distant cousins, exchanged small town small talk for a while before Joe got back to business. "Say Ian, I saw a quite a few cameras around here. Did you put those in recently?"

"We've had one at the front gate for a while. I put the others in Friday, when the tourists started snooping around. Why do you ask?"

"I was going to have Herb install some cameras around his place. Someone put that hammer in his garden shed. If anyone tries to plant anything else on his property, I want it recorded. Can you help him with that?"

"Sure, I bought two extra cameras last week, so we'd have spares. I could put them up at Herb's right now, if you want. The back of their cottage is already covered by one of my cameras, since it is on the edge of the park. We can cover the rest with the other two."

"Can you hide or disguise the cameras, Ian? If someone tries to plant something, I want to catch them with the camera. If they're aware of the cameras, they may try something elsewhere."

"I think so. Ben's been putting bird feeders around the park. He's hung them from trees. If I put the cameras on the feeders and attach a few branches to them, no one will notice. If Ben's still here, I'll ask him to help."

Herb thanked Ian. "We appreciate your help and support. You don't know what it means."

Joe interrupted. "Yes, thank you Ian. Unfortunately, I've shared more about the case with you than I should have. I'd like to ask you not to say anything about what we've said with anyone and not to post about it anywhere on the Web."

While Ian started to set up the cameras, Herb walked Joe to his car and thanked him again. After Joe drove off, Herb picked Della up from Albert's cottage and took her home. When she saw him, Della gave Herb an enthusiastic greeting that included a lot of licking and jumping. When Herb got her home, Della searched the house looking for Dot. "She's not here," Herb explained to the dog, while giving her some of her favorite treats. "I suppose Joe won't mind me telling you," He then went on to tell Della everything that had happened over the past few days while he made himself a light supper. He then took a shower and went to bed. Della paced around the cottage for hours, expecting Dot to return. Finally, she gave up and jumped onto Dot's side of the bed where she slept until Herb got up the following morning.

* * *

The killer had a busy day on Monday, so didn't get a chance to check the Crime Spartans site for news on the Coopers until later in the evening. There were a number of posts with information about the charges against Dot and comments about the release of Herb without being charged. There were even some pictures of Dot being escorted to the courtroom and of Herb and his lawyer getting into a car. *How did Herb get off? The hammer was in his toolbox. You would think they would charge him with conspiracy with Dot, at the least.*

The voice interrupted. *"Don't panic. Read through every-thing on the website and check the local news sites. Perhaps they'll charge Herb later, once all of the forensics tests are done. We may have to help the police find some more."*

The killer scanned through all of news websites and read everything new on the Crime Spartans website. *I just can't believe it. They've released Herb without any charges, but at least they're charging Dot with first degree murder. Given the choice, I'd rather it was him that was still in a cell at the jail. Now that Herb's home, presumably with their dog, it'll be more difficult to plant evidence on the property.*

"You'll find a way," the voice prompted. *"Pick some more of the water hemlock when you get a chance and put it in a plastic bag, like before. I have an idea of how to get it into the Cooper's cottage without anyone suspecting. Get some sleep, and we'll talk more tomorrow."*

The next day was another busy one for the murderer, but time was found in the late afternoon to go to the Beulah library and post on Crime Spartans. The killer created an account with the name Della that included a copy of a picture of the Cooper's dog that Dot had posted on her Facebook page last year.

Once the username was set up, the following post was made. "Herb's doesn't know how to cook, and poor Dot is stuck in jail until this nonsense of her being charged is resolved. It would be nice if some of our neighbours in the park stopped by our cottage over the next few days to leave a casserole or some-thing else for Herb to eat. I'm sure Dot will be home soon, but, in the meantime, I don't want Herb starving. When you come over, don't forget to bring a treat for me."

Over the next few days, a number of people from the park and a few from the bridge club dropped off prepared meals for Herb, and of course, treats for Della. When it was obvious the posting on the Web had worked, the killer made another trip to the swamp to collect some more hemlock.

Elsie made a cottage pie with beef and mashed potatoes and took it over to Herb's cottage. *I'm not going to be afraid anymore,* she thought to herself as she walked over. *If he tries anything, I'll fling the casserole dish at him.*

Elsie had never really talked much with Herb before. When she and Babs were at a bridge table with Herb and Dot, any small talk was between the women. Because of this, Elsie was at a loss of what to say the Herb. She needn't have been.

After thanking Elsie for the cottage pie, Herb asked Elsie about the bridge hand Elsie had played when he had accused her of cheating. "I'm sorry I was such an ass at the bridge club the last time we played. I'm taking all kinds of medications, and they have some strange effects, especially with my temper. That said, I was wondering why you bid that hand the way you did. Now that I've had time to think about the hand, it was ingenious. You know you scored that hand better than anyone else in the club."

"The truth be told Herb; it was a mistake. I put down the wrong bidding card and before I could correct my mistake, Dot bid, and then you started your shouting. It was a wonder we won the hand."

They both laughed and Elsie found herself doing something she thought she would never do. She accepted Herb's invitation to be his partner at a regional bridge tournament on Saturday, assuming that Dot was not released by then.

Other visitors from the park included Max, who brought some sandwiches from the East Shore Market; Xander, who brought over a vegetable quiche; Reverend Parker, who brought macaroni and cheese; Ian, who brought some beef stew that Elizabeth had made; and Nigel, who brought a chicken curry dish. Several other park residents brought dishes and Albert invited Herb and Della over to his cottage for hamburgers he cooked on his grill. By the end of the week, Herb's refrigerator was full. Surprisingly, nobody asked Herb about the post that brought them to Herb's cottage. Everyone assumed that either Herb had posted it or that somehow Dot had access to a computer.

The killer brought over a prepared meal when there were other people at Herb's cottage. While everyone else was fussing over Della and Herb, the killer put the plastic bag with the hemlock in the freezer, under a carton of butter pecan ice cream. The killer remembered that Dot loved ice cream and that Herb didn't.

During the week following Dot's arrest, life at the park adjusted to the new normal. Most people didn't believe Dot had killed Babs and Bonnie, but there was still uncertainty lingering. When Derek was having lunch with his wife on Thursday, he expressed his thoughts and those of most of his neighbors. "Perhaps the sheriff got it right this time, but what if he didn't?"

Ian continued to spend a lot of his free time with Elizabeth, staying at her apartment every night since Dot's arrest. They started thinking about moving into Babs' cottage together once the ownership of the cottage passed to Ian. They had no idea when that would happen, but they were content to wait until the probate process ran its course.

Every evening, over a bottle of wine, they reviewed the new posts on the website. The arrest of the Coopers spiked the number of visitors and then Herb's release led to even more to posts. Posters to the site who felt that one or both of the Coopers were guilty posted every imaginable thing about them. These posts included everything from pure gossip to actual facts about their lives together, their veterinary practice, and a host of clues the police would be obligated to investigate. These clues included comments about Herb's interest in herbal medicine and assisted suicide, Dot's negative statements about Bonnie's lifestyle, Herb's anger with Babs and Elsie about bridge, and additional details of Dot's previous assault conviction. A former fraternity brother from Ohio State said that Herb was involved with a satanic group that tortured pledges hoping to join the fraternity.

There were also positive comments about the pair, mainly focusing on their love of animals and their veterinary practice. A number of people praised them on how well they cared for Della and for other pets owned by Beulah Crest residents.

Every day, there was a posting or two from Della. At first, the posts thanked everyone who dropped food off for Herb and treats for the dog. Later in the week, Della became more suspicious of Herb in her posts. "Herb's not himself. I don't think he killed anyone, but what if he did?"

On Thursday night, Della posted that she saw Herb put something suspicious in the freezer. "Herb doesn't know how to cook, but he does know how to take things out of the freezer and put them into the microwave. Yesterday, I saw him put something strange in the freezer. It was something he took out of his pocket. I couldn't tell what it was, but I could see its color. It was green. I wonder if it was more hemlock."

Elsie read the post about the freezer on Friday morning. At first, she thought nothing of it, but for some reason, she couldn't let it go. As she was preparing a pot of chicken soup, she thought to herself, *I'm done gossiping and worrying about what other people do. Why did that post make me think the worst about Herb and Dot? I've agreed to play bridge with Herb tomorrow, so I need to let it rest.*

Later, after having a bowl of soup for lunch, she filled several plastic containers with the remaining soup and put them in her freezer. She then headed down to the Maples nursing home to run the bingo game. The lady who usually called the numbers was down with laryngitis, so Elsie volunteered to cover for her.

All afternoon, Elsie couldn't concentrate, and her thoughts kept coming back to Herb's freezer and what he could have put in there. *Who was posting as Della? Herb wouldn't incriminate himself and surely, Dot didn't have access to the Internet from her jail cell. Could it be the actual killer who's posting this nonsense?*

On the drive back to Beulah, Elsie told herself to just leave it alone. If there was anything to the posts by Della, surely the sheriff would sort it out. As she pulled into her driveway, she had another thought. *The sheriff can't do anything if there's something in Herb's freezer. He won't be able to get a warrant to search the Cooper's cottage based on postings of a dog on the Internet. Anyway, he already had the place searched after he arrested them last week.*

Finally, Elsie's impatience and curiosity got the best of her. She took the containers of chicken soup out of her freezer and walked over to Herb's cottage with them. When Herb tried to tell her that he had enough food to last a week, Elsie invited herself in. "I'll put these in the freezer while you make us a cup of coffee. We should talk about what bidding conventions we'll use if we're going to play bridge tomorrow." Della, who enjoyed the stream of visitors lately, welcomed Elsie by putting a paw on her thigh.

Herb, who had spent the day working with the lawyers, and then with Dot, was tired, but he invited Elsie in. Maybe talking about bridge would help him relax a bit. As he put the coffee on, Elsie put the soup in the freezer. As she moved various casseroles to look around, she saw the plastic bag with the hemlock and thought to herself. *That can't be hemlock. I know what it looks like, but I've never seen it frozen before. It could be seasoning or something from the garden.*

Elsie's thoughts were interrupted when Herb said, "How about a piece of pie, Elsie? Max brought one over from the Cherry Hut?"

"I'd love a piece," Elsie answered, while thinking. *This is nonsense. This man has hemlock in his freezer and I'm having coffee and pie with him.* Then her thoughts shifted. *Wait a minute old girl. You told yourself that you weren't going to be frightened any more. Sit down and talk to the man and see if you can learn anything. Get yourself a glass of water and tell him you won't have any coffee because of the caffeine. No need to take chances, just in case he's brewed the same thing Bonnie drank.*

Fortunately, Elsie was expert enough at bridge that she didn't need to concentrate much while Herb went over the bidding conventions he liked to use. After agreeing to use the conventions Herb suggested, the new courageous Elsie found herself asking a question. "Herb, have you seen that Crime Spartan website lately?"

"Not since I was released. Our lawyer is monitoring it for anything that might be of use. Why do you ask?"

Elsie got up and walked over to the freezer and motioned Herb to follow. She opened the freezer, lifted the butter pecan ice cream, and then pointed to the plastic bag with the hemlock. "Do you have any idea what this is, Herb? It's frozen, so it's hard to tell, but it looks like hemlock to me."

"I've never seen hemlock, frozen or fresh, so I wouldn't know. I can't tell you when it was put there. I never saw it before."

"Well," Elsie responded. "Either you or Dot poisoned Bonnie, or someone planted it there to incriminate you. Where's your computer?"

"Over there on my desk."

They both walked over to the desk and Herb let Elsie log onto the Crime Spartans site. Elsie scrolled through the posts. "Let me show you what's been posted lately."

When he first saw the posts from Della, Herb laughed. "Della, sweetheart. No wonder everyone's been bringing casseroles over." Della barked playfully when she heard her name and then put her head on Herb's lap. Herb petted Della's head while thinking and then finally asked Elsie, "Who's this Della? Our Della's a smart dog, but she's useless at the keyboard. I know it can't be Dot either, or anyone posting for her. She doesn't have access to a computer, and the only people she talks to are me and the lawyers."

Elsie sensed that Herb was genuinely baffled. She thought for a moment and let her instincts tell her to believe Herb. "I think whoever posted as Della, wanted a crowd dropping off casseroles so he could join them and plant the hemlock in your freezer."

"That's pretty devious, don't you think?"

"If that's what happened, it's even more devious than that, Herb."

"What do you mean?"

"When I first saw the post about the hemlock in your freezer, I thought the sheriff would also see it and come over here and search the place."

"He could be on his way over here right now. Shouldn't we get rid of it, before he gets here?"

"I don't think he'll be able to get a warrant to search your cottage based on the posting of a dog on the Internet. Even he's smart enough to realize that."

"So."

"I think the actual killer, assuming it's not Dot…"

"It's not."

"Anyway, the actual killer posted the comment about you hiding something in the freezer, hoping a nosy neighbor, like myself, would pop over with another casserole, find the hemlock in the freezer, and then call the sheriff, who would then have sufficient cause to search your place."

"Oh, my! That's a lot to swallow, Elsie. Do you really believe what you're saying? I can't think of anyone who is that twisted, can you?"

"No, I can't say that I do."

"What should I do? I'm so worn out and stressed over poor Dot, I just don't where to turn, and now this. I'll just throw it out." Herb got up and headed toward the kitchen."

"No, wait," Elsie called out. "It you touch the bag, you'll leave fingerprints on it, and your DNA. Why don't you call the lawyer who's handling your case? I hear he's pretty good. He'll know what to do."

Calvin and Joe were working on the case Friday evening when Herb placed the call. Joe answered on the first ring of his cellphone. "What's up Herb? I was just about to call you."

"Have you seen the posts on that website about something in my freezer?"

"I have, Herb. That's why I was about to call you. Is there anything in your freezer that looks suspicious?"

"Yes, there is. My neighbor, Elsie Taylor, found a plastic bag with what she thinks may be hemlock. She thinks someone planted it there."

"Have you or Elsie touched the bag?"

"No, neither of us have."

"Good. Now, I don't want you to do anything until I get there. I'll be there in about an hour, with someone who can verify the identity of the plant. Can you do that?"

"Yes, of course. Elsie and I can talk about bridge until you get here. We'll stay out of the kitchen."

"Ok, we'll be there as soon as we can."

Elsie overheard the conversation Herb had with lawyer and was glad he was getting sound advice and that the lawyer was coming over. When Herb hung up, she told him so and then got up to leave. "Herb, all of this has got me a bit rattled and has set off a headache. I think I'm going to head home, take some aspirin, and lie down. If your lawyer wants to talk to me, have him stop by."

* * *

The killer could see Herb's cottage outside the kitchen window. Elsie was observed walking over to Herb's and going inside. *I knew Elsie wouldn't be able to resist taking a look in Herb's freezer. All that talk of hers about not being a gossip anymore. I didn't believe a word of it, did I?*

The voice answered. *"Of course, you didn't. I wasn't sure about your idea to set up an account on that webssite using the name of Della, but I have to say, it was a good idea and it worked. There were so many people taking casseroles over there it was easy for you to join the crowd and leave the hemlock."*

Thanks. We can expect the police to arrive at any time now. Look, Elsie is leaving Herb's cottage. I'll bet the first thing she does when she gets home is call the sheriff.

"Let's watch. He should be here pretty soon."

I hope so. Elsie does have a reputation as a gossip though. Perhaps the sheriff won't listen to her.

"He'll listen to her, because he wants to. He's after a conviction and publicity, not the truth. You know that as well as I do."

You're right of course. I don't like the man, but he does serve our purposes.

* * *

Calvin was driving, so it only took the lawyer and paralegal 45 minutes to get to Beulah. On the way, Joe called Marv Portman, a friend who was a retired botanist. Marv, who's an expert in native and invasive species in Michigan, lived in nearby Honor. Calvin and Joe picked him up on the way to Heb's cottage. Marv had seen the Crime Spartans website, so he was glad to help.

"That's Queen Anne's Lace," Marv told Calvin, Joe, and Herb when Joe pointed to the bag in the freezer. "I don't even need to take it out of the bag to tell you. This is a sample of what is commonly called wild carrot."

"Are you sure?" Joe asked.

"Quite sure. See the stem? On hemlock it's smooth and has little purple spots. Notice the hairy texture on these. This is definitely not hemlock. Occasionally, someone makes the mistake, with deadly consequences, of eating hemlock, thinking it's a wild carrot. Of course, the flowers and leaves are also similar, but easy to differentiate."

Joe thanked Marv and then turned his attention to his client. "Herb, I'm going to call Nick Townsend and asked him to come over. Are you OK with that? He's an honest cop on I want it on the record what we found here and when."

"I suppose, but why? Do you think the killer planted it here? I know it wasn't here when they arrested us. The freezer was almost empty when the casseroles started arriving and the police searched the place last week."

"I don't know why it was put there. Perhaps someone thought it was hemlock and is trying to implicate you, or perhaps it's just a nasty prank."

"As if Dot and I don't already have enough trouble."

Calvin made a fresh pot of coffee while Joe called Nick Townsend on his cellphone.

When Joe got off the phone, he told the others the detective would be there in a a few minutes. "Herb, before the detective gets here, can you make a list of who visited in the last week?"

"I think so. I kept track after the first few so I could send thank you cards."

"Good," Joe answered. "If you can, put down when they visited and if they had access to your freezer."

"It could have been anyone one of them. Elsie was the first, with a cottage pie that was quite good. I ate it that evening, so it never got frozen. Everything that came later went into the freezer. Elsie was just here and discovered the, what did you call it? Oh yes, the Queen Anne's Lace, in my freezer. I suppose she could've put it there herself, this evening. She's a good bridge player, so she's smart. Do you think she's that devious?"

"I think she's nosy and a bit lonely," Joe responded, "but not devious or dangerous."

Before Joe could say anything more, they all heard a knock on the front door of the cottage. Herb answered the door and let Detective Townsend and Deputy McGregor come in. After introductions were made, Nick asked Joe to show him the hemlock.

Marv interrupted the detective. "It's Queen Ann's lace, Detective. Don't worry, I didn't touch it. It was obvious just by looking at it through the plastic bag."

Everyone walked into the kitchen and watched as Nick opened the freezer. "There's a lot more stuff in here than when I searched last week, Herb. So, where's this bag with the... oh wait, I found it. This bag wasn't here last week," he exclaimed, as he put on a pair of latex gloves and picked up the plastic bag. "I agree, Marv. Looks like wild carrot. Any Boy Scout could tell us that."

"What does it mean?" Herb asked.

"I don't know," the detective answered. I'll send it to the crime lab and see if there are any fingerprints or any DNA matches to any of the other evidence collected in this case. I'm inclined to think it's a prank, but let's see if the lab folks find anything. I'll put a rush on it, so hopefully we'll know if there's anything here before the preliminary hearing."

Joe responded. "Thanks Detective. We all appreciate your help. We didn't call the sheriff because, well..."

"I know," Nick commented, "but don't ask me to say more."

* * *

Still in the kitchen, the killer saw the visitors to Herb's cottage. *That's not the sheriff. It's that lawyer from Traverse City who's representing Dot and Herb and that guy from his firm I saw on their website. Who's the other guy? I've never seen him before. Maybe another lawyer? What are they doing there?*

The voice interrupted the killer's thoughts. *"Don't worry. It's just a coincidence. The lawyer or one of his associates were at Herb's place yesterday and on Monday. They have to prepare for the court hearing next week."*

I suppose, but I thought Elsie would've called the sheriff by now. Maybe I should walk over to her place and have a coffee with her. I'm sure she'll tell me if she saw anything and if she called the sheriff.

"I'm sure she would, but do you want to call attention to yourself? Elsie is smarter than you think. She may sense that you have something to hide if you barge in and start asking questions. Give her some time to act. If she saw the hemlock, I'm sure she'll call the sheriff. She won't be able to sleep until she's done something."

Oh, look, a police car with two people in it are pulling into the Cooper's driveway. You were right, we could count on Elsie. She must have called the sheriff's office. Oh, no, it's that detective, Nick Townsend and the woman deputy.

"What's wrong with them?"

Oh, it's just that if it were the sheriff, he'd be sure to take Herb into custody. He'd want the publicity.

"I'm sure your right, but Detective Townsend is an honest and professional cop who will handle the evidence, so it won't be thrown out by a judge on a technicality. The sheriff is useful to a degree, but he has a lot of his arrests dismissed because of his carelessness."

The killer took another look out the window. The detective could be seen leaving with the deputy. They weren't taking Herb with them, but the deputy was observed carrying a small evidence bag. *Well, at least they're taking the hemlock. I wonder why they aren't arresting Herb.*

"They're going to check the bag with the hemlock for prints. They released Herb because his prints weren't on the hammer, so I suppose they're shy about holding him until they have something conclusive. You wore gloves when you handled the hemlock and put it in the bag, didn't you?"

Yes, of course. I also put them on when I took the plastic bag out of my pocket and put the hemlock in the freezer. There'll be no fingerprints of mine on the bag. Hopefully Herb picked it up and left some of his prints, or perhaps, Elsie did.

"Hopefully, he did. Meanwhile, it might be a good idea to post what you've seen this evening on the Crime Spartan site. If the public knows they've taken more evidence from the Cooper's cottage, there might be more pressure to arrest Herb, and we might even get lucky. If Elsie's prints are on the plastic bag, maybe they're arrest her as well."

The killer drafted a post to the Crime Spartans site that would be made as soon as the library opened in the morning. The post from Della said, "I don't know what Herb is up to with Elsie, but she's been at our cottage a lot lately. Yesterday, the police came and took whatever Herb put in the freezer with them. They came right after Elsie was there. I heard the police say something about it being hemlock. I hope Albert will let me live with him and Greta if they take Herb away to prison with Dot."

Happy with the post, the killer went to bed. *I think I'll sleep well tonight, knowing our plan to incriminate Herb appears to be working. If they arrest him, I'm sure they'll charge him, and Dot, with the murders of both Babs and Bonnie. Now, I can start working on a plan to take care of Max and Elsie.*

CHAPTER 11
Best Made Plans...

The weekend and the next week remained quiet at the park, with no further violence. Other than a post about the new evidence taken from the Cooper's cottage, nothing new of substance was posted on the Crime Spartans site. There was, of course, more gossip on the site, some of it rather vicious.

At first, none of the people posting could come up with a good reason why Herb or Dot would want to kill Bonnie. It didn't take long for more wild accusations to appear. Someone speculated that Elsie wanted Bonnie out of the way because Herb had a fling with her last year. "I saw Elsie over at Herb's cottage twice last week. If anyone in the park would know if the rumor about Herb's fling with Bonnie was true, it would be Elsie," The post concluded, "If Elsie and Herb wanted to be together and if Dot had to go, Bonnie would also need to be eliminated."

The fact that Herb and Elsie played bridge together received a lot of attention at the bridge club and online. There were gasps and pointing of fingers when the couple sat down together as partners. Several posts, some with photos, were made to the Web during and shortly after the bridge session. Some speculated that Herb and Elsie murdered Babs so they could be partners and others speculated that perhaps there was more to their relationship than just bridge. Others wondered if they set up Dot to get her out of the way while another person commented that Herb and Elsie were better bridge players than Dot and Babs, and they would be tough to beat if they partnered at state and regional tournaments.

While the gossip about bridge, infidelity, and hemlock was going on, the defense team, the prosecuting attorney, and sheriff's department continued the tedious work or preparing for the preliminary hearing. Residents of the park and the friends and family of the victims were interviewed by both sides. Alibis were checked and rechecked and the backgrounds of the suspects and victims were investigated.

The prosecution, with the help of the sheriff's office, took a different approach than the defense lawyers when combing through all the information posted on the Crime Spartans site.

Deputy Kathy McGregor knew more about social media than any of the other members of the sheriff's department. She had personal accounts on all of the major social media sites and also had accounts on a number of crime related sites, like Crime Spartans.

Once the sheriff got word of her expertise; he gave her specific instructions. "Draft a list of every accusation, lead, or statement about evidence related to Herb or Dot Cooper posted on that damned Internet. Also, anything about the personal lives of the two victims. I want an updated copy of what you find on my desk the first thing every morning."

Every morning, after reading through the list, Sheriff Van Dyke assigned members of the department to investigate the validity of the posts. Everyone was assigned a list of tasks to investigate. Nick Townsend, who was the only officer actually qualified to lead the investigation found himself without any officers to support him, since everyone in the force was running around the county verifying posts from mostly unidentified people, and a golden retriever named Della.

The defense team took a somewhat different approach as they went through the posts on the Web. An Internet forensics expert was brought in as a consultant. He monitored the Crime Spartans site, but in addition to creating a summary of posts for Joe and his team to investigate, he did an analysis of the posts. Eighty percent of the posts were from people who did not give their true identity.

The forensics expert tried to hack into the Crime Spartans website to determine the true identity of people who posted, their locations, and the identity of the people who owned and managed the site. Unfortunately, he found the site to be one of the most secure he'd come across and was not able to break through their security.

Unable to break into Crime Spartans, he brought in a language expert who analyzed the posts from a linguistic stand-point. The expert found that a large number of the posts made under a number of different accounts, including Della's, were very likely made by the same person. These included posts about the hammer in the Cooper's shed, the request for neighbors to bring Herb casseroles, the hemlock in Herb's freezer, Herb and

Elsie's plot against Dot, and accusations against a number of people in the park.

Unfortunately, only a few of those posts were made while Herb was in custody, so the linguistic information couldn't be used to help clear him. Since many of the posts were made while Dot was in custody when she didn't have Internet access, they might be used to identify the actual killer, if his identity could be found.

While both sides were preparing for the trial, Ian and Elizabeth spent almost every evening pouring through the postings on the website. Ian moved more of his clothes and personal items to Elizabeth's apartment since he was spending most of his free time there. They talked more about moving into Babs' cottage, but Ian wasn't comfortable thinking about the move until he was sure her killer was identified.

Elsie enjoyed the company provided by Babs' cats, Chocolate and Fudge and the cats seemed to be happy at Elsie's cottage. Because the cats has a temporary home, Ian didn't feel compelled to move into Babs' cottage in a hurry.

On Thursday afternoon, the pre-exam conference was held in Angela Berg's office. The prosecuting attorney, Angela Berg, met with Dot's lawyer, Joe Quandaro to determine if they could negotiate an agreement before the preliminary hearing on Monday.

Joe argued for dismissal, based on the limited amount of evidence. He also argued that the posts on the website indicated someone was trying to frame the Coopers for the crime by posting information about the hammer and the hemlock and by inviting neighbors to Herb's cottage so more false evidence could be planted.

Unfortunately for Dot, Angela Berg didn't budge. She felt she had enough evidence to have Dot bound over for trial. DNA results would be available soon and she expected these would provide enough evidence to convince a jury, once the case made it to trial. Also, she wasn't sure how much weight, if any, to give to posts made anonymously on the Internet.

On Friday evening, Ian and Elizabeth went through the Crime Spartans site again. As owners of the site, they were analyzing how many people were visiting the site, how many registered, and how many clicked on the advertisements that were on the website pages. Angela was focusing on the site metrics, while Ian got distracted by reading through the posts made to the site.

While scrolling through the site, Ian made a comment that got Elizabeth's attention. "I'm still not comfortable making all of this money from what happened at the park, but it would pay for a great wedding. We could hire the Accidentals to play. They're a great band, and I love that electric cello she plays."

Elizabeth almost dropped her wine glass but didn't say anything. She just waited to see if Ian would realize what he just said and wanted to see his reaction, if and when, he did. She'd learned that Ian often spoke without thinking of what he was saying and when asked to repeat what he had just said, he would often say something completely different.

Elizabeth lost her chance to ask Ian to repeat the comment about the wedding when he changed the direction of the conversation. "Elizabeth, do you think Connor is up this late? Let's give him a call."

Wondering why Ian wanted to call one of their partners she asked, "Why? It's almost midnight, but yes, he'll be up. He never goes to sleep before dawn."

"Look at these posts to the site I've highlighted. No, wait a second, I'll copy them all and put them all together on the same screen." Ian then filled a screen with almost all of the same posts the linguist at the law firm had thought to be from the same person.

"What's going on?" a frustrated Elizabeth asked.

"Just read through these and tell me what you think."

Elizabeth took a few minutes and read though all of the posts and then paused for a moment to think. Something about them stuck out, but she couldn't put her finger on what it was. "There's something strange here," she mumbled. She was still distracted by Ian's earlier comment about the wedding.

"Take your time," Ian prompted. "I want to see if you come to the same conclusion that I did."

Elizabeth dropped her wine glass and screamed. "They're all from the same person. He's Canadian, or maybe British. They use several different usernames, but they're all the same person. Even Della, the dog."

Ian rushed to pick up the wine glass and clean up the spill as he asked, "Why do you think he's Canadian or British?"

"Look at the spelling, Ian! Colour, flavour, and favourite, for example, all include the letter u. That's how most of the

English-speaking world spells, with the exception of us in the United States."

"I thought the posts were all from the murderer, but I couldn't put my finger on why. They all just seem to have the same writing style and tone, but perhaps it's the spelling as well."

"Do you think it could be Nigel or Spencer? They're British."

"I hope not. I like them. They're great to work for and have done a lot for me and the community. I'd hate to think it's them, or, for that matter, anyone from the park."

Is there anyone else from the park from England or Canada, or somewhere else where they spell like that?

"No one with an accent like Nigel or Spencer. Can you tell if someone is Canadian, by the way they speak?

"Some of them put 'eh' at the end of every sentence, but I don't know enough Canadians to say if all of them have an accent. Anyway, why did you want to talk to Connor?"

"I want him to find out where this guy was when he made these posts. If they're all made from the same place, I think we're right that they're all from the same person and perhaps, we have our killer. I'm guessing he's using a computer in a library or a coffee shop so his posts can't be traced to his personal computer or home."

"No need to bother Connor, Ian. He's already set up an app to track where users are when they sign in. Hold on a second, I'll run these usernames."

"While you're doing that, how about the Accidentals for the wedding?"

"What wedding?"

"Our wedding. Didn't I just ask you to marry me?"

"No, you didn't. You mentioned there was money for a wedding, for the Accidentals, and also how you liked their cello."

"I suppose you're right. Hold on a minute and let me get something." Ian got up and searched through his pockets. When he couldn't find what he was looking for, he ran out to his car. He came back a few minutes later with a bunch of roses and a small box. He knelt in front of Elizabeth and said, "Let me try again." He then opened the small box and took out the ring that belonged to his great grandmother. He presented the ring and the flowers to Elizabeth and asked the big question. "Elizabeth, will you marry me?"

"Now that you're asking, of course, I will." A tear or two rolled down her cheek as he put the ring on her finger.

"Awesome," was Ian's response. He then ran out to the car again, returning a minute later with a bottle of champagne. There was no further talk about the murders for the rest of the evening.

The next morning, while pouring coffee for herself and Ian, Elizabeth remembered the report she ran last night that contained the location of where the posts were made with the usernames used by the person they suspected. One of the posts was made from a library in Traverse City. All of the rest were made at the library in Beulah.

While refilling the sugar bowl, Elizabeth asked, "So, now that we know where these posts were made, what do you propose we do? I'm not saying that you are all that skilled at making proposals, but I'd like to hear what you want to do."

Ian smiled and winked at Elizabeth. "I got the answer I was looking for, so I'll suggest that my proposal skills are quite refined. Anyway, I'm thinking we hang out at the Beulah library and see who's using the computer there."

"That could work, but it may take a while and neither you nor I have the time to hang out, as you put it, until he decides to post. You're late for work as it is, and I have too much on my plate right now. With all of the hits the site is getting, I have a lot of work keeping it going."

"Hold on, Elizabeth. Were the posts made at random times or were they made at the same time of day?"

"Let's see. The one made in Traverse City was made in the morning. The other posts, the ones made at the Beulah library, were made right after the library opened or late in the afternoon, just before the library closed."

"That makes it easier. I can go down there every day at those times and see if I recognize anyone. If it's someone from the park, I'll know them."

"If it's someone from the county, you'll know them. I don't know there's if anyone in the area you don't know."

"I suppose you're right about that. You're also right that I could be spending a lot of time at the library until I see the killer, especially if he's smart enough to let sleeping dogs lie and let Dot, and maybe Herb, go to prison.

"I think I have an idea of how we can move things along more quickly. How about if we post something that will frighten the killer and make him respond?"

Ian leaned over and gave Elizabeth a kiss. "You're not only smart, but you're also devious. What do you have in mind?"

"How about if we create a new user. Let's call him Justice. No, wait a minute. That's not personal enough. Call him Archangel Michael. My sister's super religious and talks about this angel a lot. Maybe that alone will shake up killer."

"Ok, so what should this angel say?"

"Hold on, let me think," Elizabeth remarked while getting up to refill both of their coffees. When she sat back down, she continued. "Ok, to get him involved, let's have the archangel respond to Della with something like, *Della, I thought golden retrievers were smart and loyal, but here you are writing off Dot and Herb. Does Albert give you better dog biscuits than the Coopers?*"

Ian interrupted. "Cute, but not enough. He'll just think it one of the many jerks posting nonsense. Maybe someone who doesn't like dogs."

"You might let me finish, sunshine. Archangel Michael goes on to say, *I saw who killed Babs and I saw the same person picking hemlock down near the swamp. It wasn't Herb or Dot. By the way, I never did like dogs. I'm more of a cat angel.*"

"Meow!" Ian playfully clawed at Elizabeth like a cat before continuing. "Seriously, I think it will get a reaction. I'm just afraid of what his reaction might be."

"What do you mean?"

"What if he kills someone else in the park after reading this? Perhaps he already suspects he's been seen by someone and this forces him to act again."

"I'd be devastated if anything like that happened. How about if we add, *I was visiting someone at the park when,* just before he goes on to say he saw who killed Babs."

"That's better. This could spark a reaction but not set up anyone in the park. Hopefully it'll drive the killer to quickly post again though. That said, do we really want to do this? Maybe we should just tell the sheriff what we know." As Ian was speaking, his phone beeped, reminding him he had a meeting with Nigel, Spencer, and a contractor at the park in 30 minutes. "Oops, I've got to run. I'm going to be late. Can we hold off deciding on this until tonight?

"Sure. It's probably a good idea to think about this anyway. I'll see what Connor, Roscoe, and Megan have to say in the meantime. Now, go to work."

While Ian was on his way to the park on Saturday morning, Nick Townsend was meeting with Angela Berg, the prosecuting attorney, in her office. They usually didn't meet on Saturdays, but murder cases didn't happen all that frequently in Benzie County and the preliminary hearing was on Monday. Angela had some questions, and Nick agreed to meet her in her office if she brought doughnuts and coffee. It was a standing joke with them that the prosecutor didn't get any cooperation from the sheriff's office without a doughnut bribe.

As Nick was getting the doughnuts out of the bag, both of their phones signaled they each had a text from Charlie Turner, the medical examiner. "Don't like bothering you on a Saturday morning, but I've got some interesting results. Call me."

"That's Charlie, too nice for his own good," Angela commented as she read the text. "Did you also just get a text from him?" After Nick nodded, Angela called the medical examiner on her speaker phone. When she got him on the line, she told him that she also had Nick on the speaker.

"I'm glad I've got you both," Charlie answered. "I have a little mystery for you that might muddle your case a bit."

"What've you got, Dr. Turner?" Nick asked. "If you blow up this case, the sheriff will go ballistic. It's not a pretty sight, but if truth be told, it's fun to watch."

They all laughed before the medical examiner continued. "I knew this one would come down to DNA. First, there's the hammer, the weapon used to kill Babs Tucker. The DNA tests confirm the blood on the head of the hammer is from her. There're also fragments of her brain tissue mixed with the blood."

"Thanks for that extra little detail, Charlie," the prosecutor commented. "I think I'll pass on the doughnuts I just bought."

"Sorry, I didn't realize you were eating. Anyway, there was a surprise finding under the dried blood. There was one other DNA sample. It looks like it came from perspiration from someone with oily skin who handled the hammer by the head."

Angela interrupted with a question. "How admissible will this evidence be with one DNA sample on top of another?"

"Not a problem? The latest software can identify five different samples with a high degree of confidence. I can't tell you when the sample under the blood was placed there, but I can tell you there were two and only two samples on that part of the hammer."

Nick took a turn at interrupting the medical examiner. "Now I suppose you are going to tell me that the other sample on the head is not from Dot or Herb Cooper."

"Definitely, not a match, Detective. The only DNA from one of the Cooper's is on the handle of the hammer. It was left with Dot's fingerprints."

"At least that's something," Nick commented.

"I'm not so sure," was the response from Dr. Turner. "The placement of her fingerprints indicate they were from when Dot Cooper picked up the hammer from the toolbox. Her hand wasn't positioned to use the hammer to hit something. Also, there were no other fingerprints or DNA on the handle."

Angela interrupted. "Hold on a minute. We have a hammer in her possession, and that hammer was used to kill Babs Tucker. Dot or Herb wiped the hammer handle before putting it in the toolbox, so that's why there was only the one set of prints."

Charlie asked, "So why didn't they wipe the blood from the hammer head?"

"Whose side are you on, Charlie? I still have enough to take to this the preliminary hearing. The second DNA sample on the head of the hammer could have been from anyone and could have been there for ages, so it doesn't make any difference to the case, unless... Wait a minute. You've got something else, Don't you?"

"I do."

Nick interrupted, "Let me guess. You found the same DNA on another piece of evidence, something linked to Bonnie Campbell's murder."

"Good guess, Detective. You're right. I do like working with smart people. I'd like them even more when they let me get a word in."

"Right. About what, exactly?" Angela asked.

Dr. Turner answered. "You recall Bonnie Campbell's hemlock laced coffee mug the park manager found in the sink at the coffee shop? There was a teaspoon in the mug with a fingerprint. We didn't get a match on the fingerprint, but whoever left it had oily skin, so we got a good DNA sample. Whoever left the print on the spoon was same person who left their DNA on the hammer head before it was used to kill Babs Tucker. The DNA is not a match to either Dot or Herb Cooper. We ran the sample through the database and there isn't a match to anyone in the system either."

Nick laughed. "The sheriff will go ballistic. He wants this solved quickly and it doesn't look like that is going to happen."

"I've got one more finding, Nick. It's from the wild carrot found in the Cooper's freezer yesterday."

"Do they have the same DNA as the hammer and spoon?" Angela asked.

"They do. There were a few drops of perspiration on the plants and also on the plastic bag."

Angela commented. "This isn't good for our case. That bag wasn't in their freezer when the cottage was searched after Dot and Herb's arrest, was it?"

"No," Nick answered. "I supervised the search myself. I think the DNA is telling us that someone is trying to frame the Coopers, and that someone is probably the killer."

The medical examiner shared a few more details before he rang off. As Angela hung up her phone, Nick looked at the remaining doughnut with a pleading·look. Angela nodded for him to take it. "I've still got the comment about blood and brains on my mind. Go ahead and eat."

After Nick devoured the doughnut, he asked, "Well?"

"Well what? I can't take what we've got to the preliminary hearing on Monday and expect to get Dot bound over for trial. We're going to have to release her. The two murders are linked, and the evidence points to someone else who is yet unidentified. Joe tried to tell me that yesterday."

"I hate to say it, but I agree with you. I read through all the crap on that website last night, and someone is playing us like a fiddle."

"I know. I also went through it all after Joe highlighted the posts he felt were made by the same guy. Someone even posted using the Cooper's dog's name asking for neighbors to bring casseroles. When the neighbors did, it looks like he joined them and left what he thought was hemlock in the freezer to incriminate Herb and Dot Cooper."

"He's a manipulative bastard, for sure, Angela, but what if there are two different people at play?

"What do you mean?"

"Bonnie Campbell was killed with hemlock, but Queen Anne's Lace, otherwise known as wild carrot, was left in the Cooper's freezer. Did the killer make a mistake and put the wrong plant in the freezer or is someone else just playing a game here?"

"I don't know, Nick. It looks like more work for your team to sort this all out. Meanwhile, do you want to tell the sheriff that I'm dropping the murder charges, or should I?"

"Oh, let me. It's been a tough week and I need some entertainment. Not that next week will be any better. I still don't have any idea how we're going to catch this guy."

"Nick, Dot Cooper still has the assault charge for striking Deputy McGregor. We can still hold her on that, at least until Monday, when we can revisit her bail."

"I talked to Kathy about the case on Friday. She doesn't want to press charges if we don't charge Dot with the murder. She said, "If Dot's innocent, she didn't do anything I wouldn't do in the same circumstances.""

"I can't let that charge go, but under the circumstances, I won't press for a custodial sentence. I'll get with Joe Quandaro to see if we can negotiate a plea that he and I can live with."

The sheriff was in Flint for the weekend for a wedding, so he didn't learn anything more until the preliminary hearing on Monday morning. The judge almost held him in contempt of court when he screamed and threw his hat on the floor when the murder charge was dropped.

The hearing was short, with Dot pleading guilty to a charge of disturbing the peace. Another hearing would be held later for sentencing on that crime, but she was granted bail. Since the charge of murder was dropped, the DNA results were not disclosed in court and were therefore not released to the public.

The other piece of information not released to the public was the email Elizabeth and Ian anonymously sent to Nick

Townsend and the prosecuting attorney early Monday morning, after they posted the comment from Archangel Michael to Della. The email contained all of posts they felt the killer had made using different usernames, the reasons they felt they'd identified the killer, and the times and locations where the posts were made.

The murderer heard about Dot's release before Herb pulled into their driveway with Dot. Someone posted the news on the Crime Spartans website with pictures of Dot hugging her lawyer in front of the court building. Someone else posted the text of the press release from the prosecutor's office that said the charges were dropped because there was insufficient evidence.

Upon hearing the news, the killer started to panic, with all kinds of thoughts coming to mind. *How on earth could they release her? They caught her with the hammer. Did I leave some DNA or fingerprints somewhere? I was so careful.*

The voice interrupted her thoughts. *"Even if you did, they don't have your DNA or fingerprints on file anywhere. Now calm down and let's think this through. Why don't you take a walk and get away from the park for a while? If you're there when Dot gets home, you might react inappropriately and give yourself away. You shouldn't see her until you've calmed down."*

The murderer was walking down the steps to the lake as Herb and Dot pulled through the gate of the park. *I've got things on my calendar today, but I need to focus and get my emotions under control. I'll send a few texts and cancel everything I had planned for today.*

The killer almost fell down the stairs while texting, but eventually made it safely down to the lake. While turning left on the lakeside trail at the bottom of the hill, the voice returned. *"I'm here. Now I want you to take a few deep breaths and focus on something you can see. Look, there's a deer in George Baxter's front yard over there. Look, he's eating something in George's vegetable garden"*

The killer did as the voice instructed and eventually calmed down. *Ok, I think I'm in control again. I'm going to take a long walk and think this through. What could have happened? Did they find new evidence or did the prosecutor just think the evidence I provided them wasn't enough?*

The voice returned. *"That's something you'll need to find out. When you get home, you'll want to talk to Herb and Dot, and most of the other people at Beulah Crest. As you know, there are no secrets in the park. You'll find out what happened."*

I could just wait a day or so and stop over at Elsie's cottage. She'll have gathered all the gossip by then.

"Of course, you'll want to talk to Elsie, but you need to talk with the others as well. Elsie lost a close friend and is frightened. She'll probably be emotional and won't be objective. Go to the coffee shop this afternoon and listen to what people have to say, not just about Herb and Dot, but also about what they have seen and heard over the past two weeks."

That's good advice. I need to know who they think the killer might be, and if they suspect me.

"Now what about visitors to the park? You saw the post made early this morning by someone who calls himself Archangel

Michael. He says he was visiting when he saw you kill Babs and later, he saw you picking hemlock. Who do you think it could be?"

Nigel and Spencer don't live here, so they technically aren't visitors, but I don't think it could be them. It could be Xander's sister, Katie, who was visiting from Germany. Would she leave the country after witnessing what I did to Babs without contacting the police? I don't think so. She's a doctor.

"You're right, it wouldn't have been her. You have to wonder why anyone would keep silent about what they've seen, and then post something like that on the Internet."

It is strange. Maybe they want to blackmail me.

"That's a possibility. It could also be some kid just trying to make trouble. No one has tried to contact you."

There's one more possibility.

"Oh, what else could it be?"

It really is Archangel Michael, and he's seen what I've done. Perhaps he doesn't think I should have taken on the responsibility of clearing the community of unworthy people. Perhaps I've gone too far.

"Do you really think so? I'm disappointed if that's the case. I've been here to support you as you do what you need to do. Do you really think the real Archangel Michael, the one in heaven, makes posts to the Internet?"

Of course not. I'm being silly, aren't I? You can hear divine voices in your heart and mind, like I do. You don't find them posting on the Internet. I can use the Internet though, to move things along. I have an idea of how to respond to this clown who calls himself Archangel Michael.

The killer and the voice went back and forth on the topics of Dot, Herb, and Archangel Michael. After two hours of walking along the trail, a plan developed. Over the next few days, the killer would talk with and listen to the other residents of the park to learn why Dot had been released and whether anyone had actually seen anything. Crime Spartans would also be followed to learn of anything new.

Of course, planning would continue on how to eliminate Max and Elsie. Depending on what was learned from the other park residents, the killer would decide if anyone should be added and who was next on the list.

While the killer was walking and thinking about the case, Dot was settling in after her release from the county jail. Della was excited to see her and welcomed her home with a lot of affection. Over the next few weeks Della never left Dot's side.

After a long hot bath, Dot decided to make a late lunch for herself and Herb. Wondering if Herb had been shopping, she looked in the refrigerator and freezer and called over to her husband. "Herb, you mentioned that a few of the neighbors brought over some casseroles, but this is ridiculous."

"They just kept bringing the stuff. I couldn't say no. I told you about the posts on the Internet made by someone calling themselves Della. Once people saw the post, they felt compelled to help."

"Why don't you give the neighbors a call and invite them all to an impromptu party this evening over at the Mouse House coffee shop. I'll heat this stuff up, and we can take it over and feed everyone. I feel like celebrating."

"Are you sure? Whoever planted that hammer in our garden shed might come."

"I hope they do. I'll be watching and listening to see if I can figure out who it is."

"You're a tough old girl, Dot. Whoever the killer is, he picked on the wrong person when he went after you. I'll start calling folks right now."

When Herb finished calling the neighbors, Dot asked him a question. "Herb, before we head over and celebrate, I need to ask you something. While I was in the bathtub, I read through the posts on that website on my tablet. There were quite a few about you, Elsie and your bridge partnership. Is anything going on that I should know about?"

"Nothing. You're my partner for bridge, and everything else, forever. Elsie was down because of Babs, so I agreed to play bridge with her. We only played once."

"I hope so."

Herb gave Dot a hug, which prompted Della to jump up and start licking them both. "You know it's so. That said, I learned something funny from her while we were talking. Do you remember that bid she made that prompted me to lose my temper?"

"Six hearts, if I recall correctly."

"Yes, six hearts. Anyway, Elsie said she accidently grabbed the wrong bidding card. She meant to bid four. You responded quickly with a pass, so she didn't have time to say anything or retract her bid. Then I went on to make a fool of myself."

"As long as you're my fool, I'm OK."

A small crowd responded favorably to Herb's invitation to celebrate Dot's return to the park. Elsie, Xander, the Parkers, Albert, Ben, Nigel, and Spencer. Ian would be there with Elizabeth. Of course, Della and Greta were also invited.

The mood in the coffee shop was subdued, since everyone knew a murderer was still at large, but curiosity got the better of everyone, so they came. Ian took the opportunity to introduce Elizabeth to everyone as they came in the coffee shop.

Dot was the center of attention as everyone asked questions about her arrest, her time in jail, and how she got released. Having spent the last week alone in a jail cell, Dot welcomed to company and didn't mind answering the inquiries from her neighbors. There was a question on everyone's mind that Dot couldn't answer. If Dot wasn't the killer, who was?

When Ian asked about the preliminary hearing and why they decided to drop the charges, Dot answered as best she could. "Joe, our lawyer, came by the jail on Sunday afternoon and told me the murder charges would probably be dropped and the assault charge would be reduced if I pled to a lesser charge. He said it had something to do with the fact that the only fingerprints on the hammer were from me when I picked it up. He said the prosecutor didn't share much else because she didn't want anyone else to know about the other evidence they had collected. I got the feeling they are close to catching someone else."

Reverend Parker asked, "Do you think they've got the actual killer identified?"

"Joe seemed to think they did. Otherwise, they wouldn't have let me go so easily. He thought it would all come down to DNA samples and the like. His partner, a nice lady named Pearl, thought there were quite a few clues on that website, and she felt the killer was probably posting there, along with everyone else."

"Do you really think the killer is posting there?" Derek asked.

"Now that you ask," Dot answered, "I think Pearl's right. Someone, using the name Della, got most of you to bring over the food we're enjoying here. One of the people who brought the food also planted a plastic bag of hemlock in our freezer."

"When I saw the posting on the Web from Della, I thought something was fishy," Elsie commented. "I went over and looked in Herb's freezer where I saw it hidden under the ice cream. When I told Herb, he called his lawyer. The lawyer then called Detective Townsend, who came over and took it away.

"Did you handle the bag of hemlock?" Derek asked.

"No. The police came by my cottage today and took a DNA sample from me. I'm guessing they found fingerprints or DNA on the bag. Since I never touched it, I was happy to let them take my prints and a swab from the inside of my mouth. I wonder if they could make everyone in the park give a sample. That would certainly make things easier."

Herb interrupted. "Here's the funny part. It wasn't even hemlock. Whoever put it there made a common mistake. It was Queen Anne's Lace, a wild carrot. It looks a lot like hemlock. Dot thinks it was a prankster, but I think the killer is just stupid. In addition to leaving the wrong plant, I think he also left a fingerprint or DNA on the plastic bag, and that's why they released Dot."

The killer, trying not to react to what was being said, listened to the conversation and occasionally asked questions. Nothing conclusive was said, but the risk of being identified was getting higher. *I'll have to do something. If what I'm hearing is true, the police could come knocking on my door at any time.*

The killer's thoughts were interrupted when Ian called out to the group, "Say everyone, I'd like to make an announcement." Ian was about to announce his engagement to Elizabeth. When the room went quiet, Ian noticed that Ben wasn't in the group. "Has anyone seen Ben? He's as much a part of the park as anyone. I'd like him to hear this as well."

Herb answered. "I talked to him just before I called you, Ian. He said he'd be right over. He was just finishing up planting some flowers at the top of the stairs to the lake. Why don't you try calling him on his cell?"

Ian was concerned. Ben was never late when free food was on offer. "I'll try." Ian picked up his phone from the counter and called Ben, but there was no answer. "That's funny. Ben always answers his phone." Ian then called out to the crowd. "Has anyone else seen Ben? He doesn't answer his phone."

Xander answered. "Hortense, Derek, and I all walked past Ben as we were walking over here. He told us he'd be right over. That was quite a while ago. Herb and Dot also talked to him. They were right in front of us."

Meanwhile, the sheriff's office was in a state of chaos, and had been all morning. When the sheriff returned to the office after the preliminary hearing, he had what Nick later described as, a meltdown. He charged into Nick's office and started throwing things and ranting about the incompetent deputies on his force, the stupid prosecuting attorney, and the judge who allowed the charges to be dropped and who then threatened him with contempt charges.

At first, Nick tried to get the sheriff to calm down, but he eventually decided to let the tantrum run its course. Nick's desktop phone was the first victim as the sheriff hurled it across the desk, narrowly missing Nick. Almost everything else on Nick's desk eventually ended up flying in various directions, as did a chair and the coat rack. A crowd of deputies gathered outside the door to watch the show, with none daring to enter. Everyone had seen the sheriff in a rage at one time or another, but this was the worst anyone had ever seen.

When the tantrum finally subsided, Nik picked up a chair for the sheriff and invited him to sit down. "Sheriff, if you're finished destroying my office, how about we talk about the case. I think I have an idea of how we can catch the killer."

The sheriff, who could see his re-election hopes fading, agreed to listen. "Ok Nick. What are you thinking?"

Nick shared the information in the email Ian and Elizabeth had sent earlier and the DNA and fingerprint information he received from the medical examiner.

The sheriff had a response that didn't surprise Nick. "It would be so much easier without the Internet and all this DNA crap. When I find someone with the murder weapon in their hands, I should be able to send them to prison, end of story." The sheriff then noticed the one thing in the room he didn't manage to throw, a box of doughnuts on the file cabinet behind Nick's desk. "Give me a doughnut, and tell me what you want to do. Also, get someone in here to clean up this mess."

While a couple of deputies cleaned up the clutter, Nick poured the sheriff a coffee and gave him two maple glazed doughnuts. While the sheriff finished off his first doughnut, Nick started to explain his plan. "It appears the killer posts quite a bit to this Crime Spartans website from the computer at the Beulah library. We have a list of the names he uses when he logs into the site."

"You mean the same person can put stuff on that site using different names?"

Nick tried to hide his frustration at the sheriff's lack of intelligence as he answered. "Yes, Sheriff. The way the site is set up, anyone can set up an account or a number of accounts."

"So?" the sheriff asked. "I'm not going to have a deputy sit in the library all day and watch who uses the computer. Even if I did, the killer probably knows most of the deputies and would walk out if he sees one."

"You're probably right Sheriff. They don't have any security cameras in library, but we can get the village to put one outside the entrance. We can put it on top of the adjacent building where it won't be noticed. If we pay for it, the village will let us. I already talked to the village president."

"What good will that do? We can't question everyone who goes into the library."

Nick couldn't believe the sheriff couldn't connect the dots without help. "Sheriff, when someone posts to the website, the time and username of the person posting is included in the post. As you know, Deputy McGregor is keeping a close eye on that site. All we have to do is look at the video at the times when the posts are made using one of the suspected accounts. We can have the video fed to our office here."

"Why not just put a camera in the library?"

"It might be seen by the killer. Also, Agnes the librarian, is a big privacy advocate. She would fight us on putting a camera in her library, and word would get out what we were doing."

"Oh, for crying out loud."

"I know, Sheriff, but once we know who it is, we can follow them. Agnes sees everyone who goes into the library and uses the computer. Once we have the video, the postings from the Web, and a statement from Agnes that she saw the person in question at the computer, we can get a warrant to search the home of the person who posted and to get their fingerprints and DNA."

"I'd rather just pull them over and beat a confession out of them, but I suppose your way gives us a better chance of a conviction. Go ahead and…"

The sheriff and Nick were interrupted when a young deputy ran into the office. "We've got another one Sheriff."

"Another what?" the sheriff shouted. "Don't you know how to knock on a door before barging into an office?"

"Sorry about that Sheriff. Another murder over at Beulah Crest. Ben Weldon, this time. He's the groundskeeper over there."

"I know who Ben Weldon is, you idiot," the sheriff barked. "What else do we know?"

"Not much. They found him at the bottom of the stairs. There was a 9-1-1 call from the Beulah maintenance supervisor who said he found Ben, dead, at the bottom of the stairs. That's all I have."

"Good God in heaven," the sheriff shouted as he got up and headed for the door. "Come on Nick, let's get over there and find out what's going on. I knew they shouldn't have released that woman, or her husband."

CHAPTER 12
Distractions

"**G**o down Lake Street to Crystal Avenue," the sheriff yelled to Nick. "That idiot said Ben was at the bottom of the stairs." The chatter on the police radio confirmed the location. Two deputies and an ambulance were already there when they arrived. A crowd of locals and tourists were crowded along the edge of the lake and along the trail.

When the sheriff and Nick made their way through the crowd, they found Ben on a stretcher. An IV drip was already going, and Ben was kept immobile by a head brace. He didn't appear to be conscious.

Nick knew the paramedic, Steve Evert. Steve had his hands full, so they talked while Steve and his partner loaded Ben into the ambulance truck. "How's he doing Steve? When we got the 9-1-1 call, we were told Ben was dead."

"He probably would be dead, or crippled for life, if that jackass maintenance guy from the village hadn't been stopped by those three over there. He was going to move Ben and could have cut his spinal cord. I can't say for sure, but Ben may have broken his neck as he went down the stairs." Steve pointed to Dot, Herb, and Derek, who were talking to the sheriff.

"Is he going to make it?" Nick asked.

"It depends on the head injury. He's got a pretty nasty bump. We'll take him to Paul Oliver in Frankfort where they'll make sure he's stable, and then he'll be flown up to Traverse City in the helicopter."

"Any chance I can talk with him, Steve?"

"It's going to be a while. He mumbled a few words and I got him to move his toes, and that's it. We've got to run."

Nick stepped back as Steve's partner closed the rear doors and the truck raced away. Nick walked over to where the sheriff was talking with people from the park. Nick got there just in time to hear Derek Parker tell the sheriff, "I can't believe it. That big slob from the village wanted to pick Ben up and put him in his truck. If he did that without a neck brace, Ben could have been crippled, for life."

Herb interrupted. "He wouldn't listen to Derek, or any of us. When he saw that Ben was alive, the jerk bent down to pick him up. The three of us, and Ian, then grabbed the big ox and held him until the paramedics arrived. We could hear the sirens by then, so we knew they'd be here soon."

"And get this," Dot added. "He says he wants to press charges against us for assault because we grabbed him. If it's the last thing I do, I'm going to get that jackass fired."

Before the sheriff could react or make a stupid decision, Nick intervened. "Ok, everybody, please calm down. The important thing is that Ben is alive and is being taken to the hospital by trained paramedics. Right now, I'd like to talk with you each individually to learn what happened and what you each saw."

The sheriff decided to let Nick handle the interviews. The tantrums earlier in the day at the station and the courthouse seemed to have worn him out. "Nick, go ahead and talk to these people. I'll go talk to that idiot cousin of mine who works for the village. I'll make sure he doesn't press charges. We don't need more bad publicity."

Nick nodded to the sheriff, appreciating his decision to back out of the questioning. He started with Derek Parker, who seemed to be the least emotional of the group. He led the dentist to a picnic table near the shore. On the way, he asked Deputy McGregor to join them to take notes.

"Dr. Parker, can you tell me what happened?"

"I can't say how Ben ended up at the bottom of the stairway, Detective. A group of us were up at the Mouse House celebrating Dot's release. She and Herb brought all of the casseroles over that were left by the neighbors to share. Ian was about to make an announcement and noticed that Ben hadn't arrived. I don't follow park gossip, but even I know that Ben never misses a free meal."

"What was this announcement?"

"I haven't a clue. Hortense would probably know. Maybe something about the park or maybe he is going to marry the girl he was with. Anyway, Ian tried to phone Ben, but didn't get an answer. Given the recent events at the park, we were all concerned. Hortense suggested someone should go check on Ben since we all had just seen him at the top of the stairs planting flowers on our way over to the Mouse House."

"So, who went out to check on Ben?"

"We all did. Albert was the first out the door, with Greta, and then everyone just followed. It looked like Ben had finished planting the flowers. We assumed he was still nearby because his truck was still there. Then, Greta and Della broke loose and ran down the stairs. We all followed the dogs down and that's when we saw Ben at the bottom of the stairs with that lummox from the village standing over him."

"What happened next?"

"The guy from the village, I don't know his name, called 9-1-1 and told them there was a body at the bottom of the stairs. I heard him say there was another murder. While he was making the call, Herb and I took a closer look and saw that Ben was still breathing and had a pulse. I shouted that he was alive, and Hortense called for an ambulance. Herb put his jacket over Ben to keep him warm and Dot talked to Ben, encouraging him to hold on while the ambulance came."

"So, what about him?" Nick asked, pointing to the maintenance supervisor who was talking to the sheriff.

"He's strong, I'll give him that. Too bad he's stupid and stubborn. It took three of us to keep him from picking Ben up after we realized he was alive. I suppose the guy's heart was in the right place, though. He wanted to get Ben to the hospital as quickly as possible."

Nick talked to everyone else who was at the Mouse House and all of them said about the same thing. No one saw how Ben ended up at the bottom of the stairs. There are lakefront cottages on either side of the stairway, but their owners were not yet up for the season. The few people standing nearby hadn't seen Ben fall or anyone suspicious in the area. There were just local residents and a few tourists taking a walk along the lakeside trail.

While Nick was questioning people, deputies taped off the areas at the top and bottom of the staircase with crime scene tape. Nobody would be able to access the area or use the stairs until the crime lab people did their work. After talking with everyone at the bottom of the stairs, Nick and Kathy drove up to the park in the deputy's car. The park residents went up the stairs belonging to the condo development adjacent to the park and walked home on a trail through the forest between the two properties.

By the time Nick and Kathy got to the park, the crime lab technicians had arrived. After several hours of searching and examining the area, nothing conclusive could be found. Nick's garden tools were in his truck and the flower bed work looked complete. Fingerprints were taken from his truck and tools. Several people used the stairway every day, so prints taken there would be of little use.

The only thing found on the platform at the top of the stairs was Ben's cooler. Residents of the park told Nick that Ben always took the cooler with him when doing jobs around the park. It usually contained a few cans of beer and some sandwiches. The open cooler contained an empty beer can and one that hadn't been opened. A torn empty sandwich bag was found a few feet from the cooler in the flower bed.

There were a number of footprints in the area. Casts were made, but Nick held out little hope that anything would be learned from them. There was nothing at the site to suggest that Ben was pushed down the stairs or that he wasn't. If there weren't already two unsolved murders in the park, Nick wouldn't have investigated further, unless Ben himself claimed there was an attempt on his life.

After questioning the remaining residents of the park, Nick headed down to Paul Oliver Hospital in Frankfort. The emergency room doctor confirmed that Ben had a severe head concussion and several broken ribs. There also appeared to be a fracture of one of the upper vertebrae, so the actions taken to immobilize Ben were valid. As expected, Ben was flown to Munson Medical Center in Traverse City, where they were better equipped to handle his injuries.

When Nick called Munson Hospital, he was informed that surgery was scheduled to relieve pressure on Ben's brain and Ben would probably be in an induced coma until the swelling had a chance to go down.

On the way back from Frankfort, Nick remembered the cameras Ian had installed at the park, so he headed to the Mouse House. When Nicked walked into Ian's office, he found Ian, Nigel, and Spencer reviewing the tapes. Not hearing Nick enter, they were startled when Nick asked, "Anything useful?"

"Not much," Ian answered. "The way the cameras are angled, you can see if anyone approaches the stairway from the park and you can see if anyone goes up or down the stairway from about the fifth step down from the top. Unfortunately, there is no coverage of the platform at the top of the stairs."

"Show him what we do have," Nigel told Ian.

Ian worked the keyboard and mouse and a video from the camera aimed down the stairs started to play. "Here it is," Ian commented. A few seconds later, Ben could be seen falling down the stairs, headfirst. He rapidly fell out of view of the camera.

"Play it again," Nick instructed.

Ian played the video over again several time before Nick asked, "What do you see, gentlemen?"

"He seems to be going fast, as if he were running when he fell," Spencer answered.

"Or, was being chased," Nigel added.

"Exactly," Nick answered. "I don't know why, but I think we'd see something different if he were at the top and just tripped. I'll get someone from the crime lab to look at it who might be able to tell us more. Is there anything else from the other cameras?"

Ian answered. "Nothing. Just the usual people coming and going. There's no one approaching the top of the stairs, other than Ben, at the time of his fall."

"Ian, scroll the video back for an hour or so before the fall. Let's see if anyone who doesn't live here has been in the area."

Ian did as the detective asked, but there was nothing unusual until Spencer spotted a reflection from something that appeared to be someone's eyes. "Hold it there Ian. It looks like someone is crouching down in the forest, watching Ben."

Ian stopped the video and wound it back a few seconds before freezing it. When he zoomed in, everyone saw what Spencer had spotted and then laughed. It was Arthur, the fox, siting in the shadows watching Ben. "That fox is getting too tame," Ian commented after he stopped laughing. "I'll have to tell Elsie to stop feeding him."

Nick commented. "Looks like no luck with the video, at least from what we've seen. Ian, send me over a copy of all the videos from these cameras and the others in the park for the last few days. Maybe we'll get lucky and spot something unusual."

Nick and Kathy walked around the park and questioned a few people who hadn't been around earlier, but failed to learn anything new. Park residents who had been at the potluck lunch came by the Mouse House to pick up their casserole pans. When they got there, Albert told them he'd put the dirty pans and dishes in the dishwasher, and they could pick them in the morning.

The killer was stressed to the point of near panic over the day's events and had to do something to calm down. Without any specific plans, the killer got in the car and headed out of the park for a drive. As soon as the car was past the gate, the voice returned. *"What a day it's been. How are you holding up?"*

The killer answered by thinking, *Not very good, but better, now that you're here. I just don't know what to think about all that happened today. This morning I was devastated when I heard that Dot was released and then someone tried to kill Ben. He's not even on my list. I don't know what to do now.*

"It's too bad about Ben but think of the opportunity we have here."

What opportunity. I like Ben, and, he's not on our list.

"No, he's not, but you have a very firm alibi for when Ben was pushed down the stairs. We can shift the blame for Babs'

and Bonnie's murders to whoever tried to kill Ben and make sure everyone thinks the three events and people are connected."

Max wasn't with us at the Mouse House. I could say it was him. He's on the list, so if they arrest him, that's one less for me to take care of here at the park.

"You can still post something on the Internet, today. Head over to the library. You have just enough time to get over there before it closes. I'll help craft a message when you get there."

The killer got to the library about 20 minutes before closing time, so there was plenty of time to make the post. There was no record of who made the post because Agnes, the librarian, was out sick and Jenna, the part-time student employee, was texting on her phone while the killer was using the computer. The camera on the adjoining building didn't get installed because the village maintenance supervisor went home after the incident with Ben.

The killer felt rushed and anxious driving over to the library, but a sense of peace took hold after logging into Crime Spartans. The voice helped, suggesting a new username and message that was quickly posted to the Web. "I am Archangel Raguel, the angel of justice, vengeance and redemption. I saw who pushed Ben down the stairs."

The killer paused for a few seconds as Jenna walked past. After seeing how Jenna was preoccupied with her phone, the rest of the message was drafted and posted. "It's the same man who killed Bonnie and Babs, Max Silver. This colourful character is not what he seems. I ask everyone who sees this message to do me and yourself a favour. Do whatever is necessary to keep him from doing this again."

Confident the message would mobilize park residents to action, the killer returned home and waited for the neighbors to help with Max. *He wasn't at the top of my list, but he saw something. So, it's best if he's the next to go. If all goes well, the investigation will get refocused away from me and onto Max, unless, of course, someone else takes action before the police do."*

Neighbors at Beulah Crest, and many others, responded to the posting, but not in the way the killer expected. The post that caused the greatest stir in the community, and the one that put the killer in a state of panic, came from far away. It was from Naomi Banks, a communications and language student at the University of Queensland in Australia. She had been following posts on Crime Spartans as part of her research on the impact of the Internet on the English language.

Naomi posted on the site for the first time after reading the killer's last post. "I can't watch this nonsense any longer, so I'm posting here. I'm not a detective nor am I with the police. I'm just a language student in Australia. Archangel Raguel, Della, and several of the other usernames on this site are from the same person. We've written a program that looks at patterns in written English. Perhaps it's obvious to some of you already because these posts are the only ones from your area using Oxford English, but my algorithm confirms they are all from the same person. Unfortunately, our algorithm only indicates if the posts are from the same person, not if that person is telling the truth. Personally though, I think this is the same person who killed Babs and Bonnie. I hope your police investigate this."

Within an hour of Naomi's post, there was a flood of other postings on the site. Cherry Picker logged in and again named a suspect. "Is everyone blind? It's Reverend Parker. She's a control freak who's become unhinged since retiring. How Derek puts up with her is beyond me."

Derek responded, using his own name. "How dare Cherry Picker name my wife. What evidence does he have? If I find out who he is, there'll be hell to pay."

Elsie also came to Reverend Parker's defense. "Hortense is a saint. When I was taken to the hospital, Hortense was there when I woke up and has been there for me ever since."

Numerous other posts agreed with Naomi that the posts were made by the same person, but there was disagreement on whom the killer might be. Nigel and Spencer got the most posts accusing them because of the use of Oxford English. There were quite a few posts from the same members of the bridge club who posted earlier, implicating Elsie and Herb. One person suggested that Ben killed Babs and Bonnie and then tried to kill himself by jumping head-first down the stairs.

Ian and Elizabeth didn't get a chance to read through the posts until Monday evening. Ian was held up at the park all afternoon while the police were there, and Elizabeth had two exams to take at NMC. When they got together at Elizabeth's apartment, Ian read the posts aloud while Elizabeth warmed up some leftover pasta in the microwave and poured the wine.

After Ian read the post from the killer inviting park residents to take action against Max, Elizabeth gasped. "Ian, people are using our site to incite violence. We have to do something."

"I know." Ian's hand was shaking as he used the mouse pad to scroll through the posts. "I'm ready to shut the whole thing down. I mean shut it down right now, before something happens. The money we're making is nice, but we don't need it. Would you be OK with closing it down, at least for a while?"

"I'm not sure, Ian. I really think the site can be used to solve the murders, but we have to do things differently."

"What do you mean, differently?" Ian asked, while helping himself to some spaghetti. Still unsteady, he dropped a meatball that rolled off the table and onto the floor. "What could we do differently?"

"First, you need to clean up that mess and then chill out a bit. We're not going to get anything done if you don't calm down." Elizabeth handed Ian a paper towel before continuing. "We need to watch what's being posted more carefully. All five of us who own the site should take turns watching what's being posted and delete posts like the one just made by Archangel Raguel. I've been watching, but I can't be in front of my computer screen all of the time."

"That's not enough Elizabeth. We can still miss something if we get interrupted or distracted. A post that could lead to violence would be seen by too many people before it could be deleted by one of us."

"How about if we have all posts delayed for 30 minutes before they appear to the public. This would give us a chance to catch dangerous posts and delete them before anyone sees them; I can program the site to do this."

"I'm still not sure. There's still a lot of risk here."

"I agree, but we could be feeding everything that gets posted to the police, even the posts we delete."

Ian held up his hand. He'd been scrolling through the site as they were talking. "Hold on a minute and come take a look at this." Elizabeth leaned over and read through the post from Naomi and the posts accusing various people of being the murderer.

"That's a harsh one accusing Reverend Parker. I went to her church when I was a kid. My mom liked her."

"What did you think of her?"

"I never thought about her one way or the other. Sunday school was fun, but the rest of it was a bore. When my parents got divorced, I moved in with my father and stopped going to her church."

"Do you think she could be the killer?"

"Maybe Bonnie?"

"Why Bonnie?"

"Because her killer used poison. I don't want to sound sexist, but poison is a woman's weapon. It's less violent. Babs is another story though. Women just don't go around hitting other women in the head with a hammer. We either have two killers, which is unlikely, or it's not Reverend Parker."

"Hold on, we're getting off track here. We need to decide whether or not to shut down our site."

"I say we keep it going, but delay posts from appearing until they are reviewed by one of us. I also think we should make sure the police see everything we have, including where the posts are made and who made them, if we know."

"That's goes against our site pledge of confidentiality."

"I know, Ian, but seriously! Do you think anyone believes anything on the Internet is confidential? We may have to revise the policy."

"I suppose. We still won't know the names of people who post, unless they say who they are, and even then, they could be using a false name. We just know the IP address, which tells us the location of where the post was made."

"We're figuring this out as we go, Ian. How about if we keep the site up, review everything before it goes online, and you follow up with that detective to make sure he's reviewing everything we send him."

"Before we talk more about that, let's delete that post about Max, right now."

Elizabeth agreed and opened her laptop and logged into the site as site administrator. As she deleted the most recent post from the killer, she told Ian, "It looks like 80 people logged in after this was posted."

"That's not good. We'll need to call Max and alert him."

"I'll print all of the posts, including the one about Max, and a report of the known location of the posts that we can give to the detective."

"If we want to be sure Detective Townsend uses this, I'll need to give it to him in person. I hate to do it, but I think we have

to, which means the police will know we own Crime Spartans.
Are you OK with that?"

"I don't like it, Ian, but I don't think we have much choice.
Why don't you call him right now and ask if he can come up
here this evening? We can talk to him together."

Ian called the detective and then called Max to alert him
to what was posted on the Web.

Elizabeth overhead Ian talking. When he hung up from
the calls, she asked, "Well, what did they say. You were on the
phone with Max for quite a while?"

"Detective Townsend will be here in an hour. Max saw the
posting before we took it down. His son saw it and called from
Denver and told him about it. Max said his son talked him into
flying out to Colorado for a few days. He didn't want to go, but
his son insisted. He's got a flight tomorrow morning."

"It's probably just as well. It just takes one of the people
who saw that post to be unhinged to put Max in danger. Maybe
you should call him back and suggest he stay somewhere else
tonight. He could stay here, or maybe at the Mouse House."

"His son already thought of that and booked Max a room
for tonight at a hotel near the airport in Traverse City. Max
didn't argue. His flight's at 5:30 in the morning, so he would
have stayed near the airport regardless of the circumstances. He
was just about to leave for Traverse when I called."

"I just had another thought, Ian. Why don't we check out
this student in Australia, what's her name?"

"Naomi Banks."

"That's the one. If she's for real, we should let the detective know about her. Maybe she can help." Elizabeth took back her laptop and did a search on Google where she found a number of links for Naomi. "Looks like she's legit. She co-authored a paper on the language analysis algorithm and a bunch of others on similar topics. Hold on... here's a link to her LinkedIn page."

"What's it say?"

"She's finishing a PhD in linguistics and has a Masters in English literature. She did an undergraduate in English with a minor in criminal science. All from Australian universities. Looks like a pretty smart lady."

"If it's actually her and not someone using her name."

"Her phone number is on her LinkedIn page. Let's give her a call. How do you make a phone call to Australia?"

"I don't know. There's a country code for Australia, but I don't know what it is. Try using the Google phone app with the number on her LinkedIn page to make a video call. If she answers, we can see if she looks like the pictures on her webpages."

Naomi did answer and her face matched the person photographed on her webpage, her LinkedIn page, and on the linguistics department webpage at her university. After introductions were made, Elizabeth asked, "Naomi, can your program tell us anything else about the person we think is the killer, other than he posted using several different names."

"Now you're getting at the fun part of my research, the part my research advisor is reluctant to have me publish yet. We still don't have the data to conclusively prove the accuracy beyond identifying if the writing sample belongs to the same person."

"What else might your program be able to tell us?" Ian asked.

"It can't tell you much with the samples I have. I'm just giving my opinion. If you can get your suspect to write a longer post on your site, I can have my program analyze it, along with the other posts from the same person."

"So, what's your opinion and what more might you be able to tell is with a larger sample?" Elizabeth asked.

"This more my intuition as much as anything else given the sample size, but I think he, or she, has a university degree in a non-technical field. I'm thinking sociology, psychology, or humanities. By the style of their writing and the words, phrases, and spelling used, I'm speculating the writer may have grown up in the UK, but I'm thinking it's more likely he was raised in Canada but has lived a long time in the United States."

"So, what if we can prompt him to write some longer posts to the website?" Ian asked.

"Our program should be able to tell you their sex and estimate their age. It's nothing that would hold up in a court or that could be used to issue a warrant for an arrest, but perhaps the police could use the information to target their inquiries."

* * *

Back at Beulah Crest, the killer looked out of the kitchen window and watched helplessly as Max put a suitcase in the trunk of his car and drove off. *Damn, he must have seen my* post. I wish one of my neighbors would've acted faster and taken care of him. He's leaving, at least.

The voice returned. *"Please, watch your language and settle yourself down. There's no reason to panic or to use profanity. When word spreads that Max has left, people will suspect he's running because he's guilty. Do you still have the prepaid cellphone you used to text the sheriff?"*

Yes, of course. Why?

"Why don't you send a text to that pompous sheriff and tell him Max is leaving town because someone on the Web has evidence he's the killer? Also, tell him you saw Max push Ben down the stairs. Maybe we'll get lucky and the sheriff will run Max off the road or shoot him in a chase."

We can only hope, but it's more likely the sheriff will hold him for questioning for a few days and then they'll release him, just like they did with Dot.

"Perhaps, but we should be able to do something. Now think. Isn't there anything you could put in or near Max's cottage to incriminate him?"

We tried that with Herb and Dot. It didn't get us anywhere. Hold on a second... I did do something I shouldn't have a few days ago. I took something we might be able to use.

"What did you take?"

When I was over at Herb's putting the hemlock in his freezer, I saw the keys to his garden shed on the kitchen counter. Earlier that morning, I noticed he'd put a lock on the shed door.

"So, how did you know the keys belonged to the lock on shed?"

There were two keys on small keychain sitting on the counter, with the receipt for the lock from the hardware store down in Frankfort.

"Don't tell me you took them?"

Only one. I have it right here, along with the receipt. I could hide it in a flowerpot on Max's deck and tell the sheriff to search Max's place for the key when I send him the text.

"So, why would Max hide a key to Herb and Dot's garden shed?"

When I text the sheriff, I'll also tell him Max was planning to kill Herb and Dot and hide their bodies in the shed.

"Ok, go ahead and send the text. At the least, it'll cause some confusion at the sheriff's office and give us more time to plan what we need to do next. After you send it, I think it's a good idea to get rid of that phone. If it's ever found in your possession or in your cottage...."

I know, it would be too risky to keep it, but hold on a minute. I have another thought.

"Oh."

We still want Herb and Dot out of the park, don't we?

"Yes, but it looks like the courts aren't going to help us with them. You'll have to take care of them yourself, at some point once the dust settles."

Given that Max has fled, he won't be saying anything to the police, at least for a while. So, he's not a risk for the time being.

"So?"

I'd rather focus on Herb and Dot. I don't want them around here.

"What do you propose?"

How about if I send the text implicating Max, as we discussed, but rather than destroying the phone, I put it in Herb and Dot's tool shed. I could leave the power on so the police can track its location.

"Are you sure you can get into their tool shed without being seen? Didn't Herb put cameras up around his cottage? Don't forget, Ian also installed several cameras around the park."

As usual, you're right. It would be hard for me to hide the phone without being seen while sneaking into the shed.

"So, don't sneak. Pay a visit to Herb and Dot tomorrow morning, and when you're there, leave the phone behind in some inconspicuous place. Don't forget to wipe it clean of fingerprints. Several of the neighbors have already stopped by their place to offer their support. You'd be just another friendly neighbor."

Good idea. I think we have a plan. I'll send the text to the sheriff just before I visit Dot and Herb in the morning and then, when I log onto Crime Spartans later in the afternoon, I'll mention that I saw Herb shouting at Max and that Max disappeared shortly afterwards.

"You're weaving a tangled web, so you need to be careful. Make sure you have a story about where you've been and what you've been doing memorized before the police come around to question people in the park again. You don't need to worry about the sheriff, but Detective Townsend is smart enough to see any inconsistencies in what you tell him."

* * *

Nick laughed when Ian told him about how he, Elizabeth, and the others owned and ran Crime Spartans. "I should have guessed. I remember now you told me about setting up a crime tracking website after you came back from computer camp in high school. That was when you thought you wanted to be a police detective. I never imagined you'd keep it going this long."

Elizabeth interrupted. "Ian, you never told me you wanted to be a cop."

Ian leaned over and gave Elizabeth a kiss. "There are all kinds of secrets about me you haven't discovered yet. The 'I want to be a cop phase' lasted for about 3 months. It was before I wanted to race motorcycles and after I wanted to be a history teacher."

Detective Townsend let Ian and Elizabeth go back and forth teasing and kissing each other for a moment before he asked for their attention. "Ok, you two. Before you tell me about your wedding plans, let's go through this website and why you are telling me about it now."

"How did you know about the wedding?" Ian asked. "We were going to announce it today at lunch, but never got a chance."

"I'm a detective, sunshine. All I have to do is look at you two. Now what's new with the website. We've been watching it. What are we missing?"

Elizabeth told the detective about the posts they deleted, what they learned from Naomi Banks, and then reminded him that all but the first post from the person they suspected to be the killer were made at the Beulah library.

"I should get a court order to shut your site down, but I'm guessing you would fight that, and the publicity would make staking out the library a useless exercise."

"Detective," Elizabeth answered, "We are willing to shut down the site if we need to, but I think it can be used to find the killer. We'd like to post something that will encourage the killer to give a lengthy response. Naomi thinks her program can tell us more from a larger writing sample."

"More of what?" Nick asked.

"Hopefully the killer's age, gender, and possibly their occupation. If he decides to post from somewhere other than the Beulah library, you'll have a better idea who to watch and follow."

Ian interrupted. "Elizabeth, let's show Detective Townsend the post you've drafted."

Elizabeth handed Nick a copy of what she had written just before he'd arrived. "Detective, please read through this and tell us what you think. If you don't want us to post this, we won't, but we think this will get the killer to post again. If he does, you'll have another chance to catch him if he uses the computer at the Beulah library and Naomi's program might be able to tell us more his background."

Ian poured Nick a cup of coffee while the detective read through the post:

Dear Archangel Raguel, Della, or whatever you choose to call yourself today. I am the Archangel Michael. As I expect you know, I am the leader of the army of God. Our mission is to fight against the forces of evil. Usually, I can see into the heart and soul of people and can tell if they are working on the side of light or on the side of darkness.

I know who you are, and I know what you've done, but I still don't understand why. I see a good person who is harming other people. Please, help me and my fellow angels understand why you've taken it upon yourself to kill people who appear to be kind and God fearing. Also, I need to know who has given you this task and what else you are planning to do. What is your ultimate goal?

I await your response. If I don't hear a truthful response from you by the end of the day, I will be compelled to take action to stop you.

Nick finished reading what the couple wanted to post to the website and handed the copy back to Elizabeth. "You two really want to post this? Thanks for everything you've told me, but this is going too far. I'm a cop, one of honest ones. I can't be doing this kind of nonsense. If this post leads to an arrest and the defense finds out I asked you to post this, they could get the case thrown out."

Elizabeth refilled Nick's coffee before responding. "Detective, you didn't ask us to do anything. We called you, told you about the website and shared information about who is posting on it and where the people who make the posts are located. Confidential informant. Isn't that what they call us on TV detective shows?"

"Yes, but this isn't a TV show. It's Benzie County."

Elizabeth held up her hand to stop Nick from continuing. "I realize that, Detective. This is rural Northern Michigan, where a confidential informant is likely to be a friend of the police officer conducting the investigation. In this case, she happens to run a website that many of the people in the community are using. You didn't ask us to do anything. Tomorrow morning, someone using the name Archangel Michael will post a message on the website aimed at someone who he believes to be the killer."

Nick was about to interrupt again when Ian spoke up. "Tomorrow morning, you'll go to the office like you usually do. While you're having coffee and doughnuts with the sheriff, whatever deputy you have watching the Internet will come running into your office to tell you about the latest post from Archangel Michael. Since you didn't ask anyone to post such a thing, you'll be surprised and angry that such nonsense is on the Internet, but then you'll issue instructions to the deputy based on the post from the archangel and the information you anonymously just received by text from someone who works at Crime Spartans."

"Wait a minute, you two," the detective shouted. "Who's running this investigation, anyway?"

"You are, Detective," Ian and Elizabeth replied in unison.

Nick started laughing. "Ok, I give up. I'll use what you've given me and whatever else you learn from your site, and you'll remain anonymous. Not for your sake, but for mine."

"And since you don't know who we are and didn't ask us to post anything, you can't be blamed for using our site to entrap your suspect," Elizabeth added.

It was almost midnight when Nick left Ian and Elizabeth and headed home. He wasn't sure how comfortable he was using Crime Spartans to help solve the crime, but as he drove home, he decided to give Ian and Elizabeth another day or two before he pulled the plug on their website. He wasn't sure how he would do that, but as he thought about it while driving home, he came to the conclusion the threat to tell Nigel, Spencer, and the other residents of Beulah Crest about Ian's involvement with Crime Spartans would be enough to force Ian to end Crime Spartan coverage of Benzie County crimes.

CHAPTER 13
Angels

The next morning, the killer woke early, feeling more confident than yesterday. There was now a plan to incriminate Herb and Dot. True, it was upsetting that the neighbors didn't act quickly to take care of Max, but he had left the park, which was the objective of the last post to Crime Spartans. Before going to bed last night, the killer hid the key to Herb and Dot's garden shed in the flowerpot on Max's deck.

The visit to Herb and Dot's cottage went well. On the way over, the text incriminating Max was sent to the sheriff. Dot was out taking Della for a walk, so the killer found Herb alone on their deck, reading the morning paper. Herb offered a lemonade, but when it was obvious that getting up was painful for Herb, the killer offered to get a drink for both of them from the kitchen. While in the cottage, the killer put the phone in Dot's large purse which was hanging on the back of a chair in the dining room.

After a short conversation that was mostly about recent events and how well the community was pulling together to support Herb and Dot, the killer left. There was still much to be done, so there wasn't time to linger at the Cooper's cottage.

Hopefully, the sheriff would arrive soon with a warrant to search for the phone.

The Internet was down earlier in the morning, so the first thing the killer did after getting home was to check the Crime Spartans website. The post from Archangel Michael got the killer's attention. Not knowing what to do or how to respond, the killer expected the voice to return, but it didn't. *Where are you? I'll take a walk along the lake. I'm sure I'll be able to hear you if I can get away from this awful park for a while.*

The killer headed down the stairs to the lake and turned left toward the boat ramp. *Where are you? I need your help. Who are you? Archangel Michael wants to know. If I don't give him an answer by tonight, he'll send his army of angels. I'm not bold enough to think you're God, but I thought perhaps you were my guardian angel.*

The killer kept walking and hoping for a response, but the voice didn't return. Walking past the boat ramp, where some tourists were putting kayaks into the water, a sense of dread took over. *I'll have to decide what to do next on my own. I'll keep walking until I think of how to respond to Archangel Michael. Hopefully the voice will return and give me some guidance.*

It was still early in the season and a weekday, so the killer didn't see anyone else after passing the boat ramp. It was a beautiful spring day, with blue forget-me-nots blooming on either side of the trail, but the killer took no notice. Trying to keep a clear mind so the voice could be heard didn't work. The voice was silent. While crossing the Frankfort Highway, the killer thought the voice said something, but it turned out to be the radio of a car heading toward Beulah. *If I don't hear from the voice soon, I'll have to decide for myself what to do. Could Archangel Michael really be speaking through the Internet? All the churches used the Internet when that virus was going around, so maybe.*

The rest of the walk into Elberta was a blank. Exhausted, the killer walked through the door of the small coffee shop, sunburned and exhausted. Killian, the owner, greeted the killer. "You didn't walk all the way from Beulah Crest, did you? It looks like you've gotten a bit too much sun."

"I had something on my mind and didn't notice how far I'd walked until I walked in here. How about a large iced tea instead of my usual coffee?"

"Sure thing. Anything I can do to help?"

"No, Killian, I don't think so. A friend who had been helping me with a project appears to have backed out. I was just sorting out my next steps. I think you're right about the sunburn, though. I'm not in any state to walk back home."

"Was Sarah still sitting outside eating her ice cream?"

"Yes, I absent mindedly waved to her. Why?"

"She's waiting for the Benzie Bus to take her up the condos next to where you live. It should be here in a few minutes."

The bus pulled up just as the killer walked out of the coffee shop. Sarah and the killer were the only two passengers on the bus, which was actually a Ford van run by the county transit authority. On the way home, Sarah filled the killer in on who had returned for the season in the condo complex and shared everything she'd heard about the murders.

Sarah, who knew almost as many people in the county as Ian, could remember the exact date and time of events that happened since she was a child. The last thing Sarah mentioned was the only thing that was news to the killer. "I just got off the phone with Theresa when you came out of the coffee shop. You know her. She's a nurse up at Munson Hospital.

"Of course. She married Alex Cosgrove last year.

"That's her. Anyway, she said Ben woke up and told the police his fall was an accident. He was chasing Arthur."

"Arthur?" the killer interrupted.

"You know, Arthur, the fox Elsie is always feeding. Ben was chasing Arthur, who had taken his sandwich, when he fell, head-first, down the stairs. He woke up at 6:45 this morning."

The killer had to concentrate on not overreacting to Sarah's last comment. "I'm glad he's ok, Sarah. I hope he gets home soon." Nothing else that Sarah said could be remembered. Fortunately for the killer, Sarah thought sunburn and fatigue were the reason for the killer's inability to say more.

If the voice doesn't tell me otherwise, I'll have to be honest when I respond to the archangel. I just wish he'd speak to me directly, rather than posting on the Internet. Perhaps the voice I've been hearing is already doing battle with Michael and is too busy to speak to me. I hope he's not been hurt.

While the killer was having a difficult day, Nick's day got off to an early, but good start. As he was having breakfast with his wife, he received a call from Munson Hospital in Traverse City. Ben's condition had improved surprisingly fast and he was conscious and able to talk.

Nick arrived at the hospital at the same time as Constance, Ben's wife. After letting his wife fuss for a few minutes, Ben chased her away. "Connie, go get yourself some coffee so I can talk to this cop. I'm fine."

After Connie left, Nick sat in the chair next to Ben's bed and started asking questions. "How are you feeling Ben? You look pretty rough."

"Head hurts like hell, but the doctor says I'll be able to walk and talk. I'll have to wear this damn neck brace all summer, though, so Ian will have to get someone to keep the park in shape until I can get back to work. Speaking of work, what are you doing here? Don't tell me there's been another murder at the park!"

"No, everything is fine. I was wondering how you fell. There was a post on that website saying someone pushed you."

"Nothing so dramatic, Detective. I was chasing that damn fox Elsie is always feeding. Arthur, she calls him. I put my sandwich on top of the cooler to answer my phone, and he runs up and grabs it. I chased him away and I tripped on the platform and down I went." The nurse, who came in the room to adjust Ben's IV drip, overheard Ben's remarks and then laughed.

Less than an hour later, Nick walked into his office carrying a box of doughnuts he picked up at the Honor Market on the way back from the hospital. As he was pouring a coffee, the sheriff walked in looking proud as a peacock. Smiling broadly, the sheriff told Nick, "Pour me a cup and hand me a doughnut. We've got something to celebrate."

Nick poured the sheriff a coffee and pushed the box of doughnuts across his desk so the sheriff could grab one. "Help yourself, Sheriff, and tell me what we're celebrating."

The sheriff grabbed a maple frosted doughnut before responding. "We got him. The Beulah Crest killer. They took him into custody at the Traverse City airport trying to catch a flight to Denver. There was a post on that damn website and I also got a text this morning implicating him for trying to kill Ben, so I asked the police up there to keep a watch at the airport."

"Who are we talking about, Sheriff?"

"Max Silver, of course. I always thought there was something fishy about that guy. He's originally from New York, you know. I've never trusted New Yorkers."

Nick took a chocolate doughnut from the box before responding. "He didn't try to kill Ben, Sheriff."

Before answering, the sheriff took another doughnut. "How do you know that? If you came into the office a little earlier, maybe you'd be the one who could take credit for the arrest."

"I wasn't here because I was at the hospital talking to Ben, who regained consciousness this morning. No one tried to kill him. He fell down the steps while chasing a fox. It was an accident."

The sheriff choked on his doughnut and ended spitting a mouthful of doughnut and coffee over the top of Nick's desk. When he finally got his voice back, he uttered, "What do you mean it was an accident? I've got two witnesses who said they saw Max Silver push Ben down those stairs."

Nick held off responding while he cleaned his desk and while he tried to maintain his composure. When he finished clearing the mess, he asked, "Who are those two people, Sheriff? Do you have sworn statements from them?"

"Of course, I don't. Give me another doughnut. You made me choke on the last one." As Nick again passed the box of doughnuts across the desk, the sheriff continued while he handed Nick a printout from the Web and a printout of the phone text. "When we track down who sent these, we'll get a statement from them."

Nick read the sheets given to him by the sheriff and then shared the printout he was given by Ian and Elizabeth. "Sheriff, someone from Crime Spartans sent me this. According to their expert, the killer is posting on the site using a number of different names, including the one who pointed the finger at Max Silver, Archangel Raguel. He made nearly all of his posts from the Beulah library. I'll wager he's the same guy who sent the texts."

"Can you sure about what this guy at Crime Spartans is telling you? I'd love to wrap this up and arrest that arrogant history teacher. He's Jewish, you know. I thought they all left Frankfort years ago."

"What's that got to do with it, Sheriff? And yes, I'm sure. Ben was quite lucid when I talked to him and he insists then he fell while chasing a fox. Have you traced the owner or location of the phone that was used to send you the text?"

"I've got Kathy working on that right now."

As the sheriff mentioned the deputy's name, she walked in the door. "Sheriff, I don't have the name of the owner of the cell, but we've tracked its current location."

"Well?" the sheriff shouted.

"It's at Beulah Crest. The cottage lots are pretty small over there, but it looks like the phone is in the Cooper's cottage."

"I knew it," the sheriff shouted. "I knew it. Give me another one of those doughnuts and some more coffee. They never should've let either one of them go."

"So, you agree that Max Silver didn't try to kill Ben?" Nick asked.

"Ok, ok, don't rub it in. I'll get a lot of bad press for arresting Silver as it is. He's apparently pretty popular up at Interlochen. Let's go over and find that phone. I'd like to hear what that weasel Herb Cooper has to say."

Nick got up to join the Sheriff who was already heading out of the office. Before saying anything, Nick took a few seconds to calculate how many doughnuts the sheriff just ate, while he regained his composure. He decided it was four, plus the one splattered across his desk. Finally, in control, he calmly said, "Let's hold off making any arrests until we look at that phone. OK?"

"Fine, Nick. I'm sure once we see what's on that phone, we'll be able to arrest those two. You do the talking and I'll watch. I want to see the look on your face when you realize you're wrong."

Nick and the Sheriff headed over to Beulah Crest in Nick's car and Deputy McGregor followed with another deputy in her car. When they arrived, Herb and Dot were sitting on their deck with Della. Della enthusiastically greeted Nick and Kathy, but she growled when the sheriff approached. Dot gave the sheriff a cold stare, but asked calmly, "What can we do for you?"

Nick answered. "We're looking for a phone that was used to send a text to the sheriff this morning. Could we take a look at your phones?"

"Do you have a warrant?" Dot asked. She then turned to Herb. "Sweetheart give Joe a call. I'm sure he'll tell us you need a warrant.

"Holy mother of Jesus," the sheriff shouted as he took his phone from his pocket and called the number that was used to send the text. A few seconds later a phone could be heard ringing from inside the cottage. "We'd like to see the phone that's ringing right now. It was used to send a text to me this morning."

"That's not my ringtone," Herb commented.

"It isn't mine either," Dot added. Dot got up and headed toward the open door. "Fine, Sheriff, I'll get you the phone, but our lawyer will hear about this." She came back a minute later carrying the purse with the ringing phone.

As she started to open the purse, Nick asked, "May I?" as he put on a pair of latex gloves. She handed him the purse and watched as Nick pulled out the still ringing phone.

The sheriff was about to grab the phone, but then remembered telling Nick he could do the talking. He decided to remain silent while Nick was proven wrong.

Nick touched the phone's screen and it lit up. There was no password. He then dismissed the sheriff's call and opened the most recent text that was sent from the phone and read it aloud. "I saw Max Silver push Ben down the stairs. If you check his cottage, you'll find a key to Herb and Dot's garden shed. He planted the hammer there."

"See, there it is," the sheriff shouted. "Max Silver tried to kill Ben and Dot saw it. Why didn't you just call me, Dot?"

"You may call me Dr. Cooper, Sheriff, not Dot. As for that text, I didn't send it, and I don't know where that phone came from. It certainly isn't mine, nor does it belong to my husband."

Herb interrupted, addressing Nick while turning his back on the sheriff. "Detective Townsend, while Dot was taking Della for a walk this morning a few of the neighbors stopped by to offer their support. They've been checking on us since Dot got released. One of them mentioned that Ben came out of his coma and told the police his fall was an accident. Is that true?"

"Yes, it's true, Herb. I talked to Ben this morning. It looks like he is going to recover. Who told you about Ben?"

"Derek Parker. He didn't mention who told him about Ben."

Deputy McGregor, who had been standing in the background taking notes interrupted. "Detective, are there any other messages or calls on the phone?"

Nick scrolled down to the only other message. "There's only one more, Deputy."

"So, what does it say," the sheriff shouted.

"The hammer used to kill Babs Tucker is hidden in Herb Cooper's toolbox," Nick answered while trying very hard not to lose his temper with the sheriff.

"There it is," the sheriff yelled. Max sent that text from a phone he put in Dot's purse, excuse me, Dr. Cooper's purse, to make it look like she was trying to place the blame for Ben's fall. He forgot to erase the earlier text he sent to try to frame the Coopers. He's the one behind all of this."

"Hold on, Sheriff, Herb shouted back. "It doesn't make sense. Just about everyone in the park has stopped by in the last day or two and had the opportunity to put the phone in Dot's handbag, but not Max. I don't think he's been here." Herb turned to his wife before continuing. "Dot, have you talked to Max?"

Dot answered, before the sheriff could interrupt. "I talked to him yesterday morning when I was walking Della. I often stop by his cottage and chat when I'm out with her. Now that you mention it, he hasn't come by our cottage since I've been back and no, he hasn't had access to my purse."

The sheriff was getting angry. He wanted to arrest someone and get this whole thing wrapped up, so he shouted angerly, "Dr. Cooper, if Max wasn't in your cottage this morning, who was? That text was sent this morning."

"Dot answered. Just before I left with Della, Albert came by with Greta and then Elsie stopped over to leave some brownies."

Herb continued when Dot paused. "Then after Dot left, Hortense stopped in for a few minutes. She seemed upset about something but didn't stay long enough to say what. Then Derek came over, thinking that Hortense was still here, and then Ian stopped by for a minute to say hello and ask if he could do anything to help."

"Good God," the sheriff shouted. "It's like Grand Central Station in that cottage of yours."

After writing down everything she heard, Deputy McGregor asked Nick, who was still holding the phone, a question. "Is there a history of phone calls placed from the phone, Detective?"

"Hold on, let me look. This phone is different than mine." Nick fumbled with the phone for a minute before continuing. "Here it is. Several calls to hotels and restaurants in London, all made a year ago."

"Ontario?" the sheriff asked. "My sister married someone from there."

"No, the one in England."

"I knew it," the sheriff exclaimed. "It's those two who own this park. I should have arrested them as soon as I heard those foreign accents of theirs."

Just then Nigel and Spencer pulled up to the cottage. They were on their way to the Mouse House to meet with Ian when they saw the police cars. They got out of their car and walked up to Herb and Dot's deck. "Is everything OK?" Spencer asked. "We just heard the good news about Ben. Did someone else get hurt?"

"Everyone's fine," the sheriff answered. "Come up here. I have a few questions for you two."

Not having much choice in the matter, the park owners joined the others on the Cooper's deck. Neither of them had much trust or respect for the sheriff, but at least a crowd was there to witness whatever the sheriff might do. "How can we help?" Nigel asked.

Nigel's upper-class British accent rubbed the sheriff the wrong way, so he responded with an aggressive tone. "Does this phone belong to either one of you?" As he was asking the question, he grabbed the phone from Nick and handed it to Spencer.

"So much for fingerprints or DNA from the phone," Nick mumbled to Deputy McGregor.

Spencer looked at the phone before responding. "It doesn't belong to either of us. It's one of those cheap prepaid phones used by tourists and people who don't have good enough credit to get an account with a phone company. Who does it belong to?"

"I'll ask the questions," the sheriff answered. "Where have you two been all morning? Have you seen anyone else here at the park?"

Spencer answered. His accent didn't upset the sheriff as much as Nigel's did. "We had an appointment with an insurance agent in Beulah and then stopped in at L'Chayim for a bagel and coffee. We haven't seen or spoken to anyone at the park since yesterday. What's this all about?"

"It's about the texts sent from that British cell phone you're holding. Go ahead and read them. Since you two are the only two British people here, I suspect one of you are responsible for sending them."

Spencer looked at the texts and then handed the phone to Nigel. While Nigel read through the texts and looked through the call history on the phone, Spencer responded to the sheriff. "Sheriff, someone is manipulating your investigation with these texts and what's being posted on the website. As for the latest text, Nigel and I were at L'Chayim when it was sent."

Before the sheriff could respond, Nigel interrupted. "You can call over to the deli and check. We had a long discussion with the owner about the merits of scones vs rugalach. Meanwhile, did you notice when the calls were made with this phone? They were made last summer."

"So?" the sheriff asked.

"You might want to ask around and find out who made a trip to London last year. If you'd like, I could call someone back home who might be able to trace where and when the phone was purchased and possibly the identity of the buyer."

"Who are you going to call, Mr. Piddlemarsh? This is nonsense."

Spencer answered before Nigel had a chance. He thought it was time to intimidate the sheriff a little. "Nigel, who is known as Lord Piddlemarsh at home, is a member of the Intelligence and Security Committee of Parliament."

Nigel interrupted. "It's ok, Spencer, I'm not going to get in a fight with the sheriff." Nigel then turned his attention to the sheriff. "Nigel is correct, Sheriff. I can't tell you about my specific responsibilities because of the Official Secrets Act. Let's just say I am well connected in the British intelligence community."

"What is this nonsense, Piddlemarsh?" the sheriff shouted. He turned to Nick. "Detective, arrest these two for obstruction of justice, wasting my time, or whatever else you can come up with to lock them up."

"Hold on a minute," Nick replied. "Ian was telling me about these two. They're fairly low key here, but apparently, they're big shots where they come from. If Nigel can get the owner of the phone identified, we can solve this case. Think of the headlines. Benzie sheriff partners with Scotland Yard to solve the Beulah Crest murders."

The sheriff took a few minutes to think it over before he responded. "I do like the sound of that." "Ok, Piddlemarsh, see what you can find out."

Nigel wrote down the phone number of the cell and agreed to make some calls as soon as he got home. "Sheriff, a detective from Scotland Yard will give you a call sometime tomorrow with whatever information there is about this phone."

"I'll believe it when I see it," the sheriff grunted as he grabbed the phone from Nigel and walked away from the cottage. Everyone else left Dot and Herb's deck shortly afterwards.

Back at the station, the sheriff threw another tantrum. When he walked into Nick's office, there weren't many objects to throw because Nick had put almost anything that could fly in a drawer or cabinet. Nick offered the sheriff the last of the doughnuts, which seemed to settle him a bit. After washing down the doughnut with cold coffee, the sheriff sat down. "I need this solved, Nick. If I lose the election in November, I'll probably have to be an animal control officer again. Oh, how I hate dogs."

Nick did his best to silence a laugh. In a way, he felt sorry for the sheriff who was in over his head. "Don't worry Sheriff, we'll get this solved. I'm expecting some more DNA results for the lab tomorrow and we'll assign deputies to follow each of the people who stopped by the Cooper's cottage this morning. Also,

Agnes called back from the library. She'll let us know if anyone uses the computer today to post to that website."

"I hope you're right."

Nick was afraid the sheriff might cause some more damage to the case so he decided to ask him to do a task that would keep him out of the way for a while. "Sheriff, we don't have enough manpower for everything, and I need someone with your keen instincts to conduct some interviews, on the off chance that killer has an accomplice. Could you help with that?"

"Of course, who is the suspect?"

"Interrogate might be too strong a word to describe what I need help with, Sheriff. I'd just like you to talk to the members of the bridge club down in Elberta who've posted to Crime Spartans."

Nick handed the sheriff a list of names before continuing. "I need to know if anyone of them have a close connection to the people who visited Herb and Dot this morning. There are no bridge games today or tomorrow, so you'd have to visit them at their homes, which are all over Benzie and Manistee counties. If there's an accomplice, they'll be much harder to catch because they probably didn't leave behind any fingerprints or DNA. If you can find the accomplice, it will play well in the press."

Nick was relieved when the sheriff accepted the task that would keep him out of the way for at least a day or two. Hopefully, the investigation could proceed in an orderly fashion and a suspect could be arrested soon.

Meanwhile, the killer was anxious over the risk of being arrested and the unknown consequences of angering an archangel. After returning to Beulah Crest, the killer took some aspirin. Not sure whether it was from the sun or exhaustion, the killer had a headache. *I'll lay down for a while. Hopefully, if I can get some rest and get rid of this headache, the voice will return. Otherwise, I'll have to answer Archangel Michael on my own.*

When the killer awoke several hours later, panic set in when the clock on the bedside table indicated the time. *Damn, the library is closed. I need to answer Archangel Michael. I can't post from here; the police could track my location. Maybe it's just as well I missed going to the library. I've been using their computer a lot and maybe the police are getting close to figuring where I'm at when I'm on Crime Spartans. Fortunately, my headache is gone, but where is the voice? I wish it would speak to me again.*

It was after 6:00 o'clock, so the killer was hungry. *I haven't eaten anything since this morning. I'll go over to McDonald's with my laptop and post from there. They have Wi-Fi. I could die from some fries. If I don't hear from the voice before I start eating, I'll have to answer Archangel Michael on my own.*

McDonald's was packed, so the killer was lucky to get the last table in the back of the restaurant. A baseball game had just finished at the township park, so both teams filled the restaurant. While halfway through the fries and hamburger, the killer paused eating and logged into Crime Spartans as Della. Under the circumstances, logging in as Archangel Raguel just didn't seem right.

It took a few minutes to get started, but once the killer got started, the response to Archangel Michael was rapidly written and posted.

Dear Archangel Michael,

I've dreaded this moment, but now a sense of calm has come over me as I know you will do what is right and just. Yes, I've posted using the name Archangel Raguel, as well as Della and some others. Since you already know who I am, there's no need to post my real name here for all of the world to see.

You asked who is telling me to do the things I've done. Unfortunately, I don't have a clear answer for you. I've been thinking about what I needed to do to purify the community for a number of years and have been planning for months, but I only developed the courage to act a short while ago.

After I started this work, I began to hear a voice. The voice could speak to me, and I could speak back, without anyone else hearing us. Perhaps the voice was all in my mind, but it's been so real and encouraging I felt compelled to listen. I don't know who spoke to me, but I hoped, and later came to believe, that perhaps it belonged to one of your fellow angels.

Today, the voice stopped speaking to me. I don't know why. I've speculated that you might have intervened and prevented the voice from speaking to me. I hope the voice returns. It's been a great comfort.

You know of the work I've done all of my life to help people. I've never asked for anything in return and don't complain that I have little in terms of material wealth or that I'll spend the rest of my life living in a trailer park. I don't need money or other items that confer status, What I desire, and perhaps need, is a feeling of accomplishment.

I've taken action because my life's work has otherwise come to nothing. Regardless of how many people I help, there are so many who are unworthy of being helped who cast a shadow on everyone who is decent. Once these people are gone, think how wonderful it will be here; like the Garden of Eden.

I'll listen to your guidance, should you decide to provide any, but in the meantime, I'll continue my work. I don't know any other way to proceed. Tomorrow, I'll have to take care of another person who is on my list. I've been letting to many things distract me, but now I know it's time to move forward. My only regret is that I mistook Babs for Elsie. I'm sure Babs would understand and forgive me. She will be missed by everyone.

After hitting the send button, the killer quickly left the restaurant and headed back to Beulah Crest to plan for what needed to be done tomorrow.

Back at the sheriff's office, Nick was keeping in close communications with the deputies who were tasked with following the people from Beulah Crest who visited Herb and Dot's cottage earlier in the day. All of them, but one, went to the baseball game in the township park and then to McDonald's. The only one who didn't go to the game joined the others at the restaurant after the game.

Agnes, the librarian, called Nick just before the library closed to tell him that no one had used the computer all day. He was therefore surprised when Deputy McGregor came into his office with news about what she saw on the Internet. "The murderer posted again, Detective. Here's a copy of what he posted. He used the name Della, this time." The deputy handed Nick a copy of the post.

Nick read the entire post before commenting. "This guy's nuts, Kathy. He's planning to kill someone tomorrow." Before he could say more, his phone pinged, indicating he'd received a text. Elizabeth configured Nick's phone yesterday to make a particular sound if she sent him a text from her untraceable phone. Nick read the text and got up from his desk. "Let's go, Kathy. Della's post was just made at McDonald's."

Deputy McGregor followed Nick out the door and shouted. "Where did that text you just got come from?"

"The same person at Crime Spartans who sent us the other stuff." The deputy tried to interrupt, but Nick didn't let her. "I know, I shouldn't take anything seriously from that site, but it's all we have at this point. Hopefully, forensics will have more for us soon."

When they pulled into McDonald's parking lot, it was obvious they wouldn't be able to identify who had posted on Crime Spartans. The restaurant was so crowded that traffic was backed up onto the highway. Nick was only able to get into the parking lot by using his siren to push past other cars. Nick parked on the grass behind the dumpster. "What the hell is going on?" he asked the deputy.

Kathy answered as she and Nick made their way to the door. "Free milk shakes. The team sponsored by the restaurant won, so everyone gets a free milkshake. It's their first victory this year."

Nick looked around once they got inside. "Most of the Beulah Crest residents are here and look at how many people are texting or sending emails from their phones. Let's get out of here, Kathy. This is a waste of time."

"Hold on a minute. While we're here, we may as well get a free shake."

Nick hadn't eaten since breakfast, so he handed Kathy some money and told her to get him a cheeseburger and fries to go along with a free strawberry shake. He walked around the restaurant while Kathy waited in line and talked to people from Beulah Crest. No one acted suspicious or nervous when he approached them. He spotted Ian coming out of the rest room and talked briefly with him. They agreed to meet later at the Mouse House to discuss if there should be a response to the post from Della. Ian said he would ask Elizabeth to come.

Nick and the deputy went back to the office to eat their food. "I got a call from the sheriff while I was waiting for the food," Kathy commented as they left the parking lot. "He was excited about someone at the bridge club. He'll meet us at the office."

"If whoever he talked to keeps him distracted while we solve this, fine. I hope you bought him some food. Otherwise, he'll eat ours."

"Of course. When I told him where we were, he told me to bring him three double cheeseburgers, some fries and two milkshakes."

When they got back, the sheriff was pacing back and forth in Nick's office. "Sheriff, why don't you join me and Kathy in the conference room to eat. I'd like to hear what you learned at the bridge club." Nick didn't want the mess that would result from the sheriff eating three double cheeseburgers in his office.

"Good idea," was all the sheriff said until he had eaten one of the cheeseburgers, not noticing the ketchup he dripped onto the table and on the front of his shirt. After gulping down one of the milkshakes, he continued. "Thanks for the food, Deputy. I was starved. Now Nick, I think I have a suspect from the bridge club I want to watch closely."

"Anyone we know," Nick asked. "Is he from Beulah Crest."

"She," the sheriff answered, "is not from Beulah Crest. I don't know if you know her or not, but she has had two complaints filed against her for disturbing the peace over the last few years. The charges were dropped by that good for nothing prosecutor. The club president and two other members suggested that she had a grudge against Babs and that she still has one against Herb Cooper and Elsie Taylor."

"What's she got against them?" Kathy asked.

The sheriff downed the second cheeseburger before answering. One of the cheese slices managed to slide off and landed on the sheriff's lap. Not noticing the mess, the sheriff continued. "Her name is Enid Buck. She lives over on Grace Road. They say she's a nasty old cow who criticizes every bridge player in the club. She had a particular dislike for Babs because Babs and Elsie were the best players in the club and for Herb because of his temper."

"Anything else on her?" Nick asked while fixated on the mess the sheriff was creating while eating his meal.

"She posts a lot on bridge related websites and blogs using her own name and probably several others. The club president says most of them are very negative and some are threatening."

While the sheriff was talking, Kathy looked up Enid's posts on the Internet on her phone. After reading a few minutes she interrupted the sheriff. "From what she posts on-line, your Enid Buck doesn't seem to be a very happy person. I wouldn't want to play cards with her. Maybe she's involved. Oh, hold on, Sheriff."

"What?" the sheriff asked.

"It says on her home page that she's at a gun show in Gaylord today. She'll be back in Elberta tomorrow to try out her new shotgun at the gun club tomorrow."

Ordinarily, the sheriff didn't like being interrupted, but he made exceptions when someone agreed with or complemented his statements. "Thank you for looking her up, Deputy. I think you're right. This lady is trouble."

Nick wasn't sure if Kathy was teasing the sheriff or was serious, but he appreciated her comments encouraging the sheriff. Nick knew tomorrow would be a busy day and wanted the sheriff occupied and out of his way. "Sheriff?" Nick asked. "Perhaps you should track down that reporter tomorrow, Jennifer Reynolds. She might have some dirt on your suspect, and you could arrange to have her present if you decide to make an arrest."

"Good idea, Nick. I'll do that. I want to talk to this Enid first, and maybe I'll head over to the gun club and see what they have to say about her before I make any decision to arrest her. I wonder how handcuffing her at the gun club would play with the press. Perhaps I'll talk it over with Jennifer."

"I'm glad you're working this line of inquiry, Sheriff. I'll be tied up tomorrow with some follow-up work over at Beulah Crest and the crime lab. Nothing as exciting as what you've got going."

"Someone has to do the detail work, Nick," was the sheriff's response just before he downed the last hamburger and headed out of the conference room. When the sheriff was out of sight, Nick and Kathy looked at each other and laughed.

After the sheriff and Kathy left, Nick headed over to Beulah Crest to meet with Ian and Elizabeth. Albert had gone home for the day, so they had the Mouse House to themselves. Ian made coffee for the small group while Elizabeth turned on her laptop computer and logged onto Crime Spartans.

Ian locked the front door so they wouldn't be disturbed and sat down at the table where Nick and Elizabeth were seated. Elizabeth brought printed copies of the killer's recent post to Crime Spartans and copies of a proposed response she and Ian had drafted. She also brought a large order of BBQ chicken wings she picked up at the Cold Creek restaurant on her way over.

Nick wasn't hungry, but he nibbled on one of the wings while reading what Ian and Elizabeth had written. It was a response to the killer from Archangel Michael.

Dear Della,

I'm using one of your Crime Spartan names to respect your request for privacy. I'd like to meet with you face to face. Only then, will I be able to determine if your actions and intent are sincere. You'll find me on the trail where you often walk, along the south shore of Crystal Lake. I'll meet you at noon tomorrow near the swampy area about ¼ mile west of the boat ramp. You'll know the area because you can hear the frogs croaking. There's a big house across the trail from the swamp, but don't worry. The owners won't be back for the season until next week. Also, don't hurt anyone until we meet.

Archangel Michael

Nick dropped the chicken wing about halfway through reading the proposed post to Crime Spartans. He briefly thought of the mess the sheriff made with the cheeseburgers before he exclaimed, "You can't put this on the Internet for everyone to see. Half of the county would be on the trail to hunt the killer or to see if there really is an archangel."

"We thought of that," Ian answered. "Each user on Crime Spartans has a private mailbox that only they can access using their password. We'll send the message to all of the mailboxes associated with the names we've identified as belonging to the killer."

"That would be better," Nick responded, "but I think perhaps you should only send to Della and Archangel Raguel. You might be wrong about one or more of the other names. We don't want to send the message to another person by mistake. Now as far as…"

Elizabeth interrupted. "No need to say it, Detective. You didn't ask us to post this, and we didn't tell you anything about it, at least not yet. To cover you, we'll send you an anonymous and untraceable email tomorrow morning with the contents of Archangel Michael's email to the killer and the killer's response, if there is one. Meanwhile, I'll send Archangel Michael's email right now."

Ian then asked, "Detective, you know the spot along the trail we're talking about, don't you?"

"I do. It's a perfect spot. Plenty of cover for myself and a few deputies to hide and observe. We'll get positioned there well before noon."

On the other side of the Beulah Crest, the killer decided to check Crime Spartans before going to bed, hoping there would be a positive response from Archangel Michael. At first, the killer was excited after reading the email. *I'll be able to meet Archangel Michael in person. I can learn so much from him. I'm not afraid because I don't think there's anything to fear from an angel. The work I'm doing is for the glory of God.*

Unable to settle down and sleep after reading the email, the killer took a long hot shower and then made a cup of hot cocoa. After drinking the cocoa and reading some favorite bible verses, the killer climbed into bed just before midnight, feeling relaxed. Just as the lights were turned off for the night, the voice returned. *"You are right not to fear Archangel Michael. He's the leader of God's army of angels and is always on the side of what's right and pure."*

You're back. I missed you so much. Where have you been?

"I've been here all along. You needed to make the decision to see Archangel Michael on your own. He'll ask you if I encouraged

you to meet with him. He will only appear if you, and you alone, agreed to see him."

In any case, I'm glad you've returned. I was going to take care of Elsie tomorrow morning, but the Archangel has asked me to wait. It's a pity because I am all set up to kill her using a handgun that I bought at a gun shop over in Alpena last year. I hope I don't need to wait too long to use the gun on Elsie.

"Why wait?"

The archangel asked me to.

"I think he is just testing you. He appreciates it when his angels take initiative. I think he wants you to join his army. This is a test"

Do you really think so?

"I know so. Carry out your plans in the same place you're to meet the archangel. Do it just before he arrives. He'll be so proud of you, just as I am."

The killer felt a new sense of confidence now that the voice was back. Lying in bed, the killer looked forward to tomorrow. It would be a day to get back on track to making the world a better place.

The killer woke up refreshed the next morning to a day that provided new hope. Other residents of the park also started the day on a positive note. Ian received a call from Ben with good news. Ben would be going home the hospital in a few days with no long-term effects expected from his fall. He would need to wear a neck brace for the summer, so Ian needed to find some temporary help to maintain the grounds until Ben's return. Nate Santiago, the kid who gave tours of the park after the murders was looking for a summer job. After talking it over with Spencer on the phone, Ian called Nate and he agreed to fill in for Ben.

Dot and Herb had breakfast on their deck, with Della, who was enjoying having both of her owners dote on her. Albert opened the coffee shop in the Mouse House and spent the morning reading the news on his tablet and talking with people who stopped by for coffee. Max came in with Xander and shared the story of his arrest at the Traverse City airport and the ride in the back of a police car back to Beulah. Max had a nice conversation with the officer who made the arrest while waiting for the Benzie deputy to pick him up. The officer was a student of Max's several years ago, so they took a trip down memory lane. After telling the story, Max and Xander got to work setting up plans for a charitable trust and scholarship funds with the money left by Babs and Bonnie.

After a sound sleep, Hortense awoke refreshed, looking forward to busy day. Derek was up early and had already made coffee and was starting breakfast when his wife padded into the kitchen in her slippers and robe.

"You're looking awfully bright and cheerful this morning. Did you sort out whatever it was on your mind, sweetheart?"

"I did, Derek. I've let too many things distract me and I've decided to move forward on some projects I've been thinking about. As I've said before, God is watching, so I need to get moving. Elsie said she would help. I going to take a walk with her this morning and get things started. Now what's for breakfast? I'm starved."

Derek didn't question his wife about what had been distracting her. He'd learned over the years that Hortense's relationship with God was something she rarely discussed with him, or anyone else that he knew of. He was just happy she appeared to have gotten over the recent events in the park and that she was smiling. He had a busy day ahead with two root canals and a crown fit, so he was glad he had a reason not to be recruited to help with her project, whatever it might be.

It was after 10:00 o'clock by the time Derek left for his office and Hortense got over to Elsie's cottage. It was warm, but she wore a light jacket. She didn't want to carry a purse and didn't need to because of the large pockets in jacket.

When she arrived, she found Elsie sitting on her deck reading the paper and having a cup of coffee. Hortense put aside the thoughts of everything planned for the day and smiled as she greeted Elsie. "Good morning neighbor. Ready for that walk. I am feeling the need for some exercise."

Elsie responded with a smile. "I am. It's nice to have someone to talk to when I take a walk. I usually only talk to Arthur when I'm out by myself. How about a cup of coffee before we go?"

"Just one cup. If I have more than that, I get a bit jittery. Speaking of Arthur, you need to stop feeding that fox. You heard what happened to Ben. Arthur is getting too comfortable around people. Besides, foxes can carry rabies."

"I know," Elsie responded, "but he's such a good listener."

It was almost 11:00 o'clock by the time they left Elsie's cottage and headed down the stairs. At the bottom, they made a left and headed along the shore of the lake, away from town.

CHAPTER 14
Not Again!

Nick was up early to get set up to catch the killer. The first thing he did was send a text to the sheriff offering to help interview Enid Buck and the folks at the gun club. As expected, the sheriff declined the offer on the grounds it would be a waste of manpower at this stage.

Nick knew the sheriff would want to be on his own for the interviews because he got word last night from a contact at the *Record-Patriot* that the sheriff had invited the reporter, Jennifer Reynolds, to follow him around because there would be a big story to report today. There was little chance the sheriff would want Nick around to share the publicity for catching the killer. Nick didn't care about the publicity; he just wanted the sheriff to be kept busy and out of the way.

Nick, Kathy, and another deputy, Logan Donaldson, set up in secluded places around the swamp by 10:00 o'clock. Nick found a spot with a good view of the trail behind a bush next to the empty house. The deputies were hidden behind large trees on either side of the swampy area. If they needed to speak to each other with cell phones, their voices wouldn't be heard by anyone else because of the loud croaking of the frogs in the swamp.

Ian and Elizabeth wanted to help at the scene, but Nick refused. He'd already stretched police procedure enough by using Crime Spartans to communicate with the person he thought was probably the killer.

Ian did provide assistance in another way though. He knew the owners of the big house on the other side of the trail from the swamp. Ian had keys to the house because he managed the property and handled its occasional off-season rental when the owners were away.

Yesterday evening, Ian set up several cameras in the upstairs bedrooms of the house that were connected to the Internet. One camera caught anyone approaching from the direction of Beulah Crest, another focused on the trail in front of the house, and two others covered the swampy area on the other side of the trail. Although Nick insisted that Ian leave the area once the cameras were set up, Ian was able to view what was happening from his office in the Mouse House via the Internet. He agreed to alert Nick if he saw anyone from Beulah Crest approach the area.

Within minutes of getting set up, Nick received a text from Ian. Xander Wolfe and Nate Santiago were approaching the site. Nate, who was on the Benzie Central cross-country team ran with Xander several times a week when the college professor was in town.

Nick alerted the deputies of the approaching runners. Thinking back on the investigation, Nick realized that Nate's mother was interviewed following the murders at Beulah Crest, but no one from the sheriff's office had talked to Nate, probably because he was a minor. Nick made a mental note to talk with Nate later if he and Xander ran past without anything happening.

The two runners ran past Nick without knowing they were under surveillance. A minute later, they were past a bend in the trail and out of sight. Both were wearing only running shoes and shorts, so there was no place for either of them to hide a weapon.

A few moments after the runners ran past, Nick received another text. Dot Cooper was approaching with her dog, Della. Dot appeared to be talking to someone as she came close. Nick wondered if she might be talking to the fictious archangel, but as she got closer, it was obvious she wasn't when he overheard Dot talking to the dog. Somehow, her high-pitched voice could be heard over the noise the frogs made. "Della, I can't believe that wacko killer, whoever he is, used your name to post things on that stupid website. If he only knew what a gentle creature you are…"

Nick didn't hear anything further from Dot as she approached the curve and then walked out of view. All was quiet, except for the frogs, until about 11:30. It was still a half hour before the time the killer agreed to meet Archangel Michael, so Nick wasn't all that concerned when they got another text from Ian. "Two more approaching from Beulah Crest. Not to worry, it's only Elsie and Reverend Parker."

Nick alerted the deputies, but he wasn't too concerned. There was no way the murderer could be the minister, and Elsie was, well, Elsie. The two women were dressed similarly, with

Elsie wearing a drab dark grey pair of slacks and an equally un-flattering light grey blouse and, of course, her flat shoes.

Reverend Parker had the appearance of a minister as she sported a pair of black slacks, a white blouse, and her clerical collar. Even though it was a very warm morning, she was wearing a light jacket. At first, Nick thought nothing of the retired minister's appearance, but something didn't seem right. "Why would she wear a jacket on such a warm day?" was Nick's first thought. Then, as she came close, Nick realized it was the clerical collar that set him on edge. Reverend Parker rarely wore the collar when not engaged in religious activities or services. The only time he'd seen her wear it since the first murder was when she was leading demonstrations in front of the sheriff's office.

Nick's concentration was broken when he felt a hand being placed on his shoulder. When he turned around, he was greeted by the sheriff, who was accompanied by the reporter, Jennifer Reynolds. "What's up Nick? You didn't tell me anything about a stakeout? By the way, your Enid Buck couldn't have done much to help the murderer. She's in a wheelchair and is nearly blind."

Nick shook hands and greeted the reporter while taking time to come up with a response for the sheriff. The sheriff wouldn't throw a tantrum in front of Jennifer, but there would be consequences for Nick and the two deputies if the sheriff realized Nick had planned things in a way to exclude the sheriff from positive publicity. Fortunately, Nick was a quick to come up with an answer. "I'm glad you're here, Sheriff. We could use your help."

"So, what's going on?" the sheriff snapped.

"We got a tip from someone this morning who works at that website saying the killer would be here to meet some angel who posted on-line. I would have called you, but we figured this was a long shot, and I didn't want to interfere with your arrest of Enid Buck."

"What kind of nonsense is this?" the sheriff shouted.

The sheriff and Nick didn't notice Jennifer discreetly move behind a nearby bush and start filming with her phone's camera. She wasn't filming the Sheriff and Nick, but rather Elise and Reverend Parker, who were having a heated discussion, while standing on the opposite side of the trail near the swamp. She couldn't hear what the discussion was about because of the noise the frogs were making, but it was obvious that both women were angry.

"It's probably nonsense Sheriff, but someone who might be the killer responded to a post saying he would meet someone who calls himself Archangel Michael, here at noon. I've got Kathy and Logan hiding behind trees at the edge of the swap. Now that you are here, Sheriff, perhaps you could help with the arrest, if there is one."

Taking notice of Jennifer filming the two women arguing, the sheriff answered. "I'll make the arrest, and you can assist, if there is one. We can take the suspect away on the department boat I used to get here. It will make a good story and shut those idiots up on the county commission who want to take away funding for patrolling the lake."

The reporter ran over and interrupted. "Sheriff, something's going on over there. Those two women are wrestling over a gun. I think Elsie Taylor is trying to kill Reverend Parker."

The next few minutes were chaotic. As the sheriff ran toward the women shouting for them to break it up, Jennifer began filming again. The sheriff attempted to pull his gun from his holster, but it got stuck in the process, and he ended up shooting through the holster and into the ground.

The sound of the shot startled Elsie and Hortense. They both paused and turned toward the sheriff. As they did, the gun they were both trying to control fired and shot the minister just below the right shulder. While blood began to spread across Hortense's white blouse, the sheriff, Nick, and the two deputies all ran toward the two women, surprisingly acting in concert with each other as if they were a coordinated team.

The sheriff grabbed Elsie and handcuffed her hands behind her back. As he grabbed her, the gun used to shoot Hortense fell to the wet grass. Fortunately, it did not go off when it hit the ground.

While the sheriff restrained the frightened suspect, Nick took hold of the startled minister as she began to fall to the ground. Nick lifted Hortense and gently placed her on the ground while Logan took off his shirt and used it as a compress to help stop the bleeding. The wound looked frightening to Logan, but it appeared the bullet missed the lung and any arteries.

While all of this was going on, Kathy called for back-up and for the paramedics. The sheriff interrupted reading Elsie her rights and told Kathy to have the paramedics meet them at the boat ramp. They would take Hortense there in the sheriff's boat.

After making the call, Kathy ran to the boat to get the first aid kit and the stretcher that were kept on board. As she ran past Jennifer, she signaled for the reporter to join her. Having captured enough video to ensure a story on the evening news, the reporter was glad to help.

Nick took hold of Hortense's hand and tried to talk with her, but she was barely conscious. The minister appeared to be calm, with a serene look on her face. She didn't hear Nick ask her what happened as she mumbled the Lord's Prayer over and over.

The sheriff had his hands full trying to get anything out of Elsie. After reading the woman her rights, the sheriff asked, "Why did you do it, Elsie? Did you also kill Babs and Bonnie?"

Elsie didn't appear to hear anything the sheriff had to say. Once she saw the blood stain on her blouse, she started to scream. She didn't scream anything that was understandable other than "No, No, No."

The sheriff tried to shake Elsie to get her to focus, but it didn't help. The more he shook her, the more she screamed. He was about to slap her face to shock her into calming down like in the movies but decided not to. Jennifer was still nearby and a video of the sheriff slapping an old lady wouldn't play well on the news.

By the time Kathy and Jennifer returned with the first aid kit and stretcher, Elsie had gone silent and appeared to be having the same sort of seizure or panic attack that she had after Babs was killed. The sheriff laid Elsie on the ground and Jennifer tried to comfort her while Kathy called for a second paramedic to meet them at the boat ramp. By the time Kathy made the call, Elsie stopped screaming and fainted.

Over the next half hour, everyone pitched in to help get Elsie and Hortense to the hospital. Nick and Logan put Hortense on the stretcher and carried her to the boat. The sheriff picked up Elsie and carrier her while giving instructions to Kathy to pick up the gun used to shoot the minister and bring it with her. Kathy followed procedure and put on a pair of gloves before touching the gun and placing it into an evidence bag.

Once on board the boat, it only took a few minutes to reach to boat ramp. The 240-horsepower outboard motor moved the boat swiftly across the calm water of Crystal lake. Once the boat left the shore, Jennifer began filming again with her phone's camera. She got footage of the boat arriving at the boat dock and of the paramedics from the two ambulance trucks loading the women and departing for Paul Oliver hospital in Frankfort. Kathy rode in the back with Elsie. The sheriff had instructed her to keep Elsie under surveillance and handcuffed to the bed after the doctors treated her.

Nick rode in the ambulance with Hortense. She didn't stop repeating the Lord's Prayer and didn't let go of Nick's hand until she was sedated at the hospital. When they arrived at the hospital, Nick called Derek and told him what happened to his wife.

The gunshot wound wasn't life threatening but Hortense needed surgery on her shoulder that was more complex than the small hospital was equipped to handle. After being examined and stabilized, Hortense was moved to the medical center in Traverse City.

Before heading back to the sheriff's office with Logan, the sheriff gave Jennifer an interview to wrap-up her story. He had Logan hold the camera as he told the reporter, "Jennifer, I think this wraps up the Beulah Crest murders. I've placed Elsie Taylor under arrest for the attempted murder of Reverend Hortense Parker and for the murders of Bonnie Campbell and Babs Tucker. The people of Benzie County will rest soundly tonight knowing the mentally unstable woman who committed these crimes is in custody."

A deputy drove the sheriff, Logan, and Jennifer back to the sheriff's department where Jennifer had left her car. On the way, the sheriff asked the reporter to be sure to include footage of the boat being used to transport the injured woman and the suspect.

It was almost 6 o'clock by the time Nick and Kathy returned to the sheriff's office. The doctors told Nick that neither woman would be able to give a statement until morning. Reverend Parker and Elsie were both given medication and were sleeping soundly. Another deputy came to guard Elsie for the night while she was handcuffed to the bed.

At 6 o'clock, the sheriff called everyone in the department into his office to watch the news report. The story was written and presented exactly as he wanted. Sheriff Van Dyke was given credit for the successful investigation, and for the arrest of the suspected killer, Elsie Taylor. No one else in the department had their name mentioned in the story. There was footage of the sheriff placing the handcuffs on Elsie and there was a clip of the sheriff piloting the department patrol boat at a high speed.

After the story ended, the sheriff turned the television off and thanked everyone in the department. "I want to thank all of you who supported me in making this arrest. This is a big win for our department and for justice in our county."

"And for your election chances," Nick thought to himself, as the sheriff then started to issue instructions.

"Kathy, get the gun to the crime lab so they can get fingerprints and track its history. Logan, call that reporter and have her send us a copy of all the video she took today and then send it all to the lab. Maybe they can do their magic and tell us what the two women were saying before the shooting. Nick, get a warrant and search every inch of that Elsie Taylor's cottage. Something about that old gossip has always bothered me. I heard she's originally from New York. You know what I think of those people. Now, am I missing anything?"

Nick spoke up. "Sheriff, Ian De Vries is the property manager for the house adjacent to the crime scene. He has security cameras in the house facing the trail. We can probably get video of the crime from them."

"Great," the sheriff answered. "Get whatever he has and send it to the lab, tonight. I want to meet with the prosecuting attorney tomorrow and get that woman arraigned as soon as possible."

Nick could have called Ian and asked for the videos, but he decided to stop at Beulah Crest on the way home and talk to Ian. It was a little after 7pm when he arrived, so he was surprised to see so many people at the Mouse House. Almost all of the residents of the park were there. Ian was in his office, so Nick bypassed the crowd and walked over to greet Ian. As he walked past the coffee shop, he could hear snippets of conversations.

He heard Dot exclaim, "Do you really think she did it?" Nick couldn't hear if there was a response.

Out of the corner of his eye he saw Max telling Xander, "I hope this is the end of it, but something tells me there is more to come out of this."

As Nick approached Ian's office, he heard one last comment from the coffee shop. It was Dot's high-pitched voice telling her husband, "Herb, it's all tied to that damn game. I think Elsie wanted Babs and me out of the way so she could be your bridge partner. Bonnie and Hortense must have seen or heard something, so Elsie had to eliminate them. If she hadn't screwed up and got caught, I'm sure she'd come after me again."

Ian saw Nick approach and got up to greet him. "Good evening Detective. I'm guessing you're here for the videos. Care for a coffee while you're here."

Nick shook hands with Ian and declined the coffee. "No, I'll pass on the coffee. I don't want to deal with all the questions from that crowd in there. Have you looked at the videos yet?"

Ian offered Nick a seat in front of the monitor and started running through the videos and he answered. "I have, Detective. I didn't catch anything unexpected. Revered Parker and Elsie Taylor stop in front of the house and start talking. At first, nothing appears out of the ordinary. Then the discussion appears to more heated and then they begin to push and wrestle with each other. You don't see the gun until they turn, but just before the gun comes into view, the shot is fired and all you can see of the gun is it falling to the ground."

Nick didn't say anything until the video reached the point where the gun was fired. "It's not conclusive, is it? You think they were fighting over the gun when it fired, Ian?"

"I don't know. I don't see either of them as murderers. Perhaps one of the women was trying to kill herself, and Reverend Parker got shot as they struggled over the gun. Unfortunately, there's no usable sound in the video. It was taken from the inside of the house. All you can hear is the gunshot and the background noise made by the frogs."

"Do the videos from the other cameras show anything else?"

"No, nothing. Only one caught the shooting. Another camera caught footage of them approaching, and the other two didn't catch anything. I'll give you everything we shot on a memory stick. Maybe you can find something I missed."

"How's Elizabeth doing?" Nick asked.

"I just got a call from her. She's doing OK. There have been a lot of posts on the website since the TV news story."

"What did they have to say?"

"Most thought the sheriff did a good job catching the killer, but a few disagreed. They commented that if the sheriff could screw up when he arrested Dot, maybe he screwed up when he arrested Elsie. A few of them thought there was a sniper in the woods, and one thought Reverend Parker was the killer. There were also some posts that the shooting had something to do with the bridge club. There were several comments suggesting that Elsie killed Babs and tried to get Dot convicted so she could play bridge with Herb."

"I heard someone mention that in the coffee shop. It sounds a bit far-fetched if you ask me. I got the impression that Babs and Elsie were like sisters."

Ian finished downloading the videos and handed the memory stick to Nick. "Here you are Detective. I agree, it sounds ridiculous. Elsie and Babs were very close. Elsie is taking care of Chocolate and Fudge, Babs' cats. I suppose it's probably a good time for me and Elizabeth to move into Babs' cottage now, so I can take care of her cats. There's no room for them in my little apartment here in the Mouse House and pets aren't allowed where Elizabeth lives."

Nick thanked Ian and turned to leave. As he left, he headed to the door as quickly as possible so he wouldn't be invited into the coffee shop. As he approached the front door, he noticed the sheriff being served a coffee by Albert. Sheriff Van Dyke was surrounded by a crowd who were asking questions. The campaign for the fall election was in full swing. Nick almost made it out of the Mouse House when the sheriff called out. "Hold on Nick. Is everything OK?"

When the sheriff broke away from the crowd and walked over, Nick answered. "Fine sheriff. Just picking up the videos Ian's cameras took from the house near the shooting."

Aware that the crowd could hear, the sheriff corrected Nick. "Near the attempted murder, Detective. Anything new on the videos?"

"Nothing to contradict the validity of your arrest, Sheriff. I'll take the videos over to the lab in the morning."

"Can't you just e-mail them over?"

"I could, but I want them to move quickly on this. Also, they have a new supervisor over there I need to meet. I want to be sure she prioritizes our case. We need everything in place so Angela Berg will prosecute, don't we?"

"You're right there. She's a tough one to convince that anyone in this county I arrest is actually guilty of a crime. Thanks for your support. Doughnuts are on me tomorrow."

Nick nodded as the sheriff turned around and went back into the coffee shop to continue his campaigning.

CHAPTER 15
Closure

Elsie awoke from the medication in the early evening to find Joe Quandaro sitting by her bedside. She was admitted to the hospital for overnight observation because the emergency room physician detected something irregular in her heartbeat. "Nothing serious," he told her, "but it's better to be safe, than sorry."

When she opened her eyes, Elsie saw the attorney sitting next to her hospital bed. She was still a big groggy from the medication, but she recognized the lawyer who represented Dot. With a raspy voice, she asked, "What are you doing here?" Before he could answer, Elsie noticed, for the first time, her left wrist handcuffed to the bed frame. "Oh, yes, the sheriff," she muttered as she looked at her handcuffed wrist.

Joe handed Elsie a cup of water. "Here, drink this. It sounds like you could use it." While Elsie sipped the water, Joe continued. "Dot gave me a call when she heard about your arrest and asked me to come by."

Elsie drank the water slowly and then responded with her usual clear voice. "I never thought I'd need a criminal layer, but obviously I do. You got Dot off and made the sheriff look like a fool in the process, so you're hired." Elsie and Joe then spent the next hour talking about what happened on the trail next to the swamp and then the bail hearing in the morning.

Derek followed the ambulance truck that took his wife from the small Frankfort hospital to the larger Munson Medical Center in Traverse City. He only had a chance to spend a few minutes with Hortense before she was loaded into the ambulance. She appeared to recognize Derek, but she didn't tell him anything about what had happened. She just asked him to join her in reciting the Lord's Prayer, which she continued to repeat. Shortly after arriving at Munson, Hortense went into surgery.

Following the surgery, Hortense awoke a few times to see Derek at her bedside, but she didn't speak until morning when she woke up alert and full of questions. "The last thing I remember is wrestling with Elsie over a gun down by the frog swamp. What happened, Derek? How did I get here?" She then noticed the bandages and that her arm was in a sling. "Did she shoot me?"

"It appears that she did, dear. The sheriff arrested her for shooting you and for killing Bonnie and Babs. I saw the story on the news while you were being operated on yesterday." Derek handed her a copy of the morning Traverse City newspaper. The story, along with pictures of Hortense, Elsie, Babs, and the sheriff filled the front page. The was also a story about the Crime Spartans website and its role in solving the crimes.

While Hortense was reading the morning paper, Nick was driving down to the crime lab in Cadillac before going into the office. The lab already had the gun from the shooting and the videos taken by the reporter. Nick was bringing the videos taken by Ian from the house windows.

There was recently a restructuring of the crime lab, with many of Nick's contacts either taking early retirement or moving to one of the other labs in the state, so Nick wanted to go in person to meet the new people and establish working relationships with them. Nick found the new lab supervisor in the office of her predecessor.

When Nick introduced himself, he was greeted warmly the occupant, Wendy Judson. "Pleased to meet you Detective. How can I help?"

"I've got some more video of the shooting yesterday in Beulah I'd like your folks to review. I'm also looking for the results from some DNA samples and fingerprints from a gun we sent over yesterday."

"Oh yes. We've got what you need." Before continuing, Wendy offered Nick a coffee and a doughnut, which he accepted. "The lab is in a state because of this new work balancing program some clown above my pay grade set up. Not to worry though, murder cases still get top priority. Hold on, Detective, you don't care about our troubles. You've got a case you want to solve."

"No problem, Wendy. Charlie Turner, our medical examiner told me about your latest reorg. He doesn't seem pleased either. Anyway, what have you got?"

"I don't think your sheriff will be pleased. Preliminary results show that the DNA from the hammer in the Babs Tucker case, the teaspoon from the poisoned coffee, the hemlock found at McDonald's, and the wild carrot found in a freezer match the

DNA found on the gun you sent over yesterday. Also, we got a match on the fingerprint in the system from that spoon and from the gun. They're from the same person."

"Hold on Wendy. I thought we didn't get a match on the spoon fingerprint."

"When you called yesterday, I took another look at the file. With all the changes going on, a new technician checked the criminal databases, but for some reason, didn't check every database we can access. I had a hunch and ran a check through the database of prints from teachers and childcare workers and got a match."

Nick could see that the lab supervisor enjoyed telling the story, but he started to grow a bit impatient. "Wendy, might I inquire as to the identity of that person?"

"I'm sorry, Nick. I do tend to babble a bit. The fingerprint and therefore the DNA, belong to a resident of Beulah Crest, Hortense Parker. We have her fingerprints because she opened up a day care center at her church a few years ago. Anyone who works in such a facility is required to have their prints taken. Isn't this Parker woman the one who your sheriff said was shot by..."

Nick interrupted. "I know, I know. You think your department has issues. Come to Benzie County. The sheriff will probably argue that his suspect, Elsie Taylor, somehow planted the evidence. Who knows? Maybe he's right, but..."

"Maybe, maybe not. That's your job to sort out with your sheriff. The fingerprints and DNA are pretty convincing. Let's go see what the media tech has on your video. I saw it this morning.

It's pretty slick. If the sheriff gets a conviction of Elsie Taylor, he could use the video in his re-election campaign."

"Don't get me started," was all Nick said in response, as they walked over to the media lab.

Darius Jefferson was sitting at his bank of screens, manipulating the soundtrack of the video, as Nick and Wendy walked into his lab. He didn't notice or hear either of them until Wendy stood next to him and pointed to something on his screen. When she did, he turned around, removed his headphones, and greeted them. "Sorry, boss, I didn't hear you."

After introductions were made, Nick asked Darius, who looked as if he were younger than Nick's son, if he had any luck determining what the two women were saying.

"It's those damn frogs. I've been trying to filter them out. I think I might be close. I just tweaked the filter. Listen to this Detective."

Nick and Wendy listened as Darius played the video. They could hear Elsie's voice clearly, but not Reverend Parker's. "Can you do anything to bring up the other voice?" Nick asked.

After making some adjustments to the filter, Darius played the video again. Amazingly, the frog croaking was eliminated, and both voices were quite clear.

Elsie spoke, right after the two women stopped in front of the swamp. "Are you tired Hortense? Do you want to stop and take a break?"

"No Elsie, I'm not tired. I wanted to stop here because I'm meeting someone."

"Who?" Elsie asked with confused look on her face. "We're in the middle of nowhere."

"Archangel Michael."

"The one from the Crime Spartans website? Who is he?"

"Yes, Elsie, the one from the website. He's the Archangel Michael, the leader of God's army in heaven. He wants to meet me."

Baffled, Elsie asked, "What are you talking about Hortense. I wouldn't trust anyone who posts on that site."

"I trust him, Elsie. He's not just someone; he really is an archangel. He appreciates what I've done and what I am about to do."

Elsie responded, but her voice was drowned out by a loud boat on the lake. "Hold on," Darius commented as he made some adjustments and then re-started the video where it had been. The boat sound was filtered out and both voices could be heard again.

"Elsie started to look frightened as she questioned Hortense. "What are you talking about? What did you do? What are you planning to do?"

Hortense spoke in a calm, but decisive manner. "I killed that tramp, Bonnie Campbell, and I'm going to kill you."

"What about Babs? Did you kill her too?"

Hortense reached into her jacket pocket as she answered. "I'm sorry about Babs, she was a mistake, but this is a war, Elsie. A war against the unworthy. Archangel Michael needs me in his battle to remove people like you and Bonnie. She was a whore, and you destroy people's lives with your gossip. Bonnie was, and you are, weeds in God's holy garden. Weeds that need to be pulled and cast aside."

Elsie's face portrayed the look of disbelief and shock. She then screamed something unintelligible as she could be seen reaching for something.

Hortense then shouted, "Give me back my gun, you wretched old shrew. I've had to put up with the likes of you for too long. So many years of turning the other cheek while people in my congregation ignored my counsel and continued to sin. That stops now. It's time to clean house." The women in the video struggled over the gun as Reverend Parker tried to justify her actions.

The next sound was the gunshot. There was a short pause and then Reverend Parker fell to the ground and the sheriff rushed into the frame and handcuffed Elsie.

Darius played the video for a few minutes before commenting. "Looks like your sheriff arrested the wrong woman. I'm glad I won't be the one to tell him. Darius didn't notice Nick's slight smile as he slid his chair to another monitor and a different keyboard that were connected to a computer with an Internet connection.

Wendy asked, "Have you got something else, Darius?"

"I just wanted to check the Crime Spartans website, boss. There was a post this morning about the bail hearing. It said Elsie Taylor was released from the hospital and would attend the hearing. I want to see if there are any updates." Wendy mumbled something about the vulgarity of the site while Darius scrolled to the last post. Regardless of Wendy's feelings about the site, she leaned over Darius' shoulder with Nick to watch the video of the sheriff in front of the courthouse fill the screen.

Nick's smile turned to a laugh as they listened to the sheriff's statement. "Benzie County is safe, now that this vicious predator is behind bars. I arrested Elsie Taylor yesterday, and today she has been denied bail. She will remain in custody until the trial. Your sheriff's department solved this crime and, with your support, I will continue to hunt down criminals like Elsie Taylor and keep Benzie safe. Thank you"

"Looks like I have some work to do," Nick commented when the video ended. "I need to share some bad news with the sheriff, arrest a minister, and get that poor old woman out of our jail. Darius, please e-mail me a copy of the video."

When Nick returned to the station, he found everyone celebrating the arrest. The sheriff ordered chicken wings, fries and potato salad from the Cold Creek and a buffet was set up in the conference room. The sheriff was eating a wing and talking to a county commissioner who stopped by to congratulate him when Nick interrupted. "Sheriff, you need to come into my office, now!"

Sheriff Van Dyke didn't like being told what to do, but the strained look on Nick's face indicated something important was going on. Optimistic that whatever Nick had to say would further enhance his career, the sheriff agreed to follow Nick.

When he got the sheriff alone in his office, Nick didn't know how to break the news to the sheriff. Instead, he opened the email with the enhanced video that Darius had sent and asked the sheriff to watch. The sheriff recognized the video as soon as it started, since he'd seen it many times before. He was surprised by the quality of the sound. "This is great, Nick. They did a great job with the sound."

Nick paused the video for a second. "Just watch and listen Sheriff. Prepare yourself for a shock." Nick then hit the play button and waited for the fireworks to begin.

To Nick's surprise, there were no fireworks. The sheriff calmly asked, "Anything else?"

Nick handed the sheriff the folder with the DNA and fingerprint reports. "That's all sheriff."

The sheriff read the reports and then calmly whispered to Nick. "Show what you have to the prosecuting attorney, and get that poor woman out of our jail. Then go up to Traverse and arrest Reverend Parker. I'll call the sheriff up there and let them know you're coming."

"Are you ok, Sheriff?"

"I'm fine, just go and do what needs to be done."

Nick was uneasy leaving the sheriff, but he left to follow the instructions he was given. Getting Elsie out of jail and arresting Reverend Parker was more important than the sheriff's emotional state. He met briefly with the prosecuting attorney and shared the new evidence. She agreed to get with the judge and have Elsie released as soon as possible.

Nick then drove up to Traverse City. He was told that Reverend Parker wouldn't be ready to be released from the hospital for a few days. So, with the help of the Grand Traverse County sheriff's deputies, the new suspect was moved to the small ward at the hospital used to house inmates and prisoners.

Hortense took the news of her arrest well. "Archangel Michael will look after me," she told Nick before they moved her to the secure ward. "He'll find another soldier here on earth to carry out his work. Where I'll be going, there will be plenty for me to do."

After the arrest, Nick questioned Derek, who had no idea that his wife was the murderer and was unaware of any abnormal behavior on her part. "Hortense is Hortense," he told Nick. "We've been married for over thirty years during which she had her world and I had mine. We've shared a life, but not our hearts." Unable to remain at his wife's side, he returned home to Beulah Crest. When neighbors stopped by ask about Hortense, he didn't answer the door.

Nick stopped off at Beulah Crest on the way back to his office to let folks know what had happened, but he found that the news of Elsie's release and Reverend Parker's arrest were already known throughout the park. Albert was the first to read the news on Crime Spartans and once he told several people who were having coffee at the Mouse House about what was on the site, news spread quickly.

Although he didn't need to, Nick decided to walk over to Elsie's cottage to apologize for her arrest and see how she was doing after her experience with the sheriff and with Hortense. On his way to her cottage, he spotted her standing near the top of the stairs tossing a leftover sandwich to Arthur, the fox. When he approached, Nick jokingly scolded her. "You shouldn't be feeding him, you know. He's getting too friendly."

"I know," she answered, while tossing the last piece of the sandwich toward the fox. "I made the sandwich yesterday for Hortense, but she didn't eat it. She was in a hurry to leave and meet her archangel. I didn't want it to go to waste."

"How are you doing, Elsie? I wanted to apologize for what happened yesterday. I'm sure the sheriff feels the same way."

"I'm fine, Detective and I appreciate the apology. I'm sure it's sincere, at least on your part. Are you sure Hortense killed Babs and Bonnie?"

"I am, Elsie. We have evidence that will stand up in court. You're safe now."

Elsie responded with a familiar phrase. "Thank you, Detective. Now, as you know, I'm not one to gossip, but did you hear…?"

EPILOGUE

Life resumed its normal rhythm at Beulah Crest, busy with seasonal residents and visitors in the summer and quiet once the leaves fell from the trees in October.

Ian and Elizabeth got married in August and lived in Babs' cottage until Chocolate and Fudge died three years later. They sold their share in Crime Spartans and used the proceeds to build a microbrewery and restaurant in Elberta. Elizabeth managed the restaurant, and Ian ran the brewery. The restaurant had tablet based electronic menus on each table that had Internet connections.

Naomi Banks, the researcher from Australia, testified on a video call at one of Reverend Parker's early court hearings. Her program correctly identified all of the usernames Hortense used on Crime Spartans. A background check prepared for the prosecuting attorney confirmed that Hortense was born and raised in Windsor, Ontario, across the river from Detroit. She did her undergraduate studies at the University of Windsor, before meeting Derek and moving to Michigan.

Nigel and Spencer sold their house on Crystal Lake, for a sizeable profit, and gave Beulah Crest to the charitable trust that Max and Xander set up with the money from Babs and Bonnie.

They visited occasionally, staying with either Xander or Max, but the harsh tactics of the sheriff reinforced their fears of the corrupt nature of the American criminal justice system. "Nice place to visit," Nigel told Ian, "but not a place where I'd want to have a home or investments."

Ben fully recovered from his fall and returned to work at the end of the summer. Albert continued to run the coffee shop for years until he became too frail to do so. After a bad fall, he sold his cottage and moved to the Maples care facility in Frankfort.

Derek lived quietly for the remainder of his life at Beulah Crest. He practiced dentistry on a part-time basis for several more years. Hortense was adjudicated incompetent to stand trial and was committed to a state mental hospital near Ann Arbor. Derek made the four hour drive every Friday to visit his wife until she passed away fifteen years after she was committed.

The sheriff did not run for re-election. He quietly resigned, and Nick informally led the Sheriff's office until he was elected sheriff in November. Sheriff Van Dyke moved to nearby Manistee County, where he set up a private security company. Four year later he ran for the state legislature and won in a landslide on an anti-crime and anti-immigrant platform. He remained in the legislature until he retired.

Joe Quandaro and his legal team helped Max and Xander set up a charitable trust to support education using the funds they inherited from Babs and Bonnie. The trust started by funding scholarships for children of migrant farm workers and financially challenged local residents. It later expanded its reach to provide grants to graduate students doing scientific and historical research.

Max lived happily in his cottage for a number of years. In addition to helping to manage the charitable trust, he continued to attend events at Interlochen and meet regularly with friends there. When his health began to decline, he sold his cottage and moved into an apartment in the same building as his son's family in Tel-Aviv.

Xander kept his cottage and used it on weekends and summer breaks. Two years after the murders, he married a colleague from his university. Her family was from Boston, so he ended up splitting his summer breaks between Beulah Crest and her family's summer house in New Hampshire.

Nate Santiago moved into the Mouse House and took over the management of Beulah Crest after he graduated from Kalamazoo College. He also became a real estate broker, and he joined the supervisory board of the charitable trust.

Elsie lived quietly and continued her habit of feeding wild animals and spreading gossip. Dot lost her interest in playing bridge and began volunteering with a legal aid charity in Traverse City leaving Herb free to establish a long-term bridge partnership with Elsie. The pair won numerous bridge tournaments, and Elsie managed to get Herb to control his temper at the table.